Best wishes to my good friends
Shelba and John Lee

Basil Moss
2-25-98

Tales of the Wichitas

WTales of the ichitas

Basil Moss

Texas Tech University Press

This book was set in New Baskerville and Della Robbia and printed on acid-free paper that meets the guidelines for permanence and durability of the Committee on Production Guidelines for Book Longevity of the Council on Library Resources. ∞

Cover photo "Wichitas Looking North from Mt. Lincoln" copyright Andrus Clark and frontispiece "Mount Scott Cloudburst" copyright G. B. Sage published, with permission, as the winners of a 1997 competition sponsored by the Wichita Wildlight Photographic Society, Lawton, Oklahoma.

Design by Rob Neatherlin

Library of Congress Cataloging-in-Publication Data
Moss, Basil, 1925-
    Tales of the Wichitas / Basil Moss.
      p.   cm.
    ISBN 0-89672-390-9 (alk. paper)
    1. Wichita Mountains (Okla.)—History—Fiction. 2. Frontier and pioneer life—Oklahoma—Wichita Mountains—Fiction. 3. Indians of North America—Oklahoma—Wichita Mountains—Fiction. I. title.
PS3563.088457T3   1998
813'.54—dc21   97-41841
                                         CIP

98 99 00 01 02 03 04 05 06 / 9 8 7 6 5 4 3 2 1

Texas Tech University Press
Box 41037
Lubbock, Texas 79409-1037 USA
800-832-4042
ttup@ttu.edu

Contents

Preface

The Red River swings east around the southwestern corner of Oklahoma and embraces a land of rolling hills and tree-lined creeks. Before the prairie was turned root-side up by breaking plows, grass rippled in waves over the gentle slopes. Bison grew strong on the nutritious stems. Today, fields of wheat, grain sorghum, and alfalfa patch the countryside. Beef cattle feed at well-filled troughs, and dairy herds loll on tended pastures. Neatly squared farms spread northeast to the land where the haze-softened Wichita Mountains rise out of the plains in sudden splendor. Their granite peaks are remnants of an ancient mountain range, which raised spires like pink cathedrals millions of years before the Rocky Mountains emerged. Those upthrusts of granite core, which the Plains Indians knew as places of safety and shelter, were named for the Wichita Indians, an agrarian tribe that once held sway nearby.

Protected from wintry blasts and hidden from their enemies, the Comanches and Kiowas wintered along the creeks in the Wichitas for centuries. They also found great spiritual power in certain natural formations scattered among those primordial mountains. After being masters of the Texas plains and the nearby mountains for a hundred and fifty years, the Plains Indians did not withdraw meekly when white settlers swept into their stronghold from the east. Between 1867 and 1874 several battles of the Red River wars raged beneath the rock-strewn slopes of the Wichita Mountains. By usurping the homelands of aborigines, white people in Oklahoma and Texas helped complete the conquest of a continent.

In the late 1870s, after crushing their final defenses, the United States Army drove the Plains Indians into the Wichita Mountains and held them there. At the same time white settlers from the East were coming into the region in greater numbers, ready and willing to occupy territory conquered in the Red River wars.

By 1925, the year of my birth, the tides of history had washed people of Dutch, Irish, English, Scots, German, French, and Swiss ancestry into the Wichita Mountains, where the Kiowas and Comanches now owned much of the arable land.

The wars were long over when I appeared on the scene, but cultural differences remained. Most of the time Indians and Anglos mixed and mingled quietly. But sometimes they collided in crashing waves of disagreement. Deriving from my life in the Wichitas and from stories told to me by my family, the tales in this volume reflect my perception of the Indian and white people who lived in my birthplace, a loosely defined area in southwestern Oklahoma known as the Mount Scott community. We were the children and grandchildren of those men and women who lived at the close of the struggle for the landmass of North America.

The earlier stories in this book mirror the lives of Kiowa and Comanche peoples as they might have been twenty-five to fifty years before I met them. My own adventures color the yarns set in the 1920s and 1930s.

Although the tales are fictitious, they reflect the feelings and wisdom that came to me in my close contact with Indian culture. The narratives are intended to entertain, but I hope they will also shed light on times and places in our history that have not been written about or studied extensively.

It troubles me that too many writers, broadcasters, filmmakers, artists, and others continue to reduce interaction between Indians and Anglos to stereotypical accounts and to present life on a reservation as the last chapter of three centuries of violent aggression.

Too little known and seldom told are the stories of Indians who survived the onslaught of the overpowering Anglos and who did not go to a reservation. Instead, they took advantage of a belated government offer and claimed farms within the great land area that had once belonged to them. These were the Indians of my childhood. Among them were artists, farmers, ranchers, ministers, engineers, athletic coaches, teachers, and college presidents.

I cannot say there weren't those Indians and those Anglos in the Mount Scott community who fit the caricatures and stereotypes, because there were. But there were others. I remember my Indians neighbors as people like us simply trying to make their way, weaving into their daily lives what ancestral traditions and customs they could. We were different, but living together made our differences less important. I hope these tales illuminate the ways in which we worked through our differences and came to accept the diversity of our community.

Basil Moss

Tales of the Wichitas

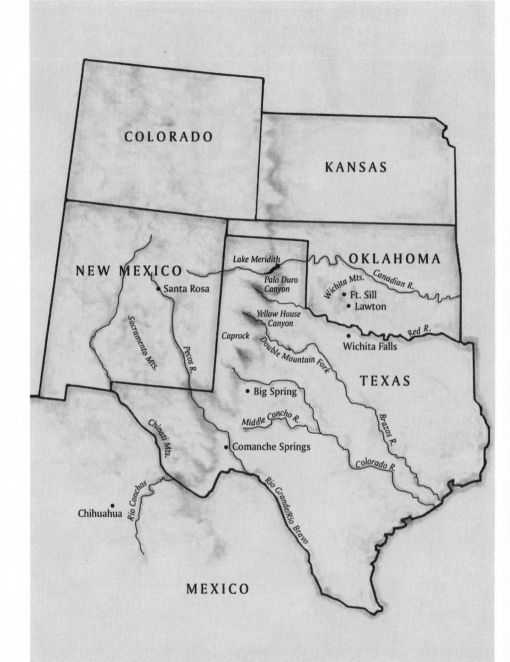

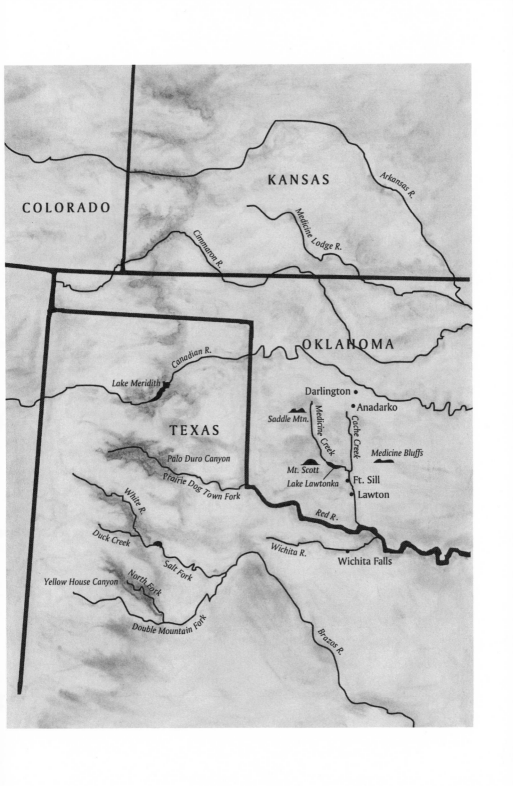

Scourge of the Plains

Tehat Hauvone moved with a lilting skip, more suggestive of a child dancing than of a pregnant woman. This was a rare moment in the life of the tall, black-haired daughter of the western plains. Her work was done and her only child, Tree Blooming, was in her mother's care. Tehat was free to wander and explore. Because the Two Mountain band of Kiowas was at Tahoka Lake, her favorite campsite, she especially welcomed the chance to roam. The season of long days and sunshine had come to the Llano Estacado, the Staked Plains. This was the time when grass grew thick and bison thrived.

On her climb up the slope, away from the lake, Tehat hummed. Although she strolled with a carefree gait, her walk was not aimless. She sought a place she'd loved since she first walked there as a child. Finally she found the spot. There on the rim of the canyon, where eroded caliche gave way to level grassland, a carpet of flowers like yellow cups spread out in front of her. Purple whorls on smaller flowers sprinkled throughout reminded Tehat of the sky when the sunset blends into the dark blue of evening. Twirling on her tiptoes she sat down at a low shelf cut into the edge of the plains by wind and rain. In the lush valley below a blue lake washed the base of a curving white cliff. Across the canyon, horses grazed on the plains. Red, black, white and brown, their bodies stood out against the green grass of the prairie. In the east, along the Caprock of the Llano Estacado, fleecy white clouds billowed into the sky like freshly washed sheep. Their line of rising traced the edge of the level grassland where an escarpment ended and the land fell a thousand feet to the Rolling Plains below. Absorbing this view, Tehat raised her arms and opened her hands. Needing room for a fullness that crowded her chest, she took a deep breath.

Her gaze lowered to tepees on the shore of the lake and she basked in peace. Languid plumes of smoke wafted up from smoldering cook-fires. The voices of other women drifted to the watcher above. A dog barked half-heartedly at some small animal invading its territory. When her eyes fell on the tepee she shared with her husband, Jessee Hauvone, Tehat's thoughts warmed even more. Nearby, stood the comfortingly familiar tepee of her father and mother, Hawk and Little Deer. Her eyes shifted to Chief Buffalo Horse's tepee. Gratitude welled up as she proudly thrust out her chin. "You did right, my chief. I'm glad you refused to sign the white man's paper and give them our beautiful home."

Tehat was thinking of a treaty signed by some Kiowas at Medicine Lodge River in Kansas in 1867. That was seven years ago. The Kiowas who signed had agreed to go to a reservation and be under the control of a white agent. They'd accepted as truth the white men's word they would never go hungry. For that promise, they gave away most of the land claimed by the tribe in Texas. By refusing to sign, Chief Buffalo Horse had made it possible for his band to go on living on the land they loved.

Tehat knew she sat in the garden of Hero, the supernatural child of the Sun by an earthly mother, who did many wonderful things for the Kiowas. Plaiting the stems of flowers she had picked, she reveled in her exquisite surroundings. A song of love rose to her lips:

> *I cherish this land of unbroken view,*
> *cleansed by the driving wind.*
> *I wish I could live in this wondrous land,*
> *with those whom I love, forever.*

While her fingers nimbly twined the yellow and purple blossoms, Tehat watched a small figure below her. Tree Blooming was climbing the slope. When she saw Tehat, she ran to her knee. "What are you doing, Mama?"

Tehat slipped the finished garland of flowers around her own neck and lifted Tree Blooming onto her lap. "I'm remembering when I found flowers like these, when I was a little girl like you."

"Teach me to make a circle of flowers like yours."

Tehat continued to hold her daughter close and showed her how to weave the stems. When they had finished another wreath, Tehat slipped the necklace over Tree Blooming's head and set her on her feet. It was time to return to the valley.

Tehat noticed a change in the east. Ominous black clouds were rising like pillars over the Rolling Plains. Foreboding caused Tehat's heart to pound as she hurried Tree Blooming back to camp.

Reassured by the smell of cooking food, Tehat laid her concerns aside in the familiar sights and sounds of the campground. She smiled and crushed a handful of red peppers into the buffalo stew she was heating. Each time she used these fiery pods, she was reminded that her husband had not been born Kiowa. He'd been captured in Mexico as a child. Nevertheless, he'd grown into a true Kiowa—in everything except his name and his taste for chili peppers. Hauvone, his Kiowa father, had named him Jessee because that was the only word he said to the Kiowas who brought him back. Even though he'd forgotten his life in Mexico, Jessee still craved the food he'd eaten in childhood. Sometimes his wife teased him, saying he only raided in Mexico to steal peppers that look and burn like coals of fire.

Tehat watched Jessee leave Chief Buffalo Horse's tepee and lead his brown and white horse toward her fire. He was a short man, his gray eyes coming only to the level of Tehat's throat. Despite his small stature, strength and vitality radiated from his muscular body. His vigorous, well-balanced steps caused Tehat to think, for the thousandth time, that he was the most masculine man she had ever seen.

Jessee fingered the flowers wreathing Tehat's neck. "I see you have been on the slope. I hope you walked carefully. You must not fall and lose my son you carry."

"I'm careful," Tehat said, resisting the temptation to say it might not be a son she carried.

Jessee nipped a bite of buffalo meat from the bubbling pot and smiled. "You remembered the peppers."

"Were you talking to Chief Horse?"

"Yes. Tsain-tai has dreamed that white men are coming from the east. Buffalo Horse sends Hard Rain Falling and me on a scout. We'll gain the edge of the plains under cover of darkness and watch from the heights at dawn."

Tehat recalled the foreboding she had felt earlier that afternoon and her blood turned cold. Fearing that speaking of a thing might make it happen, she said nothing.

Jessee finished his evening meal and went to the tepee pole where his weapons hung. He took down his buffalo-hide shield, bois d'arc bow, and quiver of arrows. Hanging the bow and quiver across his back, he slipped his forearm through the strap of the shield. He thrust his stone axe behind the belt-cord that held his steel knife and folded a blanket on his arm above the shield. Ready to ride, he ducked out of his tepee and walked to his horse. When he had mounted, his wife did an unusual thing. She ran to him and laid her cheek against his bare leg. "Guard well, Jessee. Return safe to your children and me."

Jessee touched his wife's hair. "We don't go to do battle. This is only a scout."

That night Tehat was restless. Several times she awakened to hear the wind whispering a tale of loneliness through the poles of the tepee. At dawn she rose and began her day's work. Voices buzzing like angry bees interrupted her and sent her heart racing. She dragged herself to the opening of her tepee and looked out. Two horses were coming from the east.

Hard Rain Falling rode into camp leading Jessee Hauvone's horse with Jessee's lifeless body draped over its back. Dried blood streaked both sides of Jessee's face. Men, women and children followed Hard Rain Falling to Buffalo Horse's tepee, crying out in anger and sadness. Tehat ran to her husband's body. "Oh, Jessee, my beloved Jessee. They've killed you."

Chief Buffalo Horse stepped out of his tepee and the people fell silent. Hard Rain Falling raised his chin off his chest.

"We watched on the heights above the lower prairie. North of us, two Tonkawas led six horse-soldiers onto the Caprock. When Jessee saw the Tonkawas leading our enemies to kill us, he grew angry and forgot himself. He cursed the man-eating Tonkawas and charged the invaders. All of them shot at him. One bullet found his neck. I left him there and rode south. The soldiers followed. I led them off the Caprock, down to the lower plains. Where I rode on rocks the Tonkawas lost my trail. I circled back and picked up my friend."

Chief Buffalo Horse motioned to Hard Rain Falling. "What of the soldiers? Where are they now?"

"They found their way back to the high plains. They suspect we are here."

"Break camp!" Chief Buffalo Horse shouted. "Hurry!"

Sobbing, Tehat lowered her husband's body to the ground. Little Deer helped carry him to his tepee. In a daze Tehat dismantled the tepee and packed their goods as she had done hundreds of times before. She didn't need to think to load the travois. She packed the tepee and half of their possessions behind her brown horse. The rest she packed on a travois pulled by the horse Jessee had ridden. Tehat tied his body atop those belongings.

Although Tehat was ready to leave camp as soon as any of the others, she didn't immediately fall in line. Instead, with Tree Blooming seated behind her, she rode her horse onto the plains above the cliff. Wielding her knife, she cut off the little finger and the one next to it on her left hand. Binding the stumps of her severed fingers with a rabbit skin, she glared to the east. "You no good, blue-coat sons of evil mothers," she shrieked, "you've killed my beloved Jessee and torn the life out of my body. I'll never forget who did this. Until now I've hated you in the way that all Kiowas hate you. From this day on, I promise you a hatred beyond all others. I hate you from the depths of the spirit in me. I loathe the wombs that bore you. I smear Buffalo dung on your food. I spit on your ugly white faces. I'll find a way to get even."

Tehat turned her back on the despicable men of the east and trotted her horses into the line of retreating Kiowas.

Buffalo Horse rode north, toward the mouth of the Double Mountain Fork of the Brazos River. After a while he halted. With a raised hand he signaled Hawk to come forward. "We'll pause here while I wait for my scouts. Tell your daughter there will be time to bury her husband."

"I'll do that. Then where do we go?"

Buffalo Horse looked east. "I'll trail north until I know if other horse-soldiers come behind those who killed my warrior."

Tehat, her mother, and some of the women withdrew with the travois that bore Jessee's body. When they had dug a shallow grave, the women lined the depression with a blanket and lifted the brave's body into it. They placed his bow, arrows, shield, and axe beside his right hand and covered him with a buffalo robe. Then they filled in the grave and began a song of death. Their singing was disturbed by a lone figure riding in from the east.

Buffalo Horse tightened the reins on his black stallion until the scout rode up beside him.

"What report?"

"Bad Hand is here with two hundred. He camps on the mountain river, at the east end of the canyon of yellow houses."

Hawk joined the other men to listen. "What does he say?"

"Bad Hand is between us and the Rolling Plains. He cuts us off from the lower river."

"Where do we go?"

Buffalo Horse pointed west. "On to the Llano Estacado. We'll turn back toward Cedar Lake and keep our eyes on Bad Hand."

Later that day, after he'd moved his band a safe distance, Buffalo Horse sent scouts to watch the horse-soldiers. His spies rode into a canyon from the west. Yellowed by the lowering sun, its eroded caliche walls resembled cliff dwellings in other canyons, far to the west. A scout pointed at the bluffs. "Yellow houses."

The Kiowas found a troop of United States cavalrymen camped in the mouth of Yellow House Canyon. Silently mounting the steep walls, they took up positions to watch.

Below, the soldiers worked quickly, building fires, and setting up tents. The sergeant who had led the scouting party earlier that day reported to his superiors. His official account included the sighting of two Kiowas and the killing of one. Then he joined the other non-commissioned officers and watched the men make camp.

"We shot one Kiowa and chased after the other one. The Tonks lost the trail, and we went back to where we'd killed the first one. We couldn't find his body anywhere. None of us thought dead men could walk, but some of the men got spooked. Finally, the Tonkawas straightened us out. They studied the hoofprints and told us the Indian we chased had returned and carried his friend's body toward Tahoka Lake."

Across the camp from the sergeants, two blue-clad officers stood beside a canvas-covered supply wagon. One wore the eagle emblems of a colonel. The other was a lieutenant. The colonel rested his crippled hand on the rim of a wagon wheel. "At least we've made contact, Henry. We've found the enemy and I expect to close with him soon."

Lieutenant Henry W. Lawton nodded. "Will you pursue them onto the Staked Plains?"

"Don't think so. The scouts report that the two Kiowas they ran into were from Buffalo Horse's band. He operates near the Double Mountain Fork. I intend to stay between him and the Rolling Plains and catch him if he tries to get to his home territory."

Lieutenant Lawton shifted his weight to his other foot. "What are my orders?"

"Return to the supply camp on White River and pick up corn for the horses and rations for the men. I'll patrol the Caprock south and east, then swing back to Duck Creek and meet you there."

During the days that followed, the scouts of the Two Mountain band kept watchful eyes on Colonel Ranald S. Mackenzie and his troops. The Kiowas hid in gullies and dry playa lakes and watched the cavalry search along the edge of the Llano Estacado. When Colonel Mackenzie turned east, a scout returned to Chief Buffalo

Horse. "Bad Hand is moving east and is looking for us on the Two Mountain Fork."

Buffalo Horse gathered his men. "We'll ride north to kill buffalo. I want to be in Palo Duro Canyon when cold weather comes." The chief spoke of the place north of the Llano Estacado where the head-waters of Red River had washed a deep trench in the plains. This high-walled basin would give them warmth and security. Native people had known about it since time out of memory.

While the Two Mountain band hunted buffalo on the plains, the Indians in the Wichita Mountains grew hungry and restless. Cheyenne and Arapaho who were on the warpath burned a wagon train. The Cheyenne Agency at Darlington called for help. Depredations near Fort Sill elicited the order that no Indians could come into the post unless accompanied by the post interpreter.

Learning of atrocities near Fort Sill, the President turned over management of the Indians to the army. Peaceful Indians were to be placed on rolls for identification. Hostiles who refused to surrender were to be punished.

Three days later at Anadarko, a battle ensued on ration day for the Wichitas, Caddoes, and Delawares, when Kiowas and Comanches helped themselves to the formers' rations. When a column of soldiers from Fort Sill appeared, the Kiowas and Comanches mounted their ponies and painted themselves for a fight. Colonel Davidson, who commanded the column, accepted the surrender of Red Food, a Comanche. But Red Food would not give up his arms. When the Kiowas sneered at Red Food, a skirmish broke out and the Indians charged one company of the relief column from Fort Sill. Although the battle was bloodless and lasted only a few minutes, several civilians were killed when the Indians moved down river.

The next day more skirmishes took place before the Kiowas fled upstream. Fearing reprisals, the scattered Indians sought protection from the army at Fort Sill. Within a few months, half of the Kiowas and Comanches were settled on the reservation. The rest sought safety in Texas.

Hostile Kiowas under Mamanti and hostile Comanches under O-ha-ma-tai broke for the headwaters of Red River in Texas. The chiefs approached Palo Duro Canyon with caution. Each sent outriders to check for white soldiers or unfriendly Indians. The scouts peered into the depths of the vast canyon. Far below, a golden eagle, a dark speck, spiraled over a ribbon of water. Horses, seeming no larger than sheep, grazed on the other side of the valley. Beyond the horses, tepees lined the base of a red cliff. A Comanche scout studied the tepees, then made slashing motions up his forearm, signing "Cheyenne" to the others.

When their scouts reported seeing only their friends the Cheyenne in the canyon, the Kiowa and Comanche chiefs led their followers into the protection of its depths.

A few days after the runaways from Anadarko rode in from the east, the Two Mountain band arrived at the west end of the gorge. Chief Buffalo Horse was satisfied that his band was prepared to spend the coming season in this sunken sanctuary, but he moved cautiously. Ordering the women to wait, he took Tsain-tai as interpreter and went to visit the other chiefs. At the campfires of the Comanche leader O-ha-ma-tai, they heard about the fight at Anadarko. They paid a courtesy call on Iron Shirt, chief of the Cheyenne. At last they rode to the camp of Mamanti, the Kiowa medicine man. There, Buffalo Horse asked about the wisdom of making a cold-weather camp in Palo Duro Canyon. Mamanti made medicine then stood by his fire.

"From my medicine I have learned that no blue-coated soldiers will enter this canyon."

"I thank you," Buffalo Horse said. "I'll probably camp close by."

On the way back to the waiting band, Buffalo Horse stopped his black stallion. "And you, Tsain-tai, Old Friend, what do you think of Mamanti's medicine?"

"My medicine is not strong. I cannot see or hear clearly in the clatter of these strangers, but I am uneasy. I sense we must be cautious."

Back at camp Buffalo Horse dismounted. "The women may set up camp. The medicine man Mamanti says no soldiers will come into this canyon, but Tsain-tai warns us to be alert."

While Little Deer and Tehat unloaded their goods and set up their tepees, Little Deer chatted amiably. She was pleased that Hawk had taken their daughter and granddaughter into his care. Tehat worked in silence. Although her life had gone on, her broken heart hadn't healed. She no longer cried, but her bitter feelings kept her out of pleasant conversation. Her mind dwelt only on revenge.

Once their tepees were in place, Tehat and Little Deer joined the other women of the band in preparing for cold weather. They stored buffalo stomachs filled with pemmican and rawhide bags packed with dried buffalo meat. They stacked firewood by the opening flaps of the tepees and piled buffalo robes around inside the bison-hide walls.

Late summer passed into early fall, and the Two Mountain band forgot Tsain-tai's counsel. When horse-soldiers didn't appear, they settled into safe, untroubled living in the canyon of plenty.

Far advanced in her second pregnancy, Tehat couldn't find a position on her buffalo robes that would relieve her painful back. She spent a sleepless night. At dawn she heard a gunshot. Someone was hunting early. A volley of four shots followed, and Tehat leaped to her feet. Kiowas didn't waste ammunition on game.

She rushed out of the tepee and looked down the stream. Like images of death, shadowy figures stealthily drifted into line across the lower end of the canyon. Skull-white faces contrasted with the dark uniforms of crouching men who led their horses as they sneaked into the sleeping camp. Terrified, Tehat took Tree Blooming by the hand and ran through the early morning light. The weight of her unborn child slowed her steps. As she scrambled up the canyon wall, she bloodied her hands and bare feet on sharp rocks. Pressing Tree Blooming between her body and the red clay, she clung trembling to the roots of a juniper tree.

Transformed into flesh-and-blood killers, the ghostly figures mounted their horses and with horrifying yells began crashing through underbrush. Tehat heard tree branches cracking and snapping. As the line of horses charged into view, Kiowa, Comanche and Cheyenne warriors reeled from surprise but hurried to form a line of defense. Fear tightened Tehat's throat. She knew her father, Hawk, would be among them. Firing and falling back, the Indians gave ground slowly. Although Tehat lost sight of the battle, the gunfire told her of the fighting, and above the noise she could already hear the death songs of the fallen braves.

Downriver, women and children slipped into a side canyon that opened to the south. Tehat wondered if Little Deer might have escaped with them, but dared not cross the open canyon to find out. Nailed by fear to the canyon wall, she could only shush Tree Blooming's cries. Choking on the acrid fumes of spent gunpowder, Tehat strained wildly to stare through the smoke and dust that filled the canyon.

Soldiers stormed back down the canyon and began to destroy the camp. Tepees fell, their contents broken and scattered. Soldiers dismounted and ran through the village like rabid coyotes. Snatching up anything that would burn, they threw tanned hides, tepee poles, buffalo robes, baskets, blankets, and clothes into fire. Whatever would not burn they smashed or cut up. They slashed through rawhide bags packed with dried meat and buffalo stomachs filled with pemmican. They knocked holes in cooking pots. They roped drying racks draped with fresh meat and pulled them down. This was not war as the Kiowas understood war. This was annihilation. Tehat's spirit shriveled. The actions of these terrible wild men made no sense. Taking nothing for themselves, they destroyed everything of value. Finally, the soldiers answered a bugle call and the rampage ceased. They rode away down the canyon, driving more than a thousand horses ahead of them.

Completely routed by the unexpected attack, the people left the canyon in every direction. Some Comanches followed their chief west across the Llano Estacado toward the Pecos River. O-ha-ma-tai led his band east, down the Red River, in the direction of Fort Sill. Iron Shirt took his Cheyenne north toward Kansas.

The Two Mountain band gathered in their destroyed campsite, their heads pulled down by shame. Without a mount, Buffalo Horse stood in their midst, lost and confused. In stunned silence, his men gathered around him.

Tears welled into the eyes of Walks Alone, one of the younger men. "What can we do? They've taken our horses."

Chief Buffalo Horse stared blankly until a sudden shout went up. A short, broad-chested, young brave led six horses into the circle. "Will these help?" One of the six was Chief Buffalo Horse's black stallion.

His face brightened. "How did you save them, Ge-hay-tie?"

"When the attack came, my brother and I ran to the horse herd with ropes. These six and four others we captured and hid in the small caves up the canyon. The whites never saw them."

Mounting his stallion, Buffalo Horse squared his shoulders and raised his chin. He beamed at the man called Ge-hay-tie. "You've done well. We have horses for scouts and some to help with the loads. We'll survive."

Raising his hand the chief pointed south. "In time we'll make for Yellow House Canyon. There we should find enough food to live through the winter. Tonight we sleep above the western rim of this canyon. Perhaps we can take back our horses."

Tehat walked among the wailing women who sang songs of love for slain warriors. Little Deer mourned with the others:

My daughter, hear my song of death and desolation.
Hawk is dead. Brave Hawk is dead. He fell in the first attack.
He would not give ground. He stood against the insane wolves.
He fought and died for us.

Her voice rose,

Oh hear, Great Spirit.

Hawk's death rips the spirits from our bodies. Take him to yourself, we
ask.
Let him ride a swift horse in that green valley prepared for the beloved
brave, beyond the western ocean.

Tehat joined in her mother's mourning. First a low moan and then a tearful cry filled the air as she sang her song of death.

Buffalo Horse rode into the midst of the women. "We are saddened by the loss of our friends, but we cannot take time to mourn. While the women save what they can from this camp, we must go up above and prepare to defend ourselves. If the white men see we're an organized band, they'll hit us again."

Tehat and the other women hurried back into the camp and grabbed whatever could be saved from the flames. They picked up spilled food out of the dirt. They gathered partially burned blankets, buffalo robes, and clothes. The men caught five more horses that the soldiers had missed. The Two Mountain band spent the remainder of that day sorting and packing the meager goods they had saved. They spent the night on the west wall of the canyon. The next morning, they continued to salvage.

By midafternoon they were packed and ready to leave. Gunfire beyond the canyon rim halted their departure. Buffalo Horse deployed his small force to meet a charge, thankful he'd gotten his people to higher ground. When no attack came, the chief sent men to reconnoiter. A scout returned with a chilling report. "They're killing our horses!"

Buffalo Horse touched his forehead. "They kill our horses so we can't get them back. They intend to destroy us, but they haven't finished us yet. Follow me."

Before night had closed around them, the chief had spurred the band to move. Both Tehat and Little Deer bowed under loads more suitable for the backs of horses than those of women. Having no moccasins, Tehat and Tree Blooming stumbled along on bleeding feet. "Hawk is dead," she repeated over and over, weeping. Like the mountains, he'd existed before she was born. A father should go on forever. When Hawk had taken her in after Jessee was killed at Tahoka Lake, her love for her father had grown. Now he was dead and the Kiowas were a defeated people. Tehat could see no future for herself or the tribe. The white men had destroyed her world, turning it, like dry cedar in a roaring flame, to ashes.

Suddenly she stopped, startled to see Tsain-tai, the medicine man. His eyes were lit with satisfaction. "Tehat, daughter of Hawk, you appeared to me in a dream last night."

"What would you dream of me? I dreamed of noise, blood, fire and death."

"I, too, dreamed of defeat. Yet your face appeared to me."

Tehat wiped her wet eyes with the back of her hand. "Defeat I understand. Our world is gone forever."

Tsain-tai shook his head. "Not so. As I looked on your face, a voice came to me saying you would be grandmother to a great man. Your daughter will bear a son who will lead his people into the future."

Tehat's throat tightened. Like all Kiowas she knew a medicine man spoke for the Great Spirit with wisdom and power. She glanced at Tree Blooming. "What could my poor little daughter have to do with a leader of our people?"

Tsain-tai locked eyes with Tehat. "Woman, I give credit to the ordeal we have suffered that you should question my words. You know I have strong medicine. You and all the people have had many signs of my powers. Do not ignore what I say. Your daughter will bear a son who will lead this people into a new life. Remember!"

"Forgive me, Medicine Man. I know you speak the truth and I honor your words."

"The grandson you must expect will be born near a place of strong medicine. Stars will stream over the place of his birth. A child will direct you to him."

At twilight, Tehat caught sight of Buffalo Horse on his black stallion. He beckoned the band to follow him onto the Llano Estacado, a lonely, windswept sea of grass. These staked plains stretched to the horizon. The skyline was broken only by stems of Spanish Dagger rising like survey markers in an empty land. The vacant prairies reflected the bleak despair that Tehat felt as she staggered and sweated under her load. Bluestem and buffalo grass grabbed at her knees at every step. Her leg and back muscles burned and cramped. She was tempted to give up and lie down, but fear of showing weakness in front of the other women drove her on. ·

When the chief signaled a halt at a place where tules grew in a swale, Tehat set down her load with a sigh. Tsain-tai's words troubled her. Why her? Why hadn't he dreamed about one of the men, an uncle, a grandfather, or Chief Buffalo Horse? Then an answer crossed her mind. She had spent wakeful nights planning how she would take her revenge on the men who killed Jessee. She was the one who had begged the Great Spirit for a chance to retaliate against the white soldiers who deserved nothing but torture and death. Little Deer was sitting close by and Tehat touched her knee.

"The Great Spirit has heard me. He's sending a man to lead us. We'll kill all the white people or drive them from our home. Tsain-tai brought the message. The man will be my grandson."

When the march resumed, Tehat moved with a stronger step and a lighter heart. The load on her back wasn't so heavy. The child inside her didn't weigh her down as much. A promised one was coming and vengeance would be hers.

Buffalo Horse followed landmarks known to the Kiowas since the time they first pushed south onto these prairies. Subtle changes in the trackless realm guided him as he brought his people to the verge of Yellow House Canyon. The Two Mountain band had returned to the Double Mountain Fork of the Brazos River, a stream they knew well. Before turning west to begin the ill-fated trek to Palo Duro Canyon, they had watched Colonel Ranald S. MacKenzie and his troop of cavalry near this site.

The line of weary Kiowas angled down into a small canyon. Tufts of grass dotted its sloping banks and a rivulet wound along its bottom. Clinging to cattails at the water's edge, redwing blackbirds swayed in the wind. Several ducks and a blue heron flew up from the narrow stream. With their topknots bobbing, barred quail ran ahead of Buffalo Horse's black stallion at the front of the march. Rabbits scurried and prairie dogs chattered as the marchers entered their territory, passing buffalo dung and deer droppings. The Kiowas ended their retreat from Palo Duro Canyon alongside a pool by which humans had camped for 12,000 years.

Ever alert, Buffalo Horse sent scouts down the river. Now, he watched them return. Eager to talk, the warrior Broken Nose slid his horse to a stop beside Buffalo Horse's black stallion. "We rode east and south onto the prairie. Tonkawa scouts led Bad Hand and his horse-soldiers southwest."

"Bad Hand is here? He's on us again?"

"He was here, my chief, but he's going away."

"What happened? Where did he go?"

"The Tonks spotted us and gave chase. We took them for a run to the west. The troop came after us. After a while, when they didn't find the rest of you, they broke off. Now, Bad Hand leads them away from us."

"He's missed our hiding place. All is well."

That night Tehat took Tree Blooming to the fire that Little Deer had built. On sticks over the flames, they roasted venison, a gift from Buffalo Horse.

Later, Little Deer watched Tehat fashion a bed for Tree Blooming out of a scorched buffalo robe. When Tree Blooming was settled, Little Deer touched Tehat's hand.

"We must talk."

"I know what you are thinking, Mother. We are two women without husbands. We have no one to hunt for us."

"Yes. I have been thinking about that. You remember that my brother, Night Bird, and I have not spoken since I told him he was wrong to marry that Wichita woman."

"Yes, Mother. You spoke words you thought were true, and shamed your brother."

"Tonight I've sent a message to Night Bird asking him to come to my fire. If he comes, you must speak with him."

Tehat nodded. "What shall I say?"

"You must follow his lead."

In a short while Tehat heard footsteps and stood up. Recognizing Night Bird, she looked down at her hands. "There you are, Uncle."

He looked into the darkness over her head. "There you are, Tehat, my sister's daughter. Ask your mother if she wishes to speak with me."

Tehat slipped her hand into Little Deer's. "Your brother asks if you wish to speak to him."

"Ask my brother if he has anything he wishes to say to me."

"Tell your mother I am here because a Kiowa does not shame his sister. He should not leave her a woman alone."

Little Deer went to stand in front of Night Bird, and looked at the ground. "Has my brother come because he feels sorry for me?"

"You know our father taught me to help those who deserve my help because I respect them, not because I feel sorry for them."

"I hear your words, my brother. What would you say to me?"

"I want you and your daughter, Tehat, and her daughter, Tree Blooming, to come into my tepee."

"And, what does the Wichita woman who rode double with you in the war party say?"

"My wife, Corn Tassel, sent me to speak to you."

"I honor Corn Tassel as my sister. I thank you and her for your good hearts, and accept your invitation. My daughter will speak for herself."

Tehat stood beside her mother. "Thank you, Uncle. Tree Blooming and I will be honored to be in your tepee."

"That's all right then. I'll tell Corn Tassel to expect you to join us."

Little Deer raised her eyes toward her brother's fire.

"Never mind, my brother, we'll tell her."

Tehat and Little Deer went immediately to join Corn Tassel who greeted them with embraces.

Morning found the people in the camp busy, making the most they could out of the few things they'd saved. The women in Night Bird's protection thought they had enough buffalo hides to create one tepee. They knew it couldn't be the size of any of the three they had occupied before their defeat at Palo Duro. They took the poles out of the pile the horses had pulled and laid the tanned hides out to see what they could do. Tehat had only assisted at the making of a tepee, so she followed the lead of the more experienced women. Little Deer and Corn Tassel were in serious conversation when Night Bird rode up.

"We need to set up a tepee. I'll help."

The women looked at each other. Never before had a man suggested he should help raise a tepee. They wondered if he knew how. Night Bird slipped off his horse and went to the pile of poles.

"I'll use this one as the starting pole."

Corn Tassel took the pole out of his hands.

"Husband, we are now discussing what hides to use and how to arrange them. Please let us get on with woman's work."

Night Hawk swung onto his horse. "I see I am not wanted here."

Corn Tassel laid her fingers on his moccasin.

"Do not take offense, my husband. I know you want to help repair the damage the white soldiers did. Maybe there is something else you should do."

"What's that?"

"Tehat will soon have another child, yet she has no cradle for it. If you ride along the river, you might find some fallen branches to bring to us so we might make one."

Night Bird whirled is horse around and tore off to the river. Dismounting, he stomped along the stream grabbing up fallen tree branches suitable for making a cradle. When he had gathered what he wanted, he looked for a way to get the wood back to the tepee. He was not accustomed to walking when a horse was available, and he seldom carried anything in his arms. He was riding bareback so he could not tie the wood on the horse's back. Sliping his rawhide rope off his shoulder, he tied it around the sticks and dropped the bundle on the ground. With a flip of his hand he wrapped the other end of the rope around his wrist. Swinging onto his horse's back, he slammed his heels into its flanks. Bouncing along behind the racing horse the packet of tree limbs cavorted crazily. One bounce sent it flying around a tree trunk and the rope snapped.

Massaging the shoulder that the violent jerk on the rope had all but disjointed, Night Bird realized how ridiculous he must have appeared and laughed. But his mirth was laden with frustration. Coiling his tattered rope, he picked up the wood and headed toward his tepee, a grim determination settling on his face. He'd show those women they were not the only ones who could make a cradle.

When Night Bird asked for a sheet of rawhide and borrowed Corn Tassel's awl, she was taken aback. When he drew his knife and began dressing the tree limbs, she called Little Deer and Tehat. The women watched him tie four branches into a frame, then begin punching holes around the edge of the rawhide. Charmed, they raised their voices in approval. Other people at nearby tepees heard them and came to watch. Night Bird threaded a thong through a hole he had punched an began lacing the rawhide to the wooden frame. The women wondered at his efforts, but the men laughed at him, a man doing woman's work. Night Bird didn't take offense at their laughter. He laughed with them. In this time of misery and defeat it was good to have something to laugh about again.

Satisfied that he had done a creditable job constructing the cradle, he felt no further need to intrude in women's domain. Handing his rope to Tehat who sat outside the tepee, he asked her to replait it for him.

Little Deer hurried out of the tepee, and took the rope from Tehat's hands.

"She mustn't plait a rope while she's pregnant. She could cause the cord to wrap around her baby's neck and kill it."

Night Bird faltered. "It has been so long since Corn Tassel had babies . . . I forget these things."

"That's all right, Brother . . ."

Tree Blooming ran up. "I caught a frog down by the river."

Tehat squatted beside Tree Blooming.

"Be quiet, daughter, you must never break in when older people are talking."

"Yes, Mama, but . . ."

"Shush, Tree Blooming. You above all the children must learn to follow our ways without question. You must be fit to raise a son who will be a great leader of Kiowas."

In the days that followed, Tehat heard her mother and Corn Tassel making plans for her expected baby, but she took little interest. She'd taken Tsain-tai's words to heart, and was anxious to get on with the training of Tree Blooming.

On the night her baby chose to be born, Tehat was planning what she'd ask the medicine man, Tsain-tai, to teach her daughter. The onset of her labor pains were nothing more than a distraction to her busy mind. Little Deer and Corn Tassel saw that delivery was imminent and hurried to get ready for it. Corn Tassel spread out the buffalo robe.

Little Deer asked her brother to bring rabbit skins for the baby and water from the river, then set about building a fire.

Night Bird hurried to do as he was told, stopping along the way to retrieve the cradle, which he had insisted upon fashioning himself.

When Tehat's pains grew worse, Corn Tassel suggested that Night Bird leave the tepee.

Corn Tassel and Little Deer heated large chunks of solid caliche and put them in Tehat's lap and at her back. They gave her hot soup to help her inside. After a long while, Little Deer had Tehat kneel, then knelt behind her to catch the baby.

Afterward, they laid Tehat on a buffalo robe that had been saved from the fire. Corn Tassel took the afterbirth outside to bury it deep so the coyotes would not find it.

Tehat's face lay against the buffalo robe, the stench of its scorched hair filling her nostrils. She rolled over and stared up. The holes in the poorly fitted cover of the makeshift tepee let starlight through. She lowered her gaze and her eyes fell on the cradle that had been cobbled together by a man. She thought about all they had lost at Palo Duro, and wondered if life would ever be worth living again. Then she remembered Tsain-tai and Tree Blooming. She needed to get on with her daughter's training. Her grandson would put everything right.

Little Deer laid the newborn baby beside Tehat.

"The baby is a girl. What name will you give her?"

Tehat thought about all they had been through.

"I will call her She Who Comes in Grief."

Food was scarce in the canyon of the yellow houses. Without their best horses, the small band of Kiowas could not mount a buffalo drive. Sneak-hunting buffalo, antelope, and deer didn't supply the amount of meat needed by the band. They did their best to supplement their supply with small game and roots, but hunger stalked the Two Mountain Band that cold season.

Tehat would have gladly gone hungry so Tree Blooming could eat, but Little Deer scolded, reminding Tehat that she was nursing a baby and must eat well herself.

Tehat argued. "Tree Blooming must grow strong. She is to bear a son who will avenge the deaths of my husband and father. He will lead his people into a new life. I want nothing to stand in the way of the revenge he will pour on the heads of the white men." One day, Tehat motioned for Tree Blooming to sit beside her.

"I have told you before that you are chosen to be the mother of a great leader. For that reason you above all others must always do what is right."

"I know our laws and taboos, Mother."

"Perhaps as much as any Kiowa child," her mother agreed.

"I never look straight at someone or interrupt grownups when they're talking."

"Yes. Those rules you have learned well. And you know simple taboos like never stepping over a baby or mentioning the name of someone who has died."

"I know, Mother. If you step over a baby, it will die. And we never say the names of our papas who are dead because they might have to come back."

Tree Blooming fidgeted, and Tehat put her arms around her.

"You are young, Tree Blooming but you know much. Still, there are other lessons you must learn. I have asked Tsain-tai to help with those."

In a few days the weather cleared, and Tehat looked out to see Tsain-tai in front of Night Bird's tepee. She peered out of the opening. "There you are, Medicine Man. Welcome to this tepee. What do you wish for from us?"

"You have asked me to help with your daughter's training. Send her out to me."

In a while Tehat and Tree Blooming stood in front of Tsain-tai. Carefully he inspected Tree Blooming.

"This child has been chosen. I intend that she should be an *ade*. Though that honor is usually reserved for the child of a chief, I'll put her forward to be given special consideration. Each day when the weather is good, I shall come for her, and teach her what the mother of a great leader should know. We'll begin now."

He turned and walked down the path toward the river. Tree Blooming hugged her mother, and followed him.

Tsain-tai stopped suddenly and Tree Blooming bumped into him. He laid his hand on her shoulder. "Shh."

Peering ahead, she could see nothing except tall grass and a plum thicket. While she was watching, the center of the plum thicket moved. Tsain-tai tightened his grip on her shoulder.

"It is one of the large animals we fear and honor."

"Which one?" Tree Blooming whispered in alarm.

"Hush, child. No one, not even a medicine man may speak its name unless he is speaking to someone who is named for it or is named for it himself. Its medicine is strong enough to kill any man who looks directly at it. Soon, it will break through the bushes. You must cast your eyes above its head, at the sky."

Tree Blooming could not imagine a beast so great that even Tsain-tai would fear its name. When this one reared onto its hind legs and walked into view like a man, she trembled. She quickly turned her eyes away, stepped back, and hid behind Tsain-tai. Both humans kept their eyes averted. The bear lumbered up river and out of sight.

Tsain-tai brought Tree Blooming up beside him. "You've been privileged to be in the presence of this animal. Rarely do we encounter one in the canyon of the yellow houses. Though they are of this world, we treat them with great respect. Only stupid men would kill and eat them."

Not all of the lessons were held out-of-doors. Sometimes Tsain-tai came to the tepee of Night Bird and taught Tree Blooming there. Some of his stories she knew already well, but listened nonetheless with the respect Tsain-tai was due. When he told how the creator brought the Kiowas out of a hollow log, she didn't even allow herself to smile at the part about the pregnant woman getting caught in the log, blocking the exit of any more Kiowas.

On another day they sat beside the river, and he talked to her about the Sun Dance. He used simple terms to tell about the ceremonial cutting of a tree for the center pole, the arrangements of the tepees around the Sun Dance Circle. He described the dances men do to gain power. Though Tree Blooming listened in earnest, it was more than she could absorb. When he finished, Tsain-tai took her chin in his hand and studied her face.

"Tell me child; what do you remember about the Sun Dance?"

Tree Blooming hesitated for only a moment. "When the center pole is being selected, the young men sit on their horses not looking around, but with their eyes down, quiet and respectful."

Tsain-tai rocked his body. "That is enough. If you remember that Kiowas respect the Sun Dance, I am pleased. I will repeat this lesson. Later I will teach you about the Ten Grandmother bundles, which contain the most powerful medicine known to the Kiowas."

Throughout the long days and nights of hunger and deprivation, Tree Blooming's lessons went on.

One morning in early spring, a cold wind blew down the canyon and Buffalo Horse called the men together. Standing in front of a meager buffalo-chip fire, the chief pulled his robe tighter. "We live in cold and starvation. We survive, but I cannot say for how long. The buffalo have gone away and we have no horses to follow. We can no longer feed ourselves or fight. The time has come when I must lead you onto the reservation."

The men jostled shoulders. One shook his head at the others. "We can't submit to the control of our enemies. They don't think of us as men," he said.

Night Owl nodded. "We'd rather die here on the Texas plains than be treated like animals."

Tehat and the other women listened to their words, grieving. In the end, though, Buffalo Horse prevailed and led his band to the Fort Sill Reservation.

Ordered to control the Plains Indians, the army of the United States had defeated the Kiowas, Comanches, and Apaches in battle. Now they held them prisoners on a reservation in the Wichita Mountains of the Oklahoma Territory. Soon Chief Buffalo Horse of the

Kiowas regretted his decision to take his people there. The worst fears of his men came true. Like cattle, the band was driven into a stone corral at Fort Sill. The men were not allowed to hunt or gather wood for fires, but had to exist on what little they got from the soldiers, who threw meat over the walls with pitchforks, as if they were feeding lions. Born free on the open plains, these people bore their imprisonment in abject misery. Living in closely packed and filthy conditions, many sickened and died.

After eighteen months they were allowed to leave the stockade but were guarded closely in camps they set up on the post grounds at Fort Sill. A full decade of humiliation and maltreatment passed before they were allowed to move onto the lands of the reservation around the fort.

On the reservation white people applied subtle pressure in an attempt to wipe out Kiowa culture. The United States Department of the Interior sent agents to take charge of the tribes. Christian missionaries and white school teachers were brought in. The agents encouraged the Kiowas to forget the freedom they had known as hunters and to take up farming. A few Kiowas moved into houses built by the government and tried gardening. Others, deploring sham mimicry of white culture, refused to change.

Tehat Hauvone was one of them. The memory of Tsain-tai's prophesy honed her determination to cling to the past. Untamed, she rejected life in a house and spent her days in a brush arbor beside her tent. She would not plow or garden. Refusing to enter a church, she grew angry when white missionaries tempted her children into school with food and praise, and then gave them new names. She never accepted *Maude,* the name they gave to her daughter She Who Comes in Grief. Yet when she was told that *Ruth,* the name the missionaries gave to Tree Blooming, means "I will go wherever you go," Tehat yielded to the truth in that and agreed to the change.

Ruth had already gone wherever her mother had gone, and had done whatever her mother wanted her to do. From the day Tsain-tai announced the awesome responsibility she would bear, the little girl had obeyed. Ruth had given up her childhood to sit at the knees of the elders who trained her. She had spent long hours committing the wisdom of the Kiowas to memory.

As Ruth matured into her childbearing years, Tehat continued to command her obedience. Tsain-tai's prophesy must be fulfilled. Ruth respected her mother, but she also walked the Jesus road. Accepting the stories told by the missionaries, Ruth had grown to adulthood with a foot in each world, the old and the new.

According to the calendar she saw at the school, the year was 1909 when Harry Grass asked Ruth to marry him. Wanting to come to the marriage in honesty, she put him off while she thought over his proposal. When he returned for an answer, she took his hand. "I have been chosen to be the mother of an uncommon son. The medicine man, Tsain-tai, had a vision and told my mother that my son will lead the Kiowas into a new life. I have been trained to raise a great leader."

"I don't believe that medicine-man stuff. And I don't believe in the Ghost Dance story or the peyote visions. I've not made my mind up about Jesus. But I trust you, Ruth, and I want you to be my wife. I'll never interfere with your preparations for our son."

Tsain-tai had prophesied that Tehat's grandson would be born near a place of strong medicine, a holy place of great spiritual power. Tehat was sure he referred to the Medicine Mounds, which Hawk had pointed out to her when she was a girl. He had told her that these natural formations were surrounded by strong medicine. At this sacred site, south of the Red River in Texas, bell-shaped hills rise out of the plains, looking as if they were fashioned by the hands of a giant.

Ruth became pregnant. When her time was near, Tehat determined to take her to the Medicine Mounds. She had learned that her cousin, Big Belly had gained permission to hunt antelope on the Texas plains and sought him out. "Nephew of my father, I want you to take my daughter Ruth and her husband, Harry Grass, and me to Texas. We must follow a promise made by the Great Spirit."

"I know about the prophesy Tsain-tai revealed to you. I will consider your need."

After he'd talked to the men who would be hunting antelope with him, Big Belly agreed to Tehat's request.

On the fourth night of their journey west, angry voices awakened Ruth, Harry, and Tehat. They stepped out of their tepees and found the antelope hunters gathered. Big Belly pointed up to the sky.

"Look, there!"

The trio saw a bright star overhead with a long tail sweeping across the sky. Their hands flew to their mouths.

"Medicine," Harry Grass said.

Big Belly fixed his eyes on Tehat. "Your strange errand has angered the spirit of the night. We allowed you to come with us because you said you were on a mission for the Great Spirit. But this light is a bad sign. We want you to go away."

Tehat recovered quickly. "Don't be alarmed. This light is not bad. It confirms the promise we follow. Many moons past, the medicine man, Tsain-tai, told me stars would stream over the birthplace of my grandson, who will be a great leader."

The hunters conferred, then accepted Tehat's word that the star was not bad. They returned to their tepees.

Ruth held open the tepee flap for Tehat. "I heard your words, Mama, but there is another explanation of the strange light. The white teachers have expected this streaking star. They call it a comet."

"Call it what they will, I believe it is a sign given to me when you were a little girl."

Night and day the star remained visible, a white tail streaming behind it, like mare's milk on a colt's muzzle. When Ruth gave birth to a son, the star was overhead. Tehat named him He Who Will Lead His People. Ruth called him Paul. When Ruth explained that Paul was a great leader of men in the Jesus stories, Tehat was satisfied.

Ruth held her baby close. "My Mother, the son we have waited for so long is here."

"Yes, Beloved Daughter, he has come. He has been born near a place of great medicine. The stars have streamed at his birth. The promise will be fulfilled."

"But there is another thing, Mama. Didn't Tsain-tai say a child would direct you to the one who would lead our people? I hold my son in my arms. No child has directed us to him."

"I've thought about this. When Tsain-tai first came to me, it was just after the battle at Palo Duro Canyon. All of the tribes were in confusion. He may have misunderstood some of the words of the Great Spirit—he'd told us before that his power was sometimes weak when he was among strangers."

That winter a flu epidemic swept through the community, taking the lives of Ruth and Harry Grass. Tehat took Paul and moved into the home of her son-in-law, Fred Gehaytie, and her daughter, She Who Came In Grief, known in the community as Maude.

Tehat cared for her grandson in all ways, raising him as her own. From his earliest childhood, she recited simple Kiowa legends and stories to him, preparing him to lead his people. Even after he began formal schooling at the Mount Scott community school, she continued instructing him in his Kiowa heritage. He would avenge the unspeakable wrongs done to her people in the past.

Paul was an excellent student, advancing in the community school as readily as he assimilated Kiowa customs. When Ralph Moraine, teacher at the community school, suggested that Paul should attend the Fort Sill Indian School, where better education was available, Tehat resisted. She made a special trip to the Mount Scott School. although she was not fluent in English, she knew enough to make herself understood. "Leave Paul alone, he must finish Kiowa teaching," she said to Moraine in his own language.

Ralph extolled the advantages of the Indian School until Paul was convinced he should continue his education there. He begged his grandmother to let him go. Tehat couldn't refuse a request of the promised one.

In his thirteenth year, 1923, Paul Grass transferred to the Fort Sill Indian School on the banks of Cache Creek east of Fort Sill. After he had been away for a few months, Tehat found that he no longer listened to her teachings. Although he had inherited the intelligence and physical ability of the Kiowas, he no longer took an interest in their history. He had discovered the white man's game called baseball. A natural athlete and excellent player, Paul spent every free moment on the baseball diamond.

By his fifteenth year Paul had little interest in returning home. His indifference notwithstanding, Tehat never gave up. On his rare visits home, she continued her efforts to shape him into a leader. Despite her advancing age, the Kiowa grandmother with a long memory was committed to carrying out the promise she had made forty-five years ago to the medicine man Tsain-tai.

On one of his visits home Paul became ill. Tehat and the Gehayties watched in agony as the teenage boy erupted with measle spots, the scourge of the Plains Indians. After seven days and nights of fever and choking, Paul died. Once again, Tehat's enemies had shredded her life. The white men who infested the land had stolen her beloved grandson, not once, but twice–first with a useless school-boy game and now with the disease they had brought with them.

In the front room of the house, Tehat sat on a red blanket laid over pillows on the floor. She rested her toothless face on her clasped hands and rocked her body. Tears streaked down her wrinkled face. "Tsain-tai's medicine was not strong. The promised one is dead. The Kiowas have lost their last hope. Paul will not lead his people into a new life."

Turning away from a boiling pot, Maude Gehaytie lowered her own reddened eyes to Tehat's. "Please, Mother, don't bring up the medicine man's prophecy again."

"I want my grandson buried on the Texas plains. He should lie at Medicine Mounds, where he was born under the streaming star."

Fred Gehaytie sat down in front of his mother-in-law. "We've told you, Mother, we can't take Paul's body to Texas. We can't wait for the permission paper required by the white man's law."

"I spit on the white man's law. Did my father die fighting the blue horse-soldiers in Palo Duro Canyon so we could live forever under the heels of the whites? If Hawk were alive he'd take Paul to meet the Great Spirit at home in Texas."

Fred took her wrinkled hand in his. "We know your father was brave. We are proud of the Kiowas who did battle with the horse soldiers. But this is 1925—we no longer do battle with whites. We must bury my nephew's body here in the Wichita Mountains."

Tehat left the government-built house she despised and returned to the brush-covered arbor in the yard. There, she spent the night alone.

In the cool gray morning of the following day she sat in the dirt beside a small fire. Warming her hands, she ignored the preparations going on around her. Neighbors built a long box out of pine planks left over when the house was built. Family members and friends spoke to Tehat, but she was deaf to their voices. When the Gehaytie children, Tonepah and Marie, ran into the yard and argued about who would wear a red sash to the funeral, she paid no attention. Men carried the rude coffin out of the house and placed it in the bed of a Studebaker farm wagon. Tehat looked away.

When Maude and Fred walked toward her, she faced them with hardened eyes.

"I won't change my mind. I will not go with you to bury my grandson. He should meet the Great Spirit on the plains at Medicine Mounds."

The Gehayties took their place directly behind the funeral wagon. Once more Maude beckoned to her mother, "Please, Mama, go with us."

Tehat gazed steadily at the one she had carried inside her on the day Hawk died. "The name I gave you is true. You are surely She Who Comes In Grief." She waved her hand, dismissing the mourners, and the cortege left the yard.

In a while the fire went out. Tehat pressed the end of her ash walking stick into the ground and helped herself up. She could see the funeral procession in the distance, winding its way to the cemetery. As she thought of the wagon's burden, her chest filled with sorrow until she thought it would burst. She tilted her head to the sky.

Oh hear me, Great Spirit. I cry from a broken heart, a heart shattered
on the rocks of this terrible life.
Hear me now, as I mourn the loss of my beloved grandson.
Hear me as I give up all hope for my people. We're doomed.
Without the promised one, we must disappear from the earth.

Tehat slowly began to walk the route of the funeral procession. Anger crowded in on her sorrow. Her voice dropped lower.

What cruel thing is this you've done?
Didn't Tsain-tai, your spokesman, say my daughter would bear a leader
of his people?
You've broken that promise. Death has taken him.
No more than a boy, Paul had no chance to become a leader.
I'm sorry I ever listened to Tsain-tai.

She crossed over a creek beyond a turn in the lane. Running water under the bridge magnified the sound of her death song, and the banks of the stream deflected it upward. The road to the burial grounds led up a hill past the home of the Byers, a white family. When she spotted children in the yard of the house, Tehat stopped singing. A boy and two girls stood near the road watching the funeral procession pass, Tehat bringing up the rear. The youngest, a four-year-old girl with red hair and sparkling blue eyes, felt sorry for the old grandmother. She wanted to say something kind. "Paul's dead," the small voice said simply when Tehat drew near. Uttered in innocence, the words washed over Tehat like scalding water. She sang in a high-pitched scream,

Oh hear, Great Spirit. Even this child, the daughter of my enemies,
   mocks your failed promise.
She tells the world that Paul is dead.
She could as easily say, the Kiowas are dead.
Without the promised one, we are truly lost.

The white boy and the older girl scurried away. The little redhead stood her ground. Tehat looked at her and fell silent. "You still have Tonepah," the girl said. "Your grandson, Tonepah is alive."
Raising her face to the sky, Tehat sang again.

Now this child ridicules my loss and offers another in Paul's place.
She names my grandson to fill the emptiness left when my grandson
   died.

Suddenly, stunned by the words of her own song, Tehat stiffened. This child had directed her to her grandson, Tonepah. She remembered Tsain-tai's words, "A child will direct you to him." And a wave of understanding washed over her.

Tehat dropped to the ground, felled by the thought that she had been wrong for a lifetime. In shock, she groped to understand the rest of the prophecy. "He'll be born near a place of great medicine." Tonepah had been born at Fort Sill near Medicine Bluff, a place of great medicine. "Stars will stream over the place of his birth." On the day Tonepah was born, the flag she detested, the flag of her enemies, with its stars on a blue field, had streamed over Fort Sill. Tehat sat up, brushing red clay from her hands.

Oh Great Spirit receive my grandson, Paul.
Take him to the green valley beyond the western ocean.
I see he was not the one you sent to lead the people.
Do not turn your face away from Tehat, who thought you broke a
*   promise.*
Forgive the foolish daughter of a brave warrior.
Forgive the mother of Ruth and She Who Comes in Grief.
Forgive the confused grandmother of two grandsons.

Tehat bowed her head and became silent.

Look now upon my grandson Tonepah.

Born to a defeated people, raised in the stronghold of our enemies,
*   educated in the white man's schools. You never intended him to lead*
*   the Kiowas in the old ways.*

Oh, Great Spirit, you see what I ignored.
My grandson is only a boy, but his mind is quick.
He learns easily the white teachers' lessons.
I beg you to help him use his wits
along the rocky path of white men's lies.
Guide him around the pitfalls of their cruel greed.
Be with Tonepah in all ways, I beg of you,
while he prepares to lead the Kiowas into a new life
* in the land of my enemies.*

Tauk-see and Carmen Cavarubio

Losantos Cavarubio, a square-shouldered man of fifty, opened a large leather-bound ledger on his desk. His hand shook as he dipped the pen into the inkwell and entered the date, 19 August 1900. Each day since he and his family had moved from Mexico City to northern Mexico, he had carefully performed this ritual. For nine years he had kept close account of the operation of Santa Rosa del Norte, his ranch on the plateau east of the Conchos River. His hand trembled, for this might be the day he lost everything.

The danger hadn't come from mismanagement. Losantos had fulfilled his promise. Personally watching over the herds, he worked hard to oversee the land, cattle, and horses his wife's brothers had loaned him the money to buy. He had made the most out of the semiarid grasslands. His recordkeeping had been meticulous. The problem arose from something else. Losantos was addicted to gambling. Although he consistently lost, he was sure it wasn't his fault. The answer was simple. Luck had turned its back on him.

Losantos wiped his brow. The moisture on it wasn't caused only by August heat. As he tried to blot out the fact that he had promised to pay his gambling debts on this day, he forced himself to continue working on the log.

When he heard a rider on the road, he didn't go to the window. The maid answered a knock on the door, and he still paid no attention. When she stopped in his doorway, he looked up. "Yes, Dora?"

"A letter has been left."

Losantos opened the envelope and unfolded a thick, richly embossed sheet of paper with an impressive letterhead:

Victorio Manuel Luz Bocanegra
Hacienda Serpentigero
Valle del Conchos
Chihuahua, Mexico

He grunted and touched the gold lettering. "Show-off swine."

The salutation was minimal. The note was terse. Losantos had expected it. For years this man had beaten him at cards. Now he was coming to collect. The note ended with a perplexing sentence: "Have your family present when I arrive."

Uneasily, Losantos plowed his fingers through the wavy grey hair at his temples. "My family? Why would he want my family present?"

Victorio Manuel Luz Bocanegra, *hacendado* of the valley of the Conchos River, rode at the head of twenty armed men. He sat deep in his shiny black saddle. Silver spurs gripped his knee-high black boots, their large rowels flicking the sides of his dun-colored stallion. He rode with relaxed grace; his well-muscled back balanced his powerful shoulders. The morning sun glittered on a silver-stitched serpentine design on the brim of his black hat. Though he still cut a youthful figure, his mottled hands and swollen knuckles, as well as the puffy bags under his eyes and the blue veins on his nose, hinted that he was much older. The cruel curl on his lips had nothing to do with age. It had been present long before the drooping mustache that framed it had turned grey. The patron of Serpentigero was riding to call on a neighbor.

Losantos Cavarubio heard the horses. He shaded his eyes and watched the group of riders stream onto his hacienda. The crowns of their large hats barely cleared the sign above the gate.

Losantos went to the front veranda and called his family to come receive the visitor. His wife, Pajita, was a small woman. Her black eyes were darker than her husband's, reflecting her Indian heritage. Alberto, their eldest son, stood with folded arms and showed no interest in the approaching horsemen. His grey eyes and light skin recalled his father's grandfather, who was Spanish. Manuel, his younger brother, was dark like their mother and full of mischief. He watched the thundering herd wheel toward the house and grinned. He wished he were the leader of such a troop. The oldest daughter, Carmen, was not as tall as her mother. Her black hair was drawn back in a chignon at the nape of her neck. Her well-shaped nose and upturned chin gave promise of beauty to come. Her dark blue eyes, shadowed and mysterious, focused beyond the men on the road. The middle sister, Anita, wore her reddish brown hair in twin braids that touched her shoulders. Giggling, she shoved Alberto, trying to disturb his composed imitation of their father. Rosa, the youngest, knelt and poked at bugs, which rolled into a ball at her touch. Her mother lifted her up, brushed her knees, straightened her skirt, and told her to stand still.

The mounted men executed a military maneuver and spread out across the yard. Their commander was a tall, stony-faced man who rode to the right side of Luz Bocanegra. A barefoot servant boy ran to hold the reins on his horse as Señor Bocanegra swung to the ground and returned Losantos's handshake with careless disregard. Ignoring the family, he mounted the stairs as if he owned them.

The Cavarubios followed him into their living room. Dropping into the most comfortable chair he accepted a glass of red wine and eyed those seated around him. After a sip, he lowered the glass to the arm of the chair. "Your note is due, Cavarubio."

"Señor, this is no place to talk business. Let us drink wine. We'll discuss money when my family has been sent away."

"You have no money to discuss. I want your family here because I've something to say that touches on one of them."

"What are you saying?"

Bocanegra's mouth thinned as he leaned forward in his chair. "I'll let you keep your ranch when I'm married to your daughter Carmen."

Stunned, Losantos fell back. The room exploded around him. Pajita stifled a scream. Manuel leaped to his feet and ran toward the seated man, fists doubled. Alberto grabbed his brother's arm and wheeled on Bocanegra. "My sister is sixteen years old. Do you think we'd let her marry an ancient he-goat like you?"

Luz raised a warning finger. "Have a care Little Hot Blood. There are twenty armed men at your door."

Losantos regained his senses and jumped in front of his sons. "Don't strike him!"

Pajita touched her husband's arm. "Of what does this man talk? He speaks as if he owns you."

Luz Bocanegra gave a short, sarcastic laugh. "You haven't told your family, Cavarubio? They don't know you've been using my money to keep this ranch going?"

Pajita faced Luz Bocanegra, hands on her hips. "Why would my husband use your money? We don't need your money. My brothers in Mexico City have financed this ranch."

"Señora," Luz said almost tenderly. "Your husband has gambled away their money and this ranch to me."

When his family looked at Losantos for a denial, he stared at the floor. "Señor Bocanegra tells the truth. I've lost to him time after time as we've gambled over the years. He holds the paper for this ranch and all the cattle on it."

Alberto and Manuel sank back in their chairs while Pajita leaned against the wall, her face slack. Carmen squeezed the wooden arms of her chair until her knuckles whitened.

Losantos walked to the window, pulling a handkerchief from his pocket. After several long seconds he turned around and said, "This has been a lesson to me. I intend to do better in the future. However, I must accept Señor Bocanegra's generous offer."

When Anita saw tears streaming onto her mother's cheeks, she sobbed. Frightened by the angry voices and the crying of her mother and sister, Rosa joined them, wailing loudly. Pajita picked her up, cuddled her against her shoulder, and turned on Losantos. "May the Virgin protect us! You speak of this man marrying Carmen? Our daughter is but a child."

"Carmen is not a child. For the past year I've expected some boy to ask for her hand. I would have her marry where it allows us a new beginning."

"You don't have to do this, Losantos. My brothers will lend us more money."

"You are wrong, Pajita. I have already borrowed much more from your brothers than you know. The last time I went to them, they both swore they would lend me no more." Señor Bocanegra offers me an honorable solution."

Luz Bocanegra picked up his hat and stood. "I tire of this talk. What is your answer, Cavarubio? Do I get Carmen or do you return to Mexico City with your tail between your legs?"

"You may marry Carmen."

"A wise decision. The priest who serves my family will be at Serpentigero one month from today. Bring Carmen there at that time. The rest of you are invited to the wedding."

Luz Bocanegra left the room. The Cavarubios sat in silence listening to the horsemen assemble and ride away when their patron joined them.

Carmen walked toward the curved staircase in a daze. Too much had happened. Her father had lost the ranch and she was to marry this terrible man. Her mother caught up with her and put her arm around her waist. They mounted the stairs together. At the top, Carmen pulled away. "What are we to do, Mother? I'm sorry my father has gotten into this trouble, but I can't live with that brute."

"Your father has spoken. He expects you to obey. There"s only one thing we can do. We can pray. Speak to the Virgin, Carmen."

When the servant girl announced dinner, Carmen didn't go down. Later, when the family gathered in the parlor, she didn't join them. She stayed in her room, kneeling before a statue of the Virgin Mary. Hour after hour she prayed. She poured out her heart and begged the Blessed Virgin for help.

By the time she opened her eyes and glanced out the window, darkness had fallen. In the night sky a million points of light surrounded the north star. But suddenly the room filled with light. The statue above her blurred and the face of a beautiful young woman appeared in its place. A soft voice came to Carmen saying she did right to look north; her salvation would come from there. The exhausted girl struggled to her feet and lurched to the window, startled by the apparition and the words. As she stared north, she saw a fire. Its flames swept upward into the night. People sat around it.

Then the vision changed. The head of a man appeared. The face was dominated by a large, well-contoured nose set above lips that looked like they had been carved out of wood or shaped from potter's clay. The man's short black hair tapered onto copper-colored skin at his neck. He was an Indian, a red Indian. Carmen cried out and fell to the floor.

Her mother was bathing Carmen's face when she came to herself. "Come, my daughter. You must eat. You've gone without food and water. You are ill."

"I'm not ill, Mother. I'm happy. The Virgin showed me my salvation. One of those red Indians you used to tell us about is coming to save me."

"An Indian is coming to save you?"

"Yes, Mother."

"I can't believe it. Those men were savages. They came down in such hordes that we huddled in our houses for fear of our lives. They descended on us like wolves when the Comanche moon shone."

"You've told me the stories before, Mother. I know it was bad. But the Virgin has shown me the man who is coming to save me. I'm starved. Let me eat."

Beaten into submission in the Red River wars, the last of the Comanches that Pajita remembered were herded onto a reservation at Fort Sill in Oklahoma Territory in 1878. Confined on a small parcel of the vast territory they had once controlled, the former Lords of the Plains suffered a forlorn existence. Guarded constantly and supplied with food and fuel, they had too much idle time. The men gambled, argued, and drank whiskey, when they could get it. Those miserable conditions lasted for more than a decade.

By the late 1880s the government had loosened its grip on the Comanches. They were free to move about within the confines of the reservation. Schools were built and Christian missionaries were allowed to minister to them. The Comanches were more individualistic than the Kiowas and the Apaches, who also lived at Fort Sill. For example, they were slow to embrace a group religion.

When the Indian agents encouraged them to follow the ways of white men, some Comanches took up cattle ranching. Others tried farming. But planting corn and beans didn't appeal to "the Horse Indians," as some other tribes called the Comanches.

In the mid-1890s, when it became possible for the Comanches to sell the land they lived on, some sold their holdings and spent the money. Those were left destitute, reliant on government handouts to survive. Dependency and confinement left them crushed in spirit, without a source of pride or pleasure. One outlet was open to them—a tribal campfire. There they heard stories about better days. Almost every week at Fort Sill in the Wichita Mountains, a powwow fire was held.

On the warm August night that Carmen Cavarubio prayed to the Virgin Mary, a powwow was held on Cache Creek. Like a beacon, flames from a hardwood fire swept upward. The communal blaze called to the Comanches. Their tan faces glowed in its flaring light as it danced upon them. The odor of burning oak enveloped them in its strength. Beyond them, the Wichita Mountains, night-softened, raised undulant outlines into starry skies at their backs.

Tauk-see, son of Po-tauh-see, eased away from the fire. Of medium height, he moved gracefully. His hairless face had a large, curving nose and distinctly carved lips. His short black hair tapered onto his neck.

Slipping behind the figures at the fire, Tauk-see lay down on the nearby creek bank. He gazed into the night and listened to his father's voice. Hundreds of times in his eighteen years he'd heard Po-tauh-see speak at these tribal fires. Tonight the message was the same: The golden days of the Comanches are past, but once there was a time when the Comanches roamed free on the plains of Texas and called themselves the People. They fought anyone who crossed their paths. Whites, Apaches, Mexicans, and Tejanos—all were enemies, especially Tejanos. Only the Kiowas were friends.

Po-tauh-see began to speak of the raids in which he had ridden down the Comanche trail to Mexico. "We rode by the light of the Mexican moon. We weren't afraid. Our hearts were strong. It was good to ride through the cool fall nights, taking whatever we wanted from the great haciendas of Chihuahua. We stole horses, cattle, food, women, and children. Some of us here tonight were stolen in Mexico and honored by being allowed to become Comanche. Many of our horses had beautiful grandmas and grandpas in Mexico."

Beautiful horses in Mexico! That thrilled Tauk-see. Each time his father or one of the other men talked about horses in Mexico, his mind painted pictures of mountains and prairies where great herds of beautiful horses grew strong in green pastures. He wished he could go there.

The young Comanche's thoughts were suddenly shattered by a sound sharper than a clap of thunder. He felt a prompting, as if from a voice out of the darkness; a strangeness flowed into and around him. The tenor of his thoughts shifted. No longer was it simply a matter of wanting to go to Mexico. He had to go. Jerking to a sitting position, he looked around, searching for the source of the sound he had heard. Nothing had changed. The other Comanches were still at the fire. The creek still flowed, and the mountains loomed upward as before. But inside Tauk-see was different. The prompting he had felt reverberated like a command.

As other voices at the campfire replaced his father's, telling about Comanche bravery on the warpath, Tauk-see lay back and pondered how to carry out the order he had been given. Gradually, a plan came to him.

When he felt a movement at his side, he looked up and saw his cousin, Santoso. Their resemblance was remarkable. The obvious difference was the single braid of black hair at Santoso's neck. Santoso lowered himself onto the grassy bank and stretched out.

"Here you are, Tauk-see. I saw you leave the fire and guessed you'd come to the creek."

"Welcome to the stream of dreams, where great things are planned and all things are possible."

"Very poetic. What are you talking about?"

"You know how we've always wished we could go to Mexico? With me, it's no longer a wish. A short while ago something told me I have to go to Mexico"

"Something told you?"

"A voice, a sound, something in my head, I don't know what. All I know is I have to go to Mexico. I've come up with a plan that'll get me there."

"I'll go with you. What's the plan?"

"We'll ask your father to take us."

"My father? What makes you think my father would take us to Mexico? Why not your father? He often speaks of Mexico."

"I've talked to my father. He says those days are gone. Comanches don't ride the warpath any more."

"He's right. Comanches haven't raided Mexico for twenty-five years. Our fathers are brothers. Why would my father be any different from yours?"

"I've watched To-pek-chi at the campfires," Tauk-see said. He has good memories of Mexico and the beautiful horses. He'd like to go back. Why don't we find Tenny-sau and Wo-tank-ah and then ask your father to lead us all on a raid?"

As the campfire meeting broke up, their cousin Tenny-sau, son of Sau-pit-ki, felt strong arms lock around his neck. Lips pressed against his ear. "Let's go to Mexico," Tauk-see whispered.

Tenny-sau was smaller and younger than his cousin who had collared him. Pulling out of the headlock, he swung around. "Tauk-see, what are you talking about?"

Tauk-see and Santoso told Tenny-sau their plan. He was pleased and agreed to talk to To-pek-chi, his mother's brother. Then Tauk-see ran to ask his other cousin, Wo-tank-ah, the son of Cha-pit-ki, his father's brother, to go with them.

To-pek-chi walked ahead of his wife toward his tepee. A low hiss stopped him and his son confronted him. Three nephews crowded close behind.

"What is it, son?"

"Tauk-see wants to speak to you."

Tauk-see stepped forward. "We ask something, of you, Uncle. We've been cheated. We haven't stolen beautiful horses. Lead us on a raid in Mexico."

"Impossible. Comanches don't ride the warpath anymore. Those days are gone forever."

"So they say at the campfire. But you've thought different. You've wondered what it would be like to again ride the Comanche trail. You'd like to go to Mexico for horses and treasures. We offer you a raiding party. Take us there."

To-pek-chi looked at Tauk-see with narrowed eyes, surprised at the shrewd insight his brother's son had shown. "A raiding party? You four? You make me laugh. You and Santoso have eighteen summers. How many do Wo-tank-ah and Tenny-sau have, sixteen?"

Santoso thrust out his chin. "You were fifteen the first time you went on a raid. I've heard the story many times. You held the gate open while the others drove out the horses. I can do at eighteen what you did at fifteen."

"It's different. We grew up riding the trails. You boys have grown up on this reservation."

Wo-tank-ah raised his hand. "We've grown up carrying our bows, riding horses, running, and swimming in the streams. Why did you old ones teach us to run and ride and swim if you never meant us to use what you taught us?"

"It is natural to teach boys. We don't train warriors. What you ask is out of the question. Come in, Santoso. The rest of you go to your beds. We'll speak of this no more."

Tauk-see refused to be dismissed. "Uncle, I have for years listened to you and the other men speak of riding the trails to Mexico. Your words have created pictures for me—tall mountains, cool streams and green meadows, overrun with wonderful horses. My cousins and I long to go there. Won't you please take us?"

"I have spoken," To-pek-chi said. "I've nothing more to say." Tauk-see lowered his voice, "As a child, I dreamed of going to Mexico. Tonight, I find that I must go. I beg of you, please take us."

To-pek-chi turned to leave. "I don't know why you say you must go to Mexico, but I tell you this: I'll not take you there."

Tenny-sau stepped in front of To-pek-chi. "Is the brother of my mother no longer brave?"

To-pek-chi's face was hidden in shadows, yet the cousins knew he had changed. A swelling of his chest and a sudden rise in height told them he was angry. Before, he'd been a father and uncle sending youngsters on their way. Suddenly he was a Comanche warrior insulted. Santoso quickly recognized this new man. He'd seen him before. Placing his hand on his father's chest, he motioned Tennysau back.

"He's young, father. He doesn't mean the words he's spoken."

To-pek-chi's body shook. "Get him out of my sight. All of you, get out of my sight."

Santoso wasn't sure how long he'd been in bed when his father bent over him. "Bring your cousins to me tomorrow. Before the Mexican moon comes and goes, we'll test who is brave on the trail to Mexico."

Santoso didn't wait until morning. When his father went to his own bed, Santoso slipped on his clothes, raised the lower edge of the tepee, and rolled out. Many times in his life he'd escaped this way but never with this excitement and elation. Silently and confidently, he ran down a dirt road and turned to follow a footpath through an open field. His destination was a familiar one, Tauk-see's sleeping place in Po-tauh-see's tepee. He and his cousin had often sneaked out and joined forces on midnight forays—stealing watermelons from white people's gardens, racoon hunting with their dogs, or exploring the trails and back roads of the Fort Sill Reservation.

Bouncing two fingers on the tepee pole nearest Tauk-see's sleeping place, Santoso used the signal they had devised as boys. He tapped four times then paused, then tapped four more times—the sound of Comanche dancing. At that moment a hand closed on his shoulder. He leaped to his feet and whirled around. "Tauk-see! What's the heck?"

"I was on my way to see you when I heard someone on the trail. I followed you to see who was prowling around."

"You nearly got yourself hurt."

"I'm sorry. I've been worried about the trouble we had with your father. I've wondered if I should tell him about the voice I heard. What if he thinks it was just my imagination and still refuses to take us to Mexico."

"Rest easy, cousin. My father has told me to bring the rest of you to him tomorrow. We're going to Mexico."

The cousin-friends laughed and beat each other on the shoulders. After a while they ran off to bring the good news to Tenny-sau and Wo-tank-ah.

That early morning four eager Comanches talked on the banks of Cache Creek. Obviously relieved, Tenny-sau smiled. "I was sure I'd destroyed our chances of going to Mexico. I should never have said those words."

Tauk-see touched his shoulder. "Not so. I think something you don't know about gave you those words." Tauk-see shook his head. "I don't understand it myself, but I believe that you and my Uncle To-pek-chi have been chosen to get me to Mexico."

Wo-tank-ah chewed on some beef jerky he'd brought with him. "Wherever the words came from, they've done the trick. Our uncle's mind is changed."

Santoso shrugged. "His mind didn't need much changing. Tauk-see was right. My father will be glad to return to Mexico."

Their animated exchange went on until the eastern sky grew light. At dawn the Comanche braves parted, promising to meet again in a few hours.

When the young men gathered in front of To-pek-chi's tepee, they were quiet with expectation. To-pek-chi came out carrying a pipe made of bone and red clay. He sat beside the opening of the te-pee, filled the pipe, and lit it. As he smoked, he looked beyond the heads of the young men.

When the pipe was finished, he knocked the ashes out into his hand and scattered them in the breeze. "I've thought about what you say. Tauk-see sees clear when he says I think about better days and Mexico. It's come to me in the past that maybe I should leave this place and go back to our old ways. I'm sick of hanging around this army post like a whipped dog. I live surrounded by soldiers and a line drawn on a map. The white men's charity makes me feel less than a man. I want to use my strength and mind against nature and other men."

Nods of approval passed among his listeners. To-pek-chi sensed their rising enthusiasm and raised his hand. "I cannot hurry. Many years have come and gone since I led a raid, and I must find out if my war power is strong."

When To-pek-chi became silent and looked at the ground, Tauk-see got his courage up. "How will you do that, Uncle?"

To-pek-chi did not raise his eyes. "I must go back to the beginning, back to the place where power was given to me when I was young. I will take my blanket to Medicine Bluff."

Tauk-see ventured to speak again. "We know the old ones revere that place, but where does its power come from?"

To-pek-chi looked up and shook his head. "You young men don't know because you haven't been taught—a place gets strong medicine when the Great Spirit touches it."

The young men sat in silence, waiting as To-pek-chi filled his pipe again and lit it. "Many years ago a well-known medicine man was riding with some of his friends. They rode up a hill and came to the top of a two-hundred-foot cliff overlooking a creek. The medicine man wanted to go straight ahead, so he said some magic words and rode his horse off the cliff."

"Wasn't he crushed on the rocks?" Santoso interrupted.

"No, he floated over the creek to the other side. But when he saw that his friends were still at the top of the bluff, too afraid to follow him, the medicine man rode back across the creek. When he came to the cliff, the wall split open to make a pathway. He rode up the pass and brought his friends back down. To this day, it is called Medicine Man's Pass."

Tauk-see looked around at his cousins. "We've been there, remember?"

To-pek-chi said, "We will leave for Mexico after I am sure I have the power to lead you. I will go to Medicine Bluff alone. A man must think long and hard before he goes to seek power. Meet me here in the afternoon, five days from now."

At the appointed time the four cousins met with To-pek-chi. He smoked his pipe and then told the boys about his decision.

"At Medicine Bluff I went without food for four days. Then a vision came to me. Five beautiful horses ran past me to the south. Tauk-see rode the last horse. For some reason not known to me, the Great Spirit sends the rest of us to escort Tauk-see to Mexico."

Santoso grinned at Tauk-see. Sensing the boys' excitement about the adventure, he reminded them. "Our journey is serious. We are not going to Mexico to play games. We must make preparations, and I must speak to your parents, Nephews. When I tell them I know I have the power to lead you, I do not think they will refuse me. Come here tomorrow night and I will tell you what you are to bring with you."

The next day, To-pek-chi visited his nephews' families. When he explained how he had come to his decision, Sau-pit-ki and To-pek-chi's sister Mary quickly agreed to let Tenny-sau go on the raid. His brother-in-law Cha-pit-ki was also persuaded. But Po-tauh-see raised questions.

"What foolishness is this, Brother? Why should you let young men persuade you to act against your good judgment? Have you forgotten the horse-soldiers who drove us into this place. They have railroads and telegraphs now. You won't stand a chance."

"Have you forgotten that when a thing is wanted, the Great Spirit does not count the odds?"

Cha-pit-ki was silent for a moment. "And you believe the Great Spirit wants my son to go with you to Mexico?"

"My medicine tells me so."

Cha-pit-ki looked at the ground. Finally he nodded. "Tauk-see may go."

That night, Tauk-see, Wo-tank-ah, and Tenny-sau filed into To-pek-chi's tepee. Santoso was already seated beside his father, who was facing east. Once they were seated in a circle, To-pek-chi lit his pipe and drew a breath. Blowing the smoke in front of him, he handed the pipe to Santoso. "We will observe the rules of planning a raid, as we did in days gone by."

The pipe passed around the circle. Each one blew a puff of smoke to the east. When the pipe returned to To-pek-chi, he knocked out the ashes and set it on the floor beside him. "We must plan if we want to be successful. For our journey you should wear a leather shirt and pants. Leather will protect you. In the old days we wore breech clouts, instead of pants, but back then the skin on the inside of our thighs was hardened by constant riding. Bring at least ten pairs of moccasins. Bring two blankets. The nights can be cold in the mountains of Mexico."

To-pek-chi was pleased to see how carefully the young men listened to him. "Ask your mothers or your grandmothers to dry beef and make pemmican for you. They remember how, and will be pleased to show off the old ways. Speak to your father about horses to ride. Choose the best horses your family owns or can borrow. Fit them with good saddles and large saddle bags."

The talk went on into the night. To-pek-chi told the young men about the country they would ride through and what problems they might expect.

Two nights later they came together again. To-pek-chi checked to be sure they had all the equipment he had told them to bring. The young men showed him their knives, bows, arrows, plaited rawhide ropes, army-surplus canteens and blankets. Their saddlebags were filled with beef jerky and pemmican.

Then To-pek-chi had them inspect his own packing. He showed them the well-oiled Winchester rifle in his saddle scabbard. In his saddlebag he had ammunition for the rifle and wire cutters, to use on barbed wire fences they encountered. His pipe, tobacco, flint, and steel hung from his belt on a buckskin string.

"Why don't *we* carry rifles?" Tauk-see asked.

"We go to steal horses, not to kill men. You have all the weapons that braves in a horse-raiding party should have. My rifle is only for our protection."

With everything in readiness, the young warriors were eager to go. "When do we leave, Uncle?" Tauk-see asked.

"The moon was full last night. If we leave tomorrow night, it will grow into the Mexican moon when we reach the Rio Bravo del Norte, as the Mexicans call the river that white people call the Rio Grande. The day after that we'll be in the valley of the Conchos River."

Tauk-see beamed. "So we'll ride by the light of the Mexican moon?"

"Yes," To-pek-chi said, a faint smile creasing his face.

The cousins grinned at one another. From the powwows, they knew well the story of the Mexican moon. In the time of their great-grandfathers, the Comanches tried to raise horses. Later they found it was easier to steal them in Mexico. In time, they learned it was best to raid south of the Rio Bravo in the fall when the moon was full. Then the horses were well fed, the weather was good, and the bright light let them see what they were doing. To-pek-chi's generation named that full moon the Mexican moon. The Mexicans called it the Comanche moon because when it shone, they knew the Comanches were coming. White people called it the harvest moon. It was the harvest moon all right. It told the raiders when to harvest horses in Mexico.

Amused as they were, the cousins found To-pek-chi's next words sobering. "We leave for Mexico tomorrow night."

The moon was bright on the night of the getaway from Fort Sill. Its light bathed the peaks of the Wichita Mountains, flowing into the valleys and over foothills to the south. Tree-lined creeks wound toward Red River like dark ribbons. The prairie grass glowed white. In a clearing near the west line of the reservation, ten horses stood quietly. These were tough, well-bred animals, sometimes called Indian ponies by their owners and others who admired them. To-pek-chi gathered his raiding party.

"Our problem is to pass through the horse-soldiers who patrol the reservation. They guard close since Geronimo and his Apaches came here six summers ago. The whites are afraid he'll lead his people back to the land of their forefathers in Arizona." He lowered his head and took a deep breath. "You must do as I do. Follow in a single line. Separate yourselves by the length of ten horses. Seek the shadows. If you think you've been seen, stop. Make the soldiers believe you are a bush. Moving shadows attract attention."

He raised the reins on his horse and turned its head west. On silent, unshod feet the horses carried the night riders toward the edge of the reservation.

Tauk-see rode third behind To-pek-chi and Wo-tank-ah. His heart pounded. He wanted to shout. He was on his way to Mexico where he had always wanted to go, where he had to go. He didn't make noise. Whenever they crossed an open space, he held his breath. Suddenly those ahead of him stopped. Riders were coming from the north. His chin fell. The great journey was over before it began. When the horsemen stopped To-pek-chi, his followers held still as they had been told. In a moment To-pek-chi beckoned to them to come forward.

Tauk-see's spirits soared. It was his father riding with Sau-pit-ki and Cha-pit-ki.

Po-tauh-see looked at the young Comanches with pride. "We thought you warriors might need help to get through the soldiers. We've come to ride a diversion."

To-pek-chi tightened the reins on his bridle. "You're thoughtful, brother. Your presence here, along with my friends, reminds me of the old days when we looked out for one another. I wish we could return to our past and ride the trails together."

"Those days are gone for me," Po-tauh-see replied, "but you've made your choice. Companions are willing to go with you. I'm sure you'll return with beautiful horses. I know your son and ours won't shame us."

"Ride on," Sau-pit-ki said. "If the soldiers come, you stop and let us have them. We'll take them all the way to Saddle Mountain."

To-pek-chi and his nephews continued their ride west. Po-tauh-see, Sau-pit-ki and Cha-pit-ki fell in behind. As they filed between the high banks of a dry stream, they spotted two soldiers mounted on long-legged thoroughbred-type horses riding from the east. To-pek-chi and his party moved quickly into the shadow of a high bank and stopped. Po-tauh-see, Sau-pit-ki, and Cha-pit-ki urged their horses into a hard run. They flashed by their hidden companions and followed the creek bed north. The cavalrymen charged after them. Once they were gone, To-pek-chi led his band up through a cut in the bank.

As Tauk-see came out on top he looked north. He saw five horsemen heading at breakneck speed toward Saddle Mountain. The horses of the two in pursuit wore army saddles.

Tauk-see leaned forward and urged his horse to go faster. "Thank you, my father," he murmured.

To-pek-chi rode ahead of his runaways. He had to ride cautiously to watch for fences. At the first fence he slipped off his horse and used his wire cutters. He intended to cut wires all the way to Mexico. The gaps he would leave might play havoc with the white men's cattle herds in the pastures they crossed. "That's what they get for building fences between Comanches and the places they want to go," he thought to himself. When they were well away from the reservation, To-pek-chi slowed and signaled the others to join him.

"We have a good beginning, thanks to wise friends who rode at risk for us. See that you remember what they did. We'll need each other that way before we see the Wichita Mountains again." They rode on in silence. Rolling hills gave way to flat prairie thickly covered with short-stemmed grass. Before daylight, To-pek-chi led them into trees along a narrow stream and dismounted. "No fire. If the soldiers saw us when they passed last night, others will be sent after us. We won't send them a smoke signal."

They chewed beef jerky, drank water out of the stream, and let the horses graze under the trees. They watched their back trail and studied the horizon. To the north, peaks rose out of the prairie like sentinels. In pink grandeur they guarded the western reaches of the Wichita Mountains. No soldiers came.

At dark, To-pek-chi led the young men south by the light of a half moon. In a while, the short-grass prairie yielded to a land of washed gullies. Dawn found them on the banks of a wide, eroded riverbed. The river was a narrow rivulet that knifed through a puddled expanse of red sand. "Red River. We'll cross over and hole up in those brushy trees on the other side."

To-pek-chi led them through a gap in the bank and stopped when he was in the stream. "Watch your step near those puddles. This old river can be treacherous."

The Comanches rode five abreast as they picked their way around puddles of water. Tauk-see rode on the outside downriver from the rest. He came to a stretch of red sand coated over with white sediment. When his blue roan suddenly stopped and drew back his front feet, Tauk-see did what he would have done on Cache Creek. He slapped his horse on the shoulder with his reins. The horse refused to move. Tauk-see repeated the slap, harder. The roan leaped forward. His feet broke through the white crust and he sank to his belly in the soft sand. Tauk-see jumped off his back.

"Quicksand!"

To-pek-chi was the first to reach them. He stopped his pinto well back from the treacherous quagmire. As the blue roan threshed its legs, Tauk-see also struggled to free himself.

To-pek-chi took down his rope and threw one end to Tauk-see. "Stand still and catch this! Quiet your horse."

Tauk-see caught the rope and laid his other hand on his horse's neck. The two of them grew quiet and slowed their descent into sure death.

To-pek-chi threw up a hand to keep back the others who were now approaching. "Stay there! Don't ride into it. Santoso, take Tenny-sau and cut branches of the salt cedar trees on the bank. We need many armloads. Wo-tank-ah, throw your rope to Tauk-see."

Wo-tank-ah obeyed. To-pek-chi saw that Tauk-see had both ropes. "Tie one to the girth and the other one to the saddle horn."

Tauk-see quickly did as he was told. When both ropes were secure, To-pek-chi tied his rope to his saddle horn and Wo-tank-ah did the same. To-pek-chi backed his horse away until the rope was taut. Tauk-see's roan was fighting again. "Wo-tank-ah, go down the stream and tighten your rope."

To-pek-chi's pinto set his legs and would not budge. Wo-tank-ah's black faced way from the trapped roan and refused to give ground. With two ropes on well-trained horses holding them, Tauk-see and his horse were safe, for the moment.

Santoso and Tenny-sau returned, their arms loaded with branches. Santoso realized what his father intended and carried his bundle toward the foundered man and horse. His legs disappeared to his knees and he pitched forward. "Get the branches under you," his father yelled. "Spread them out."

Santoso stuffed branches under his body until he had a secure platform. He lay on it and handed others to his trapped cousin. Between them, they created a carpet of branches. Tauk-see leaned his upper body onto it. Tenny-sau came back with more branches, and Santoso and Tauk-see piled them in front of the horse. He found support on the branches and slowly moved his weight onto them. To-pek-chi and Wo-tank-ah forced their horses back. Tenny-sau and Santoso added their strength to the ropes. Working together, Comanche men and Comanche horses dragged their stranded companions to safety.

A weary band of braves lay on the south bank of Red River. When their strength returned, they chewed jerky and drank water. To-pek-chi rose to face his men. "I told you we would need each other. We didn't get far before we proved it."

Tauk-see stood beside his uncle, his head bent. "I did a stupid thing. I drove my pony where he didn't want to go. Thank you all for saving our lives."

Tenny-sau rolled over, sat up, and looked at To-pek-chi. "You told us the Great Spirit chose us to get Tauk-see to Mexico. I didn't know the work was going to be so hard."

The young braves' leader let them rest. When they recovered, he had them check their gear and saddle their horses. "Let's move out. Our next stop is southwest of here." By the time they reached their destination, evening was fading into night. Ahead, domelike formations rose out of the plains. Not tall enough to be mountains, they were hills washed and windblown into the shape of bells.

"Comanches have long known these mounds as a place of strong medicine," To-pek-chi said. "We'll seek their protection this night." Tauk-see looked closely at the red mounds. To him they resembled pottery made by the hands of a giant and turned upside down to dry on the plains. Brown plants grew on their almost vertical sides, etching patterns into their red soil.

The Comanches passed a safe night at the mounds. The next day, To-pek-chi stayed with his southwesterly route. By late afternoon, they had come to a narrow stream. He studied the landscape around it. "This is the Wichita River," he announced. "If we followed it east, we would come to a place where there used to be falls."

"Did the Wichitas live in this part of the country?" Tenny-sau asked.

To-pek-chi shook his head. "The Wichita tribe lived east of the Wichita Mountains. The Comanches drove them out and took over their land."

"Was it a hard fight? Did you kill anyone?"

To-pek-chi bristled. "I'm not that old. That battle took place before my time, back when they called us Paducahs."

"Paducahs?" Tenny-sau echoed.

"To some of the tribes it means 'Those who wish to fight us all the time.'"

The descendants of the Paducahs bedded on the Wichita. A quarter moon shone in the west when To-pek-chi roused his young companions. "Come, let's ride. You'll like what we see today."

Their route took a westerly swing. The weather turned hot as the land crumbled into gullies, arroyos, and broken bits of prairie. His followers asked To-pek-chi several times what they would see. He put them off. They were tired and sweaty when he urged his horse into a gallop. "We're getting close now," he announced.

For a short distance the band rode through evergreen trees and rough ground and then emerged at a wide, sandy riverbed. Before they could see it, they heard the sound of running water. A spring gushed out in a stream at their horses' feet. Beginning its descent down the sloping bank, the water skipped from rock to rock, spread out on a lower shelf, and then dropped out of sight over a falls. To-pek-chi looked pensive. "I remember the noise of these falls. We called them the Roaring Falls. They may not roar, but they make a beautiful sound."

To-pek-chi led his men down the bank through juniper trees and worked his way around until they stood beside a deep basin below the falls. Five dirty, trail-weary Comanches stripped the saddles off their horses and the clothes off themselves. They dashed into the icy water and shivered in ecstasy under the falls. They splashed and wrestled and ducked each other in the pool washed out at the base of the cliff. Boisterous boys took the place of Comanche braves.

After sleeping by the falls, they awoke refreshed and ready to ride. Before dawn, they trailed southwest into grass-covered hills east of the great south plains known as the Llano Estacado.

The first rays of the sun lit the Caprock of the high escarpment that faced them. Inching down like a slowly falling curtain, the light turned the shadowed cliffs into a golden wall. The Comanches galloped toward it. That night they camped by a river whose water was so salty they couldn't drink it.

The next morning they rode further west toward the cliffs. Two mountains arched above the plains south of their path. They skirted north of a white community. Beyond the village, near the base of the escarpment, they came upon a road. Wagon ruts showed that it had recently been used. To-pek-chi dismounted and squatted, his eyes tracing the tracks up the rise. "I've heard that towns have been built on the Llano Estacado. I believe this road leads to one of them."

Tauk-see rode his horse up beside his uncle. "Do we go up?"

"No. We'll stay below the plains tonight. Tomorrow we'll mount to the Llano."

All that morning the Comanches picked their way through a maze of deep trenches, huge claw marks left in the red soil by floodwater rampaging down from the plains. Early that afternoon, To-pek-chi signaled his men to dismount and led them up a rugged incline to the flatland above.

Another less strenuous ride brought them within sight of a lake that sparkled like a blue diamond against a snow-white cliff. To-pek-chi left Wo-tank-ah and Tenny-sau with the horses and led Tauk-see and Santoso to the lake on foot. "This is Tahoka Lake— Freshwater Lake. We used to share it with the Kiowas. Antelope drink here. We'll take one for food."

The leader assigned his men strategic hiding places on each side of the lake. "My rifle might attract white people, so one of you must kill it. I'll make it easier for you if we sight any coming to water."

"How will you make it easier?" Tauk-see asked.

"Remain quiet and watch."

Shortly after the sun disappeared behind him, Tauk-see spotted five antelope on the slope west of the lake. The animals were wary. They sniffed the air and studied the water as they advanced slowly toward the hidden braves. Suddenly, they flicked their ears and turned to look at something on Tauk-see's left. He slowly turned his head to see what had caught their attention. It was To-pek-chi's rifle raised above the brush beyond the lake. Two eagle feathers tied to the barrel fluttered in the wind. The antelope, four does and a buck, stared at the strange sight for a time then began to walk toward it. These curious animals had to find out what was bouncing in the wind. The path to the attractive feathers led between two waiting Comanches.

Tauk-see nocked an arrow and lifted his bow. As he drew the bowstring to his cheek, pleasure coursed through him. He'd often shot at small game and birds, but that was play. This was real. Food for the band was needed. He pointed his arrow to where the advancing antelope would cross in front of him. When they paused to eye To-pek-chi's decorated gun, Tauk-see chose a doe and released the arrow. She dropped to her knees, but was still alive. Tauk-see leaped forward, drawing his knife. Santoso beat him to her and cut her throat.

"She was alive when I touched her. I killed the antelope," Santoso exclaimed.

"That's true, cousin. Yet both of us will have a tale to tell at the campfire."

To-pek-chi joined them. "You did well, Tauk-see."

"It was you who did well, Uncle. You know these animals."

"I'm glad you got the doe and not the male. His meat would be tough. Gut her and skin her. I'll bring up the others. We'll have roasted antelope tonight."

Later, as he chewed strips of antelope meat, Tauk-see thought about the yeast-rising bread the white women at Fort Sill had taught his mother to make. A big chunk of it would taste good right now. He also thought the meat needed a little salt. But this was the Comanche trail. Hardships must be endured.

After they ate, the companions sat on the grassy shore and watched a crescent moon rise. To-pek-chi shifted to face Tauk-see and said, "I feel that there is something you have not told me, Nephew."

"That is true, Uncle. I ask your forgiveness for not being honest with you."

"What do you wish to say to me?"

"At the last campfire on Cache Creek I daydreamed of Mexico, as I've done all my life. Then a sound almost like a voice came to me out of the night and demanded that I go to Mexico. What could it mean?"

"The Great Spirit picks its own time and place to talk to a man. You've probably been chosen to do something special in Mexico. Yes, you should have told me. What if Tenny-sau hadn't spoken out and I had gone against the wishes of the Great Spirit?"

"I don't believe you would do that, Uncle. Remember it was your own medicine that told you that you and my cousins have been chosen to get me to Mexico."

His uncle rose to his feet. "I've told you they're building towns on these plains. White people are taking the Llano Estacado. We must be careful. We'll ride at night. Mount up."

Sunrise found them still moving south over empty plains. To-pek-chi found a swale where the ground was moist. They spent the day beside it. That night they moved south again. Trail-hardened, they rode all night and well into the next day. Around noon, another line of cliffs appeared in the distance. The land ahead of them sloped into a wide valley. To-pek-chi shaded his eyes and studied several columns of smoke on the eastern horizon.

"They've built a town beside a big spring in that valley. I want to water there. We'll turn west and ride away, then after dark we'll circle back."

To-pek-chi led his raiding party in a wide half-circle west of the white settlement. At dark he brought them back over the plains to a clump of scrubby trees not far above the town. A big spring poured out into a pool at the base of the ledge where they stood. They removed the horses' saddles and let them drink. Piano music and singing voices floated over the chalky flats from the town. Kerosene lamps shone through neatly curtained windows.

The young men drank too. Then they followed To-pek-chi's example and filled their canteens. He'd explained to them that a full canteen was important on the Comanche trail. You never knew when you might have to mount fast and ride for a long time.

The renegades camped without a fire and ate cold antelope meat. To-pek-chi assigned a rotating guard to keep watch on the town.

Toward dawn, Tauk-see took his turn on the ledge. He felt the wonder of watching a town as it slept. What would the white people down there think if they knew five Comanches were hidden within a rifle shot of their homes? Would they believe the Comanches were only passing through and meant them no harm? He knew there was no question about what the white people would have thought twenty-five years earlier when his father and uncles rode the Comanche trail.

Even though they intended no harm, there were good reasons for the Comanches to be watchful. If they were caught, they'd be returned to Fort Sill, shamed and defeated. Determined to keep that from happening, Tauk-see watched and listened carefully. A night bird called mournfully. Frogs plopped into the pool. Out on the prairie, a coyote hailed the morning. Suddenly, the hair stood up on Tauk-see's neck. Something was going on behind him. Slowly he turned to face west. Two lights were bobbing through the mesquite flats they'd crossed the evening before. As they came closer, Tauk-see realized they were lanterns carried by men on horseback coming toward the spring. Tauk-see was angry with himself. He ran to

To-pek-chi's sleeping spot and touched his uncle's shoulder. "Men are coming."

"How many? From where?"

"Two. From the west. They may be following our trail."

To-pek-chi picked up the Winchester rifle and followed Tauk-see until he could see the riders. Moving slowly, the men searched in the scrubby undergrowth and thorny trees. One dismounted and held his lantern near the ground.

"You're right," To-pek-chi whispered. "They're following our trail. Wake the others."

Soon, the five Comanches were ready to ride. To-pek-chi faced a dilemma. In a few minutes the sun would rise. He wanted to follow the trail west toward the Pecos River, but if he did, they would be riding straight into the hands of the approaching men. If they took any other direction, they would be seen by early risers in the town. He spoke to his comrades. "These men seek us for a reward. They probably learned from the telegraph that we broke out and might be coming this way. Very soon they'll realize that our trail leads to this pool and be upon us. We must leave."

Caught between the town and a pair of bounty hunters, To-pek-chi made his choice. "Follow me. We'll give these white folks something to look at."

As he led his group east toward the town, the rising sun whitened the dust flat they were crossing. When the Comanches arrived at the south end of the main street, the morning sun revealed ten horses and five riders. They looked down the dirt thoroughfare lined with wooden buildings on both sides. Signs jutted out from the buildings: several lawyer's offices, a doctor's office, a mercantile store, two grocery stores, a newspaper office, a drugstore, a café, eight saloons, and a blacksmith's shop. At the far end of town, a railroad crossed the street. Up a long slope, beyond the rails, a ranch house was silhouetted against the sky.

To-pek-chi took a leather pouch out of his saddlebag as his nephews watched silently. When he removed two eagle feathers and tied them into his hair, they made quiet signs of approval.

"These two I've been granted by the tribe at the fires."

He arranged the feathers to hang on the right side of his head. "You've seen the soldiers on parade at Fort Sill. We will give this town a parade. There will be danger. Keep your heads and do as I do. Spread the line five pony-lengths apart. Tenny-sau behind me, Wo-tank-ah behind him, Santoso next, and Tauk-see to bring up the rear. If we are shot at, or I give the signal, ride for your lives. I'm going north to that ranch house on the hill. Now, sit straight and make these white people believe you belong here."

To-pek-chi was remembering other times when bold Comanches had paralyzed a white community. He hoped they could do that now.

Big Spring, a thriving West Texas town, was rousing itself. Coffee drinkers gathered at the café. Women who had come up short on breakfast makings were at the grocery stores. Several men were in the telegraph office beside the railroad. A few of the legal offices were open. Two horses, left over the night, stood at the hitching post of a saloon. Their saddles were the deep-seated ones that cowboys rode.

The owner of the café was the first to catch sight of the festivities. Pouring a counter customer a second cup of coffee, he glanced out the window. A dark-skinned man rode a brown and white skewbald horse and led a high-headed black, brown, and white pinto. The rider wore a fringed leather shirt and pants with two eagle feathers tied in his hair.

"You idiot!" the customer screamed, jerking back a coffee-scalded hand. "What in hell's the matter with you?"

The proprietor didn't answer. He was staring at Tenny-sau, who had come into view riding a bright bay and leading a sorrel with four white stockings. Following the proprietor's eyes, the customers rushed to the door.

Leaping from building to building, word of the Indians' arrival swept down the street like prairie fire. To-pek-chi watched the flame of animation spread ahead of them. The citizens of Big Spring gathered along the main street of their town to view the spectacle— five Comanches and ten strikingly colored horses. Riding a prancing white horse and leading a black, Wo-tank-ah stared at Tenny-sau's back. Santoso squared his shoulders and sat straight, looking neither right nor left as he guided his red roan and brown bay between the gathering crowds. Tauk-see did not avoid the eyes of the white people. Holding the reins of the bridle on his blue roan in his right hand and the plaited rope on his black and white piebald in his left, he gazed steadily into the eyes of one white man after the other. It was not a gaze of defiance or of fear. Tauk-see made his look say, "I belong here."

When To-pek-chi saw he had nearly made it to the railroad, he breathed easier. His plan was working. Amazed by the presence of the Comanches, no white person had taken exception to it. Then, a gunshot ripped the air, followed by two more. To-pek-chi looked back. Men on horseback were crossing the open land by the spring. The bounty hunters had found them.

The shots had the desired effect. As To-pek-chi bolted, the men in the streets snapped out of their daze and rushed for their guns. Two cowboys staggered to their horses and pulled rifles out of their saddle scabbards, their eyes blurred and their heads buzzing.

The young Comanches leaned forward, and lying low on the backs of their horses, followed their leader's charge across the tracks and up the slope. A chorus of bloodcurdling yells went up. With more than a half-mile head start, To-pek-chi's band of Comanches easily outdistanced the bounty hunters. When the astonished townspeople did not bother to shoot at them, the Comanches rapidly disappeared at the far end of the street.

To-pek-chi never slowed down. He wheeled his horse into the yard of the tall ranch house between the buildings. He knew exactly where he was going. Turning back toward the railroad, he eyed its elevated roadbed. Then he led his men under a trestle into a narrow valley, out of sight of the town. To-pek-chi slowed his horse and waited for the others. "Walk your horses. We don't want to raise dust for them to see."

Quietly the Comanches headed south. At a dry creek bed downstream from the big spring, they turned west and followed it back to the spring itself. There they scrambled behind the hill where they had spent the previous night.

Peering over the top, the Comanches watched the activity in the town. People charged around and waved their hands. Horses raced wildly up and down the streets. But no one mounted an organized chase. The bounty hunters had stopped in the street to brag about their great tracking skills and the runaway Indians they intended to catch.

The runaways sat quietly. Tauk-see glanced at To-pek-chi. "That was a good trick," he said.

"We blue-quailed them."

"Blue-quailed?"

"I learned about blue quail when we wintered near the Tonka-was," To-pek-chi explained. "Blue quail are really grey. They'd rather walk than fly. When the Tonks hunted blue quail, some of the boys hid near the place where they first saw the birds. One or two boys followed the birds in a big circle. A few quail dropped off here and there, but the rest of the group always returned to where they had started. The Tonk boys who hid themselves got good shots when the covey returned. You see, the bounty hunters should have left one of themselves here this morning."

Tauk-see nodded. To-pek-chi unbuckled his canteen from his belt and led his men to the spring. "Drink deep and fill your canteens. There are three days of hard riding between us and the Pecos River. We may have to ride it without water."

Once more he insisted they walk their horses to avoid raising dust. The trail led west over a gently rising and falling land that was covered with short brown grass interspersed with scrubby brush and stunted mesquite trees. At mid-morning the raiders cut a fence that blocked their progress.

That afternoon a stiff west wind blew. Dust seared their faces and sandpapered their eyes. The wind-whipped wayfarers stopped early and made camp under the protective ledge of a gully-wash. To-pek-chi said that smoke would be swallowed in the wind and dust, so they built a fire.

The wind and sand subsided, but the night was dark. In the hazy sky, the new moon was only a faint smudge.

The next morning as they got under way To-pek-chi warned them again to save water. "Sips only, when you must. We're still two days from the river."

A mile west of the gully where they'd spent the night, they came upon another fence. To-pek-chi cut the wire and thought again how the country had changed. Less than five miles beyond the fence, the men rode up to a working windmill. A one-inch stream of cool water arced out of a pipe into a metal tank at its base.

Wo-tank-ah splashed water on his face and scooped a handful into his mouth. "That's the shortest two days I ever rode."

To-pek-chi glared at him. "So, the whites have improved the trail. Fill your canteens. We still have a long way to go."

The horses closed in around the tank to drink and the men drank one at a time from the pipe. While waiting his turn, Tauk-see surveyed the surroundings. Two moving dots on the horizon caught his attention. "Riders!"

All heads swiveled toward the spot he pointed out.

"Ride!" To-pek-chi shouted. "Those damn cowboys have seen us."

The five swung onto the backs of their horses and charged out onto the prairie. Ahead of them, five trail-broke horses ran free. Traveling southwest, the ten horses beat the dry, powdered earth into a cloud of dust. Tauk-see looked back. The cowboys were coming on fast, whipping their horses as if they meant to catch up.

Riding in the center of the line, To-pek-chi held his horse to a steady gallop, a pace chosen for the long run ahead. Five miles west of the windmill, they came to another fence. To-pek-chi slowed his horse and handed the wire cutters to his son. When Santoso rode forward to cut the wire, Tauk-see looked back. The cowboys had not gained on them.

Beyond the fence, To-pek-chi returned the group to a gallop. On and on they rode, the horses easy in their stride. When the sun reached its zenith, To-pek-chi pulled up. "Loosen your cinches and walk your horses. We've left the cowboys behind. They probably stopped when they got to their own fence line."

After a brief halt to eat some leftover antelope, they rode on, alternating between a trot and a gallop.

They had now left the fenced ranches behind, so their progress was unimpeded. Sundown found them in a parched land without trees or water. After a short rest, To-pek-chi mounted his horse. "We'll ride in the cool of the night to keep from sweating." All night they rode. The young men were ready to rest, but their leader said no. "We'll lose body water whether we ride or lie in the sun. Keep riding."

The Comanches pressed on, occasionally sipping from their canteens. At the next sundown they came to a dry waterway that angled southwest. To-pek-chi studied the land. "This draw will lead to the Pecos River. We'll stop here for a while."

After a few hours of fitful rest, he ordered them under way again. When they didn't come to the river by the next morning, To-pek-chi guessed that they had struck the draw farther east than he thought. They would follow its dry bed until they came to water. By now their canteens were empty, and the horses especially were suffering from the lack of water. Determined to do his part, each man gritted his teeth and pushed on. Late afternoon came and still no sign of the river. The men's parched tongues grated on the dry roofs of their mouths.

A crescent moon rose, the third moonrise since they had watered at the windmill. To-pek-chi rode in the lead and suddenly raised a hand. "Quiet. Catch the horses. We're near the river. But there are people at a fire between us and the water."

When the horses had been caught, To-pek-chi handed the reins of his skewbald to Tauk-see and the rope on his pinto to Santoso. "Stay put. I'm going ahead on foot."

He worked his way closer until he saw three men sitting at a fire. Their short-cropped hair and unique leggings told him they were Apaches. He didn't speak Apache, but he did speak Spanish, a language most Plains Indians understood.

To-pek-chi shouted to the Apaches in Spanish. The Apaches stopped chewing and reached for their rifles. "Who's there?" one shouted back in Spanish.

"To-pek-chi of the Comanches. We are five who have been without water for two days."

The answer came back with a laugh. "Comanches? Without water. That's too bad. You speak Spanish well. Could you be a Mexican who tries to fool Apaches?"

Three days in the saddle, two of them without water, had dulled To-pek-chi's senses. He didn't see one of the Apaches leave the fire and slip into the night. Neither was he aware that his own men had disobeyed his orders and crept forward. Tauk-see spoke Spanish as well as To-pek-chi. When he heard the exchange between To-pek-chi and the Apaches, he huddled with the others. "These men play games with To-pek-chi. They make light of our thirst."

At that moment an Apache pressed the muzzle of his rifle to the back of To-pek-chi's head. Tauk-see watched the Apache push his uncle toward the fire. The other Apaches gathered around, laughing as they poked the captive with their rifles.

Santoso pressed close. "What can we do? We have only bows and arrows against their rifles."

With his leader captured, and the rest of them dying of thirst, Tauk-see felt lost. To make matters worse, the horses smelled water and were hard to keep still. Tauk-see looked down at his hands. He held the reins on the bridles of two horses and a rope around the neck of another. Suddenly, he had an idea for their salvation. "Line up the horses facing the fire. When I signal, charge forward."

In a few moments, the horses stood side by side. "Now!" Tauk-see shouted. Screaming a war cry and pulling the horses with them, the Comanches rushed forward. The horses took the movement to mean they could go to the water. The young men dropped the ropes and reins, and the horses crashed through the Apache camp. Fire, food, and equipment scattered in every direction. All was chaos. One Apache fired his rifle and then dived out of the way as the thirst-crazed horses rushed to the river. Tauk-see caught the Apache who had fired and laid his knife across his throat. To-pek-chi whirled and grabbed the rifle of the Apache nearest him. Still spinning, he smashed the butt of the rifle into the head of the third Apache. Covering the two with the gun, To-pek-chi made them stay on the ground. "Tauk-see, bring the other one to me."

Holding a handful of hair at the back of the Apache's head, Tauk-see kept the knife at his throat.

"Set him down with these two. Then go to the water."

The young men rushed to the river, pushed their ponies out of the way and stuck their faces into the muddy water.

"One of you build up the fire," To-pek-chi said to the Apaches in Spanish. Then, in English, he added, "Quick, now."

"You speak English," the oldest Apache said, in English, as his companion raked coals together and added small branches to rekindle the fire.

"Yes, I speak English. We live with the whites at Fort Sill. Where did you learn to speak it?"

"Carlisle, class of 1890."

When the young men had finished drinking, To-pek-chi handed his rifle to Tauk-see and went to the river. When he returned, he stopped in front of the Apache who had spoken to him. "So, you've been to Carlisle. What are you doing on the Pecos?"

"We're Mescaleros from the Sacramento Mountains. We've been without rain. Game is scarce. We came out on the plains in search of meat. What's your excuse for being here?"

"These Comanche warriors needed a chief to take them to Mexico, so I volunteered."

The fire flared. Its light revealed a wrecked camp. The oldest Apache watched Wo-tank-ah and Tenny-sau poke around in the debris. "We don't have much food. We were eating rabbit. There are two more hanging in that tree. We'll share."

To-pek-chi nudged Tauk-see, who still leveled the rifle at the Apaches. "Isn't it wonderful how a loaded Winchester makes nice people out of almost everyone?" The Comanches laughed.

"Let them up." To-pek-chi pushed the rifle barrel down. "Surely we can trust a Carlisle man, now that he knows we're not Mexican."

When the rabbits had been retrieved and skinned and the Comanches had brought cuts of antelope meat out of their saddlebags, all of the men took seats around the fire to eat. The members of the two tribes eyed each other with suspicion. A few words were exchanged in Spanish. Neither group offered their names. No one asked. It was a fragile truce.

The oldest Apache cleared his throat. "We return to the Sacrementos with little success. We've wandered south of the Pecos for a week and have not killed a deer or antelope. It hasn't rained here. This land is empty."

To-pek-chi nodded. "We're passing through. We're on the trail to Mexico."

When they had eaten, To-pek-chi and the oldest Apache talked as they moved to where the Apaches' horses were tied. In a while To-pek-chi rejoined his followers.

"The Apaches will remain here. We'll sleep down the river."

The Comanches collected their horses and rode east. To-pek-chi selected a campsite on the water. "Tie the horses well. I don't want them to go back and get mixed up with the Apache horses."

Before daylight Tenny-sau awakened the Comanche camp. "Taraza is gone. My pony got away in the night."

The others ran to check the horses. They had tied up ten; nine remained. Tenny-sau's sorrel with four white stockings was missing. The young Comanches mounted quickly and circled the camp to search for the tracks of the horse that had strayed.

To-pek-chi called them back. "I'll take you to the pony."

He led them upriver. When they came to the Apache campsite, it was empty, abandoned in the night. The Comanche leader did not stop. He found the tracks of the Apaches and followed them at a gallop. After a while he stopped and his followers caught up. He turned in his saddle. "Tenny-sau, do you know your horses's hoofprint?"

"I've been looking at my pony's hoofprint as we followed the trail. Why did they steal only one? Why not all of our horses?"

To-pek-chi looked at Tenny-sau a long time, then longer at the others. His silence confused his nephews. After a while Tauk-see nodded. "They couldn't eat ten, could they, Uncle?"

"That's right. And taking one is less noisy than taking ten. Hunting had been bad for them, and they wanted fresh meat, enough for a village. You would not expect them to eat an Apache horse when a Comanche horse was available."

Five angry Comanches followed the trail up the Pecos River. At dusk they rode out on a ledge and looked down on a large Apache camp located where a creek ran into the river. The Apaches were celebrating. Women who were busy around the fires ran in and out of their tepees. To-pek-chi said, "No wonder they haven't seen us. They're getting ready for a feast."

Tenny-sau asked, "Are we going to save Taraza?"

"We're too late. See the red and white horse hide on the bush behind that tepee? But don't worry. There's a pen full of horses beyond the camp. We'll get even."

"Those no good Apaches have eaten my best friend. I wouldn't have traded Taraza for all the horses in that pen."

As the thin moon shone over the Apache camp, the Comanche leader held his men in the hills. When the last fire was out and the last Apache had gone to his bed, food-filled and drowsy, To-pek-chi gathered his men.

"We would never get out of here with all their horses. Tenny-sau and I will slip down and steal a few. We'll leave the saddles on these we're riding. Throw them in with the others and start back down the river. When you get to the place where we camped last night, ride south by east. You'll come to Comanche Springs, a good watering hole. There used to be a fort near the springs. I don't know if soldiers are still there. If you get there before we catch up, be careful. Tenny-sau, bring your bridle and rope. Let's get you another horse or two."

The next afternoon, Tauk-see was riding at the rear of the horse herd when he heard a man shout and looked west. Four horses were bearing down on him from a nearby ridge. He called on Santoso and Wo-tank-ah to wait. It was their uncle and cousin. To-pek-chi rode a golden palomino and led a red and white skewbald. Tenny-sau rode a bald-faced sorrel and led a grey. As they drew nearer, Tauk-see saw that Tenny-sau had a long blood-clotted gash on his forehead.

"What happened to you?" he asked Tenny-sau.

Santoso rode up. "Damn! What did you run into?"

"I ran into a couple of Apaches. But they came out worse off than me—they ran into my uncle. They had me down, and one of them was going to scalp me. You can see he made a good start. My uncle pulled them off and beat them senseless with his fists."

To-pek-chi raised his hand to silence Tenny-sau. "My nephew gave good account of himself. We'd have been along sooner, but we had to convince them we were going north before we came south."

To-pek-chi and Tenny-sau saddled new horses. The band continued southeast. Tauk-see rode close to To-pek-chi. "Why four horses? It slowed you down to lead a horse as you rode. One would have replaced Tenny-sau's loss and *you* didn't need another."

"A Comanche horse is worth at least four Apache horses." To-pek-chi replied. "Besides, you heard the Apache say game is scarce south of the Pecos. You never know when a couple of Apache horses might come in handy in a place like that."

To-pek-chi led his reunited band at a trot. Night came on and the hard-riding Comanches rode by the light of a quarter moon. By the time their leader came to a stop, the moon had crossed over them to the west. A huddle of ground lights had caught his attention. "Comanche Springs is ahead, but I see a white people's town nearby.

We'll ride around it to the east and water on Comanche Creek." The raiders spent a comfortable night on the creek named for them.

The next day as they rode, mountains loomed on each side of their trail. To-pek-chi grew nervous. "There used to be a fort in those mountains up north. I've heard there's a town there now. Chew jerky and drink. I don't want to stop here."

Realizing his father was upset, Santoso rode to the front. "What is it, Father? Could soldiers still be at the fort?"

"Long ago we had a fight with soldiers from that fort. I lost friends not far from this place."

The party moved on and made camp on the prairie south of two mountain ranges. The next morning when his men complained that they hadn't had fresh meat for days, To-pek-chi eyed the pony herd, then shook his head. "We can wait. Beyond that mountain up ahead, there's a valley filled with deer. There we'll eat well."

The ride to the crest was hard, but by dusk they were in a green valley. Deer scattered ahead of them. To-pek-chi gave permission for the others to hunt and Tenny-sau was successful.

While the meat cooked, To-pek-chi pointed out the landmarks around them. He was pleased to be back in a land he remembered. "When I was here, the hills we came through today were full of escaped burros. The Mexicans called that place the Slope of the Burros. This valley will take us east to a plain north of the Rio Bravo. To the south, the Chinati Mountains stretch into Mexico. They are special."

Santoso stood at his father's shoulder. "Special?"

"Sometimes strange lights are seen in the Chinatis. My grandfathers told me they are the spirits of the Old Ones, who don't wish to leave these mountains. They often help people who are lost or in danger."

"Are they Comanches?"

"You know the Comanches came down from the north before the days of my grandfathers. No one knows when those spirits in the lights began to live in the Chinatis. The lights are sacred to people of several tribes. They are spoken of at many campfires."

After they had eaten, Tauk-see left the others and climbed a hill above the camp. He looked south at the long line of mysterious mountains that To-pek-chi had pointed out, the ones that reached all the way into Mexico. What waited beyond them? Why had he been told to go there? They had traveled far and faced many dangers, and there would be more. Had it been right for him to risk the lives of his uncle and cousins? What was so urgent in Mexico? His eyes returned to the Chinatis. He remembered the lights, the spirits of the Old Ones who help people. It seemed right to speak. "Help me understand, if you can. Why am I here?"

The moon was rising when the men lay down in their blankets. The ride had been long and they were tired. Tauk-see went to sleep thinking about the Old Ones he had spoken to. Later, in the middle of the night, something awakened him. It was a strange sensation, an insistence he had to answer. He walked out of camp, leaving his sleeping companions. Suddenly, a light pulsated where he knew there were mountains. Its orange center expanded, beating against a red disk around it. A cold fear gripped his heart. The thing he saw was not of this world. Other lights appeared. They kept going and coming and moving around. One was white. Another was red with an orange center like the first he'd seen. He was frozen as he watched the spectacle.

Then the lights disappeared in a mist. Dimly at first, then more clearly, a two-story house appeared in the haze. A latticed framework reached up its front wall. Above the trellis, light was shining through a large window, outlining a human figure, a girl.

The vision faded and the lights came back. Tauk-see ran into camp. "Come see the lights!" The others hurried to see the thing that had excited Tauk-see. The lights still shone. They dimmed and grew bright and changed from red to orange.

"They're beautiful!" Tenny-sau shouted.

Santoso squinted and shaded his eyes. "They're too low for stars. And no campfire could come and go that fast."

"Medicine," Wo-tank-ah said. "My grandmother told me about medicine like this."

To-pek-chi joined them. "You're right to call them medicine, Wo-tank-ah, if you mean good medicine. As I told you, those are the spirits of the Old Ones. We don't need to fear them."

Tauk-see continued to look at the lights, but he didn't join his cousins in their enthusiastic enjoyment of them. His mind was on something else. The girl he'd seen at the window haunted him. He went to his uncle. "Can we leave for Mexico tonight?"

To-pek-chi took his eyes off the lights. "Go easy, Tauk-see. The beautiful horses will be there tomorrow."

Ten days had passed since Losantos Cavarubio promised his oldest daughter, Carmen, to Luz Bocanegra. During that time the Cavarubio family was in upheaval. Pajita argued with her husband and begged him to change his mind. His sons repeated their mother's plea. Only Carmen was silent. She couldn't strike out at her father. She loved him, but hated what he was doing to her. Anita and Rosa clung to Carmen and their mother, fearful in the midst of turmoil they didn't understand.

When the hatchet-faced man who commanded Luz Bocanegra's troops returned to Santa Rosa del Norte and told Losantos to bring Carmen to Serpentigero, the family's disruption grew worse. Señor Bocanegra wanted his bride-to-be under his own roof until the priest arrived to marry them. Losantos hurried to comply with the tyrant's orders. Immediately he brought Carmen and the rest of his family to Serpentigero. They became guests in the first-floor bedrooms, except Carmen. She was installed as a prisoner in a large upstairs bedroom at the front of the mansion.

On the second night after she'd been imprisoned, Carmen looked north out of a wide second-story window of the palatial villa at Hacienda Serpentigero. Her eyes fell on a line of mountains, not the close ones at the edge of the plains, but those far away, up by the Rio Bravo del Norte. As she absorbed the view, an unexpected tranquility came over her. It was as if she could sense her salvation in those mountains. She went to bed and slept well.

The next morning she was awakened by her mother's voice in the hallway, where armed guards patrolled and barred any visitors. "I don't care what your orders are. I'm going to see my daughter. Shoot me if you have the nerve."

The door flew open and Pajita burst into Carmen's room. Carmen sat up and put her arms around her mother. "Please, Mama, don't be alarmed. I'm all right. Everything will be fine. The man the Virgin has sent to save me is almost in Mexico."

"Has She appeared again? How do you know the man is near?"

"She has not appeared, but I know he is coming. He's in the mountains on the Rio Bravo."

"We have only four days until the priest Bocanegra hired will be here. Let's pray that help is coming from somewhere."

"I have prayed, Mother, and my prayers are being answered."

Clouds in the east turned pink with the sunrise as To-pek-chi led his comrades toward them. Before mid-morning they had ridden onto a level plain beyond the mountains. There, the leader turned south and put his horse into a gallop.

"Come along, men. The Rio Bravo del Norte is not far." To-pek-chi, however, had missed his estimate. The Rio Grande, or Rio Bravo, as he preferred to call it, was a day's ride away. Near sundown the Comanches came to the river. The horses nuzzled into the clear water and drank. To-pek-chi looked east and west.

"We've struck the Rio Bravo below the stream I seek. We'll eat over in Mexico, then ride on to the Conchos."

The young men were ecstatic. Moved by a single urge, they beat their saddles with their knees and broke for the far bank, spraying sheets of water in the air as they went. To-pek-chi crossed more slowly, then waited while his companions raced out onto the flat south of the river and circled back to gather around him.

"Not too fast, nor too far, men. I know nothing about who patrols this part of the river."

After they had filled their canteens, To-pek-chi urged his men on. A half-moon lighted their way to a smaller stream that joined the Rio Bravo from the south. To-pek-chi called a brief halt. "This is the Conchos. We'll camp in the mountains on the other side."

First through foothills and then through steeper pine-covered slopes, the Comanche horsemen traveled. In a grove of trees To-pek-chi stopped. "Build a fire. We'll eat again."

Santoso dismounted and walked beside his father. "What about the Mexican patrols? Won't they see our fire?"

"Apaches who refused to go to the reservation escaped across the river and live in these mountains. Any Mexican soldier who sees our fire will think we are some of them.

Tauk-see overheard his uncle. "How about the Apaches themselves? They're probably as mean as those who stole our horse."

"We'll deal with the Apaches if we have to."

After they had eaten, To-pek-chi rolled out his blankets. "Rest well. We'll plan our next moves in the morning."

In the light before sunup, he called his men to the edge of the trees and showed them the stream they had crossed in the night.

"See the plain across the river? The haciendas we'll raid are over there. One of them is opposite a red pillar on the mountain south of here. We'll ride to it this morning."

The intruders rode between the river and the mountain. Wo-tank-ah saw the landmark first. "Is that the red pillar?"

"That's it," To-pek-chi said. "The hacienda is just east of here. Gather around and hear my instructions. Santoso and Wo-tank-ah will ride south until you come to a box canyon. Gather fallen trees and brush, and pile them near the opening of the canyon—enough to make a barricade that will hold horses. Stay there and, at dusk, use the flint and steel to light a fire. Tenny-sau and Tauk-see will go with me. We'll cross the river and scout out the hacienda. It will be dark when we return, but the moon is almost full, so riding will be easy. Keep the fire built up. We'll be looking for it."

The Comanches broke into two parties and rode away to carry out their assigned duties.

The moon shone brightly on To-pek-chi and his two nephews as they rode up to the fire. Santoso and Wo-tank-ah were roasting a small deer. To-pek-chi accepted a strip of venison from Wo-tank-ah and approved the brush they had piled by the entrance to the box canyon.

"There are twenty-six horses in the corral at the hacienda. When we have eaten, we'll ride down and take them."

The young braves made short work of eating. They were in their saddles long before To-pek-chi wiped his hands on his pants and stood up. When he mounted his horse, the others gathered around him.

"For years you've heard us at the campfires telling about stealing horses," To-pek-chi said. "Now we're going to use what you've learned. In the time of my father, the Comanches came down in such strength that they would capture the families on the haciendas and make the men bring the horses to them so they could pick out the best. In my time, when we were not as many, we opened the gates and drove the horses out. Still, we dared the Mexicans to come after us.

"When we were few, as we are tonight, we used a different method, one that made the Mexicans think the horses had done it themselves. That way they would not come looking for us. The tracks of our horses were covered by those of the horses we'd stolen. It is good. You'll see. We have good light tonight. Let's ride."

The Comanches rode toward a sprawling house surrounded by outbuildings. To-pek-chi reviewed the horse-stealing method they would use.

Tauk-see and Santoso dismounted and handed their reins to Tenny-sau and Wo-tank-ah. With his rope coiled on a shoulder, each brave ran swiftly toward the outbuildings. Slowing, they slipped into the shadow of the bunkhouse.

They could hear strains from guitars. Excitement made Tauk-see's voice crack. "The cowboys are making music."

They tiptoed to the corner of the long building with Santoso in the lead. Bending low, they raced across an open space to the shadow of the largest barn. Rounding its corner, they came to the horse pen. As the men climbed between rails, the horses snorted, sensing a new odor. Bright moonlight flooded the pen, making the work easier. They caught two horses and made simple bridles for them by looping the ropes around their lower jaws. Tauk-see led a chestnut gelding to the fence across from the barn. He pulled one end of the top bar off a section of fence and quietly lowered it to the ground. Santoso mounted a bay and waited on the far side of the pen. When Tauk-see waved, Santoso clamped his legs into his horse's side and rushed into the herd. The panicked horses milled around until they found where the top rail was down. Pressing against the weakened fence, they crashed through to freedom. Tauk-see held a tight rein until they passed, then rode in behind them.

Hearing the noise, the cowboys rushed out. They arrived in time to see horses scattering east over the prairie. They never saw the Comanche riders, who clung to the sides of the two horses.

One of the cowboys found the splintered fence. "Chinga! Those damn horses broke down the fence."

Another cowboy joined him. "They've scattered to the winds. We can't do anything tonight. We'll look for them tomorrow."

After a long run to the east, the horses suddenly veered north, turned by three Comanches. To-pek-chi, Tenny-sau, and Wo-tank-ah had been waiting for their companions. Tenny-sau and Wo-tank-ah led their cousins' horses. Tauk-see and Santoso dismounted, slipping the ropes off their Mexican mounts and leaping onto their own horses. The five Comanches now rode in the wake of the herd.

The young braves could not contain themselves. War cries leaped from their throats. Skimming over the land like low-flying eagles, they steered the beautiful horses through the foothills and across the river. On To-pek-chi's order, they slowed and let the horses ease into the box canyon. By the time they had blocked the mouth of the canyon with the brush they had stored nearby, morning was breaking.

The raiders ate venison and scanned the prairie beyond the river. No riders appeared. To-pek-chi joined his nephews, squatting beside the fire. "The Mexicans have not followed. They're probably having steak and eggs and drinking hot coffee. We'll stay hidden, give them a day to search for their horses. Tonight we'll hit Serpentigero, the hacienda that belonged to Luz Bocanegra."

"You surprise me," Tauk-see said as he wiped his hands on a tuft of long grass. "After twenty-five years, how do you remember the names?"

"It's easy. I read his name on a sign over his gate. Luz Bocanegra was the son-of-a-bitch who owned Serpentigero. He captured a friend of mine and cut off his head. Hung it on a post beside his gate so the Comanches would see it when we returned for the body of our friend."

Tauk-see touched his own neck. "That's horrible! I wouldn't want to die that way. What did you do about it?"

"Nothing. Luz Bocanegra kept an army of men. We were too few to attack an armed guard. The bastard has probably been dead a long time. A man that mean deserves to die young."

Luz Bocanegra, patron of Serpentigero, was angry. Suffering in the early morning after a long night of drinking, he held his head. "Cavarubio, take control of your wife. She was almost killed this morning when she broke into Carmen's room. I have ordered that she, or any of the rest of you who come near that room, are to be shot. Do you understand?"

"I understand. It won't happen again."

From their hiding place at the mouth of the box canyon, To-pek-chi and his raiders watched the sun become a flaming disk. At the moment it burned into the clouds in the west, a full moon rose in the east. The leader of the Comanches brushed his pants. "The Mexican moon has come. We'll have good hunting tonight."

At the trees beyond their camp, To-pek-chi swept a hand toward the horizon south to north on a line above the river. "Serpentigero lies to the north, east of that row of foothills," he explained. "We'll take the horses like we did last night. I'll ride with Santoso and Tauk-see to the headquarters. They'll go to the barns and run out the horses. I'll take their horses and wait north of the house. There I can watch everything. I may need to use my rifle if anyone presses you.

"Wo-tank-ah and Tenny-sau will wait until the moon is a hand's width above the horizon and then start these horses north, on this side of the river. Keep them moving at a walk. When Tauk-see and Santoso bring the Serpentigero horses, we'll turn northwest and head for the place where the Conchos and the Rio Bravo come together. Do you understand?"

Wo-tank-ah nodded. "What if we get to the Rio Bravo before you? Do we cross over?"

"No. Hold the herd at the junction of the rivers. If all goes well, we should arrive about the same time."

When darkness fell, To-pek-chi, Tauk-see, and Santoso rode east toward the river. They crossed it and took a line to the nearest foothills. They passed over a ridge and rode to the crest of another. The moonlight revealed a two-story mansion surrounded by outbuildings. A gate built of river stone arched over a road that led to the house. High rock fences surrounding the compound gave it the look of a fort.

After they had studied the house and the barns around it, the Comanches led their horses back over the hill. There, out of sight of the hacienda, To-pek-chi stopped his companions. "This will be harder than what you did last night. Once you get the horses out of the pen, you must get them onto the road and out the front gate. You'll have to open the gate first.

Santoso nodded. "We can do it, Father. One of us can catch a horse, take the top rail down from outside the pen, and then ride to the front gate before the other one runs the rest of the horses out."

They rode back to the top of the hill where To-pek-chi stood guard, loosening his rifle in its scabbard.

Tauk-see and Santoso handed him their reins and silently slipped off toward the villa. They felt for toeholds and scrambled over the rock wall around it. Once inside the compound, they hid in a clump of rosebushes on the edge of the yard. As Santoso lay on his belly and studied the barns, Tauk-see suddenly left his hiding place and began walking toward the house.

Santoso scrambled to intercept his cousin. "Where are you going?" he whispered. "The horse pens are over there."

Tauk-see didn't answer. He walked on. Santoso caught him and whirled him around. "Tauk-see, what are you doing?"

Tauk-see jerked away. "Let me go. This is why I was sent to Mexico. I must go to this house."

He walked to a trellis that rose to the second story of the house. Santoso heard voices and ran back to the roses. At an open window above the trellis, a girl appeared.

Tauk-see did not hesitate. He climbed quickly. At the moment his head cleared the window sill, Carmen Cavarubio leaned out and smiled at him.

"I've been expecting you. What is your name?"

"I am called Tauk-see. Who are you?"

"I am Carmen Cavarubio. Thank you for coming."

Gaping at Carmen in sudden recognition, Tauk-see almost lost his balance. This was the girl he had seen in his misty vision on the Chinatis. Now her delicately rounded lips and soft blue eyes were only inches from his face. Freshly brushed, her wavy black hair enveloped him in its fragrance.

Carmen moved away to allow Tauk-see to crawl through the window. With her forefinger against her lips to shush him, she pulled him to the bed and sat beside him. "I am glad you speak Spanish."

"Me, too."

"We must speak softly. Guards are at the door."

Speaking rapidly, Carmen whispered her story to Tauk-see. She told how her father had lost his ranch. "To save it I must marry an aged monster. I have prayed many hours to the Virgin Mary. I believe you are the answer to my prayers. You *have* come to save me, haven't you?"

Tauk-see could not understand every word. But he realized that Carmen was a prisoner and in danger, and that she expected him to do something about it.

Haltingly, in a language he seldom spoke, Tauk-see told Carmen about his experience on Cache Creek when the Great Spirit told him to go to Mexico. He told about seeing her, and the house they were in, while he was still in the Chinatis. The vision had made it possible for him to find her, but still he didn't know why he had been sent. He searched her eyes, but they seemed to see beyond him.

"Speak slowly, please and tell me what danger threatens you."

"In three days my father will make me marry Luz Bocanegra, a *bruto salvaje* who is four times my age."

Tauk-see raised his hand. "Luz Bocanegra. I heard that name last night. I know you are right when you call him a savage brute. He once cut off a Comanche's head and hung it on his front gate."

"That is the man. He's the most terrible man in Mexico. Can you get me away from here?"

Tauk-see felt backed into a corner, but he longed to comfort the girl. Hesitantly he took her hand. "I don't know how, but I will." He sensed the movement of the soldiers outside the door.

"You will return for me?"

"If I can."

"You're my only hope," she said, fingering the long white dress that hung by her bed. "Please come back."

Santoso watched his cousin crawl out of the window of the villa and descend the trellis. His face twitched nervously. When Tauk-see had returned to the hiding place, Santoso asked impatiently, "What have you been doing in there?"

"Talking to the most beautiful girl in the world. She's the reason I was sent to Mexico. I must save her."

Quickly he told Santoso the story. "So, the man who cuts off Comanche heads is alive. I want to speak to my uncle about him."

"And I want to steal horses. My father is out there waiting for us. He won't be satisfied with a story about a beautiful Mexican girl and a man out of the past. Remember, he said we weren't coming to Mexico to play games."

Convinced by Santoso's argument, Tauk-see joined him to follow the horse-stealing plan they had gone over the night before. But one thing was different. In the light of the full moon, Santoso found five horses in a row of stalls along the back of the barn. Attracted by the nervous milling of the others horses, they cocked their ears at him. Santoso slipped over to look in the stalls and was pleased to see that the five horses possessed exceptional strength and beauty. Before he looked for his cousin's signal that the top bar was down, he opened the doors of the stalls and turned four mares and a stallion into the pen with the herd. They were dun-colored with black manes, legs, and tails. A broad dark line ran the length of each back.

When he heard the horses coming, To-pek-chi sprang to his saddle. The herd flowed past and he rode forward to hand the reins of their horses to his nephew and son. He looked hard at one and then the other. "What kept you?"

Tauk-see galloped his horse beside To-pek-chi's. "It's a long story, Uncle. I cannot shout it between running horses. Let's drive this herd to the Rio Bravo. I'll tell it to you there."

Tenny-sau and Wo-tank-ah were holding their horses on the other side of the Conchos when the others drove in the new herd. The horses drank and settled down to graze. The Comanches built a fire.

As Tauk-see told his story, To-pek-ch's face remained inscrutable. His young cousins teased Tauk-see when he told about Carmen. Tauk-see spoke Bocanegra's name and waited for To-pek-chi's reaction. "He is still alive, Uncle. The man who cut off your friend's head is alive. He holds a young girl captive and will force her to marry him in three days. I told her I would help her."

To-pek-chi offered no comment. He sat quietly, eyes downcast. His young companions remained silent, waiting for him to speak. Finally he looked up. "I lead a party of Comanches who came to steal horses. We won't return to Fort Sill empty-handed. Luz Bocanegra has an army of men. I saw them in their barracks tonight. We have no chance to save the girl. We will leave for the north at dawn."

Tauk-see waited a respectful time. "But, Uncle, we can't ride off and leave this girl. She's in real danger. You've told us that the man who holds her is a beast. We must do something."

"There is a lesson you must learn, Nephew. There are times when a man must admit defeat. In a fight with Bocanegra, we would be outnumbered eight or ten to one."

"He has that many men?"

"There are that many at the house. He can probably call in that many more from the peons and small rancheros who occupy land by his consent. I didn't bring you young men to Mexico to see you butchered. We'll leave for the Wichitas in the morning."

"What about the order I received that told me to come to Mexico? You were worried that you might have gone against the wishes of the Great Spirit."

"We don't always understand the Great Spirit. You may have heard wrong. I don't believe I'm expected to throw away the lives of five Comanches."

The fire burned down and Tauk-see sat with his head bowed. The others let him struggle alone. At last, he spoke. "You are right, Uncle. I may not have heard anything that night on Cache Creek. I can't risk your life and the lives of my cousins. I can't help Carmen Cavarubio. She must live as her father has chosen. I'll return to the Wichitas with you."

In the pale light before dawn the next morning, To-pek-chi had his first clear view of the Serpentigero horses. He walked among the herd and rubbed his hand on the side of one horse after another. They had harvested many fine animals. Although Santoso had told him about the lineback duns in the special stalls, To-pek-chi wasn't prepared for their exceptional beauty and good breeding. "I want those five to come home with us, even if we lose all the others. We won't risk them on a rope or in a loose herd. Each of us will ride one."

The young Comanches saddled the lineback-dun mares, To-pek-chi the stallion. Then they mounted and drove the herd across the Conchos. They angled northeast to the Rio Bravo and trailed beside it until they reached the crossing they had used on their way south. Once they had crossed the river, they drove the herd onto a prairie that which rose away from the water.

Wo-tank-ah rode on the right, ahead of the herd. When a deer leaped out of brush beside his horse, he gripped the saddle with his legs and reached for his bow and an arrow. The horse lowered her body and stretched into a long, ground-eating stride. Her speed kept the rider at the deer's shoulder. Wo-tank-ah nocked the arrow, drew the bow, and sent the missile into the deer's heart.

He was a proud warrior, carrying the deer across his saddle until midday. In the shade of some trees by a spring-fed stream, he dropped the carcass and dressed it. The horses drank, then grazed on rich grass near the flowing water.

In the afternoon, To-pek-chi led the group into foothills east of the mountains they had crossed a few days before. When the horses found grass, To-pek-chi called a halt. "We'll spend the night here. Tomorrow we'll push the horses north at a run. The United States Army or the Texas Rangers probably patrol this area. The telegraph may have told them we're here."

To-pek-chi's words troubled Tauk-see. Tomorrow they would run north, and the day after that Carmen Cavarubio would marry Luz Bo-canegra. Carmen's fragrance came back to him. In his mind's eye, he traced the delicate outline of her face.

The sound of the others bedding down for the night interrupted his reverie. Spreading his blankets under a juniper tree, he stretched out and looked up through its branches. The night was clear and the stars were out. The moon was not as full as it had been the night before. The Mexican moon would soon pass and the Comanches would go home. They would leave the Rio Bravo in the morning. Tauk-see closed his eyes, but sleep wouldn't come. The voice and face of a frightened girl filled his head. The others had been sleeping for several hours when Tauk-see leaped to his feet and rolled up his blankets.

"I've got to go back," he said aloud. He couldn't leave without disturbing the others, so he made no pretense of keeping quiet as he gathered his bow and arrows and picked up his saddle. His companions awakened, grumbling and asking questions.

"I have to go back. I can't go away and leave her," he told them.

To-pek-chi rolled off his blanket and confronted his nephew. "Don't be a fool. If you go back, you're a dead man."

"And if I don't go back, I'll live my life a dead man."

"The ride will be long. You may be late. If she's been married by a priest, she'll be compelled by her faith to live with the man forever, no matter who he is."

"I've heard that about her church, Uncle. I know I must hurry. I can ride faster on one horse than I can if I ride a horse and lead another, but I'll need a mount for the girl." Sensing his nephew's determination, To-pek-chi reluctantly yielded to him.

"You've learned a lot about stealing horses these last few days. You could steal one."

"Stealing a horse would slow me down and I'd risk being caught before I get to her. There is a another way, though."

"What other way?"

"Give me the lineback-dun stallion. He'll take me there swiftly, and he's strong enough to carry two."

Incredulous, To-pek-chi couldn't stifle a laugh. Leave the lineback dun behind? If Tauk-see did not return, To-pek-chi would fail in the Great Spirit's plan for the stolen horses. But the urgency on Tauk-see's face gave him pause. Tauk-see, too, had been sent here by the Great Spirit. It shone in his eyes. Surely, it could not be wise to thwart that mission, To-pek-chi concluded at last.

"So you want my stallion. Well, take him, Nephew. At least, when I tell my brother that I left his son in Mexico, I can say I left him with the best horse we'd stolen."

Tauk-see quickly saddled and mounted the stallion. To-pek-chi slapped his nephew's thigh in a rare gesture of affection. "Watch your back trail and take care of yourself. Be sure you bring me this stallion. I have plans for him and his wives."

Tauk-see gave the lineback dun his head and let him pick his way through the hills. He didn't whip the horse or drive him to the limit. He'd do his hurrying when he was safely out of the mountains. At daylight they reached the prairie north of the Rio Bravo. Tauk-see tightened his reins and tapped the horse's sides. The stallion sprang into a long-striding gallop.

Throughout the morning he kept up his powerful gait. At the place where the Rio Bravo and the Conchos came together, horse and man drank deep.

Tauk-see rode along the east bank of the Conchos. He had to find the red pillar that would guide him to Serpentigero. The sun was overhead when he glimpsed the landmark. As soon as he saw it, he went to the river to water his horse and let him graze. He chewed jerky, drank from the river, and filled his canteen.

When Tauk-see mounted the stallion again, he resisted the urge to ride straight to the mansion at Serpentigero. Watchfully he rode northeast into the scrubby brush on the nearest foothill. He crossed it and the next one.

Beyond the crest of a third hill, he picked his way through stunted trees. Suddenly the stallion stopped. Ahead of them a large bay horse stood in the trees, the reins of its bridle lying on the ground. Tauk-see slipped his bow over his head and nocked an arrow. Swinging his leg over the horse's head, he slid silently to the ground. After creeping forward a considerable distance, he spotted a man lying on his belly. He was looking through binoculars at the mansion of Serpentigero. Tauk-see stepped closer and cleared his throat. The man dropped the binoculars, rolled to a sitting position, and reached for his rifle. Tauk-see aimed his arrow at the man's heart. "Don't do it," he said in Spanish.

The man was well built. His muscular neck, broad shoulders, and thick chest showed great strength. "Careful, my friend. Don't let that thing go off."

"Why do you call me friend?"

"I am always friends with a man who has the drop on me."

"And how long does such a friendship last?"

The man laughed. "For as long as it takes me to figure out how to turn the tables on him."

"Sounds risky, fooling people that way."

"I survive by fooling people. What are you doing here?"

Tauk-see liked the man's sense of humor and honesty. He saw no reason not to answer his question.

"I rode to Mexico with my uncle and three cousins. We came to steal horses. I learned that the man who owns this hacienda holds a girl against her will. I've come back to save her and came upon you."

The man swung his body around so that he sat more comfortably, but did not make a move toward his rifle. "So you've come to save a girl from this hacienda. If you try, you'll be dead before you get to the front gate."

"I've been through that gate."

"You have?"

"We were here two nights past. I'm riding one of the Serpen-tigero stallions."

Though he registered no surprise, the man seemed to reevaluate Tauk-see. "Even so, you have no chance to save the girl by yourself. With my help you might do it. Put down your weapon and let us talk."

"So you offer to help. Is this the way you will take advantage of me."

"You still have the advantage. Take my rifle if you don't trust me."

Stepping closer, Tauk-see picked up the rifle. The man stood and their gazes met. Tauk-see read sincerity in his eyes.

"I am Tauk-see, of the Comanches. Who are you?"

"I am Doroteo Arango, a Yaqui. We have a common enemy."

"Luz Bocanegra is an enemy to you?"

Arango's eyes widened. "You know his name?"

"I haven't seen him, but people have told me about him. Carmen Cavarubio says he's the most terrible man in Mexico. My uncle told me he once cut off a Comanche's head and hung it on his front gate. Why do you call him enemy?"

"He is one of the landowners who hold the Mexican people in poverty. He has reduced his ignorant neighbors to slaves."

"Your feelings must be strong for the Mexican people."

"I'll be president of Mexico some day—I or my friend Alvaro Obregon. If neither of us, then some other man of courage. Some day the Mexican people will be free of the yoke that the church and the landed rich have hung on us."

"If you will one day be president, why do you hide here?"

"To discover a way to get at Bocanegra."

"So you plan to attack him, but warned me not to?"

"Yes and no. I have a hundred men in these mountains, but they're on foot, armed only with hoes and machetes. As long as Bocanegra's armed guards ride in force or remain in the fortress he's made of his home, we're no match for them."

For a time Tauk-see was quiet. Then he tapped the ground with his bow, excited by an idea. "I can get Luz Bocanegra out on the plains for you."

"Do that, Comanche, and my men will pull the horses down and hand him to me. But how can you get Bocanegra out of his stronghold?"

"The horses are growing restless. Let's ride to the river and talk."

When Arango heard Tauk-see's plan, he nodded emphatically. "It will work. Come with me. We'll go to my men in the mountains. Tomorrow, you go to Bocanegra's wedding."

Arango led the way up the river. Tauk-see pointed out the red pillar and the box canyon where the Comanches had held the horses.

"My men looked in on you that night. We didn't want to attract Bocanegra's attention."

Some distance south of the pillar, Arango turned west onto a trail that slanted up the mountain. At several campsites along the way, groups of men watched them ride by. Finally they came to a large clearing where a couple dozen or so rushed out to greet Arango.

One man took their horses to be fed and watered. Arango introduced Tauk-see around the camp. "These are my men—Indians of several tribes, Mexican peasants and displaced rancheros. They're through with living under the heels of others. They will be pleased with your plan to rid them of their local terror." While they ate tortillas and beans and drank black coffee, Arango outlined Tauk-see's intentions. His followers shouted, glad and defiant. At last they would get a chance against Luz Bocanegra and his hired murderers.

Although their readiness to fight reassured Tauk-see, a new thought worried him.

"What bothers you Tauk-see?" Arango asked.

"What if they've changed the wedding? Carmen Carvarubio could be married already."

"Be easy, young Comanche. She is not married. My man, Juan Ignacio, has a daughter who serves at Serpentigero. She has told her father that the wedding will be tomorrow afternoon."

Tauk-see dropped his gaze to the ground, embarrassed. "What now, Tauk-see?" Arango prodded.

"Carmen Cavarubio showed me a dress like the white women at Fort Sill wear when they marry. If she's wearing that dress tomorrow, she won't be able to ride. Could you let me have a shirt and a pair of leather pants for her?"

Arango threw back his head and laughed, his teeth flashing white. "Of course, my friend, we'll send your girl clothes to ride in. I'll enjoy the thought that Luz Bocanegra's bride is wearing my pants when you steal her."

The Comanche and the Yaqui conferred on how the plan would be carried out. Before the sun went down, Arango took Tauk-see to the edge of the trees and pointed out exactly where he and his men would wait on the plain below. Tauk-see studied the hills in front of Serpentigero. In his mind he drew the line of flight he would follow. When they understood what each would do, the men returned to the fire and Tauk-see accepted a cup of coffee. "Doroteo Arango, my teachers at Fort Sill taught us that the Yaquis are in western Mexico. How is it that I find you, a Yaqui, in the mountains of Chihuahua?"

"Your teachers were right—the Yaqui belong in western Mexico. In Sonorro, a river is named for us. We'd be on it yet if the priests and Spanish government hadn't made war on my people when they wanted to remain free. Later, the Mexican government forced many Yaqui to leave their homeland and become slaves. Yaqui were scattered all over Mexico. Some fled into the United States. Those in the west of Mexico still fight the Mexican troops. My family was one of those forced out of their homeland. I was born in the village of Rio Grande in Zacatecas. I've come north to find men. Look around and see my success."

"I see you think of more than fighting a local butcher, Doroteo Arango. I'm glad to help."

That night Tauk-see rested well. The next morning he controlled his eagerness to rush to Carmen's rescue.

After they had eaten their noon meal, the men left the mountain in twos and threes to take their places in the grass and gullies on the plain. Arango watched them disappear. "They'll be on the plain when you need them, Tauk-see. If you don't want to be late for the wedding, it's time for you to go."

"Thank you for this, Arango. I wish you good luck. I hope you will become president of Mexico."

"Thank you for your good wishes. Some day they may tell you a man of the people is president of Mexico. If you hear that, you'll know that I didn't forget my peasants, the *villanos*. You'll know me when I take the name Pancho Villa."

Tauk-see mounted the stallion and left the mountain. He followed the river north until he was opposite the headquarters of Serpentigero, where he turned east. A rapid gallop over the foothills brought him to the slope above the house where he had come upon Arango. He dismounted and loop-tied his reins to a tree. Slipping the rope on Arango's rolled up pants and shirt over his head, he crawled to the edge of the trees. A narrow strip of open ground separated him from the road that led into the front gate. He rose out of the brush and ran to the rock wall. Scrambling over it, he headed for the nearest outbuilding. As he slipped around it to get closer to the main house, two armed riflemen stepped in front of him. Tauk-see drew his knife and charged at the men. A rifle-butt slammed into his face.

Tauk-see struggled through layers of darkness and heard men's voices. How long had he been unconscious? The men were arguing. One wanted to take him to their leader immediately. The other said they should lock him in the oat barn until later.

"Good idea. If we leave him in the oat barn, we can go on to the fiesta and get our share of the pulque Señor Bocanegra has supplied to us."

The men dragged the barely conscious Comanche to a round building. Jerking its door open, they threw him into a room half filled with oats, slammed the door, and dropped a heavy bar across it. Clapping each other's shoulders and laughing, they went to celebrate the wedding of their patron.

Gradually Tauk-see regained full consciousness. He touched his smashed cheek and rolled over to search for a way out of the storehouse. He groped around the walls but found no opening except the door. In the quiet he heard the rustle of tiny feet on the oats. Rats. Rats meant rat-holes. And rat-holes meant weak boards somewhere. He crawled around the mound of grain until he found a spot low down on the wall where the rats had gnawed their way into the building. Sticking a finger through the hole, he broke out a piece of the board the size of his hand. After three well-placed kicks, the board splintered and oats poured out on the ground. He turned his body sideways and squeezed through the narrow gap.

Tauk-see rounded the granary and heard music, singing, and laughter coming from a long building. Luz Bocanegra's armed guard were busy drinking. Bending low, he ran to the front of the mansion. When he spotted the twenty brightly decorated horses, he slowed for a moment. Their bridles were hung with paper flowers. Strips of red, white, and green paper were woven into their manes and tails. These were the mounts of the twenty men of the house guard who would escort the couple as they left on their honeymoon.

Tauk-see ran on and climbed up the trellis at the front of the house. Carmen heard him coming. Without any greeting, she grabbed the back of his leather shirt and dragged him into the room. When he stood up she put her hands on his chest. "Thanks to the blessed Virgin, you've come."

"I'm glad I'm in time." He slipped the rope on the roll of clothing over his head and handed her the bundle. "Put these on quickly. They'll be better to ride in."

Carmen went behind a screen and fidgeted as she began unbuttoning the wedding dress, but it was taking too long. Impatient and fearing a knock on the door, she stepped out and stood in front of Tauk-see. "Use your knife to get me out of this thing."

Tauk-see had cut the dress from the waist to her neck when the door opened and Pajita rushed in. "It's time—" Her hands went to her face. She screamed. An Indian was holding a long-bladed knife near her daughter's throat. If Carmen hadn't caught her, she would have fallen. "This is my man, Mother—Tauk-see of the Comanches, sent to save me."

Pajita wiped her face and stared. When she fully realized that her daughter's vision had come true, she straightened her shoulders and took charge. More work was needed to remove the dress. Pulling Carmen behind the screen, she stripped it off. As she handed the sweat-stained pants to Carmen, her nose wrinkled. Carmen pulled on the shirt and Pajita turned to Tauk-see. "Where are your horses, young man?"

Tauk-see replied, "I have only the one horse, Señora, but he is a fine stallion. He'll carry us both. I'll get him and soon be back under this window."

As he turned to leave, someone knocked on the door. Tauk-see and Carmen slipped behind the screen. Pajita opened the door to her husband. "Come along, Pajita. The priest is ready." His voice was not the voice of a happy man.

Pajita placed her hand on her husband's chest and pushed him back. "We'll be out in a moment," she replied firmly and closed the door. Tauk-see ran to the window and leaped out onto the trellis. He barely touched the crosspieces as he slid to the ground. Breaking into a long running stride, he remembered the times he'd raced with other boys in the Wichita Mountains. His father and uncles may not have meant to train warriors, but he was grateful they had taught him to run and to ride.

As Tauk-see reached the stallion, the animal snorted and threw his ears forward. The Comanche sprang to his back, and the horse caught his sense of urgency.

When Tauk-see opened the front gate and dashed into the yard of the mansion, no one was watching. The armed guards were drinking and waiting for the wedding to begin. He stopped under Carmen's window, and Pajita helped her daughter climb onto the trellis. When Carmen reached the ground, she rushed to the stallion. Tauk-see removed his moccasin from the left stirrup, and she stepped into it and swung up behind him. With a farewell wave to her mother, she wrapped her arms around Tauk-see's waist. "Let's get out of here," she whispered.

"Not yet. I promised Arango I'd bring him our enemy."

Though puzzled, she asked no questions. And when he rode the stallion to the side entrance of the mansion, she did not object. With Carmen's arms around him, Tauk-see braced himself. "Luz Bocanegra, you no-good son of a mangy she-dog, get out here!"

When there was no response he took a deep breath. "Come out Bocanegra, you no good killer of Comanches! Come out and see what I have!"

The wedding party rushed to the double doors with Luz Bocanegra and the priest in the lead. There they stopped. Luz Bocanegra's drink-blurred eyes focused on his intended bride and a Comanche Indian mounted on his best stallion. He bellowed with rage. Tauk-see rode away from the house, continuing to hurl insults until Luz Bocanegra and his men staggered to the line of decorated horses. Angry and intoxicated they charged after the lineback-dun stallion. Although he could easily outrun the horses that followed him, Tauk-see didn't demand speed from his horse. Instead he held him back to be sure the Mexicans stayed near and followed. Checking the landmarks, he found the place he and Arango had agreed upon.

Tauk-see rode west toward the Conchos, picking up the pace. He glanced right and left and found men lying hidden in the grass. Gaining the river, he crossed over and mounted a high slope, pausing to check on their pursuers. They were riding across the plain, straight toward Arango's men.

When the horsemen were in their midst, the peasants leaped to their feet and grabbed at the horses' bridles. Bocanegra's guards had already drawn their pistols and were firing into the horde of men. Many were shot, but the others kept up their relentless attack. One after another, the horses were pulled down. The rebels killed their riders with hoes and machetes. The priest was slain with the rest.

Luz Bocanegra rode at the rear of the line. When he saw his men hacked to pieces, he turned his horse around and headed back to Serpentigero. Then a large man wearing a huge grey hat stormed into the melee on a bay horse. Tauk-see pointed at him. "There's Doroteo Arango, my friend who sent you his shirt and pants."

"I see why they're so big."

Arango rode through the fallen horses and fighting men in pursuit of Luz Bocanegra. The distance between them was closing when they streaked over the nearest foothill. Carmen relaxed her arms around Tauk-see and took a deep breath in relief.

Tauk-see was satisfied. As promised, he had delivered Arango's enemy. He had no reason to hurry. He and Carmen followed the river north. Sundown found them at the junction of the Conchos and the Rio Bravo del Norte. Tauk-see stripped off the saddle and hobbled the stallion. The horse drank and then grazed north of the river. Tauk-see built a fire and handed Carmen dry jerky to chew. "We'll eat better than this tomorrow. I know a valley where the deer are fat." He unrolled his blankets and sat down beside Carmen.

"So, Tauk-see, Comanche," she said with a smile, "You've answered my prayers and followed the order of your Great Spirit. What will happen now?"

"That depends on you, Carmen. What would you like to do?"

"I can't bear the thought of leaving Mexico and my family. But if Luz Bocanegra is not dead and I go back, everything we've suffered will be for nothing. I'll be in as much danger as ever."

"We don't want that."

"It is only fair if I tell you one other thing, Tauk-see. If we go back and find that Bocanegra is dead, we could stay there, and you could become a landowner. My mother would see that her brothers set you up on the land."

Although Tauk-see was thrilled to hear her talk about them being together, he shook his head. "Your offer is generous, but I can't remain in Mexico."

"Then what do you want?"

"I must return to the Wichita Mountains. My Uncle To-pek-chi told me to bring him his stallion. If my people know that I'm alive and haven't returned this fine animal to his owner, I'd be shamed."

"I understand."

"I want you to come with me. I want you to see my family."

"I've seen your family."

"How?"

"On the night the Virgin showed you to me, She also showed me your family. I saw them sitting around a fire. I'll be glad to see them face to face."

"I'm glad the Great Spirit sent me to you."

"I'm glad you were the answer when I prayed to the Virgin."

The day had been long and Carmen was tired. With her drowsy eyes on the fire, she leaned on Tauk-see's shoulder, trusting him completely. Before long she slept. When he held her gently and eased her onto the blanket, she didn't stir.

He touched her soft cheek. Then he rose to stoke the fire and scanned the horizon. To the west rose the Chinati Mountains where the Old Ones had helped him. If he went there, would they show him his future? Did the Old Ones know what was in store for him and Carmen? He wouldn't ask. In time, the Great Spirit would answer that question. At that moment, it was enough to be happy. Tauk-see had done what he could.

Cockleburs for a Kiowa Scalp

In late 1900, after To-pek-chi had brought three of his four warriors and their lineback-dun horses home from Mexico, the government announced that the land in the Comanche, Kiowa, and Apache reservation would be given to white people. In the spring of 1901, before the reservation was opened to settlement by lottery, each member of those tribes was allowed to claim 160 acres. During the legal transactions that accompanied the transfer of title to the allotted land, the Indians were encouraged to use names that matched those of the whites. Fewer Indians used only one name.

Santoso, son of To-pek-chi, arrived at the office of the Indian agent to apply for his land. A young white man met him at the counter.

"Name, please?"

"Santoso."

"Is that your first or last name?"

"I don't understand. My name is Santoso."

"We must have two names."

"Why?"

"There are spaces for two names on this form."

Santoso scratched his head and looked around until his glance fell on his father, To-pek-chi. His face brightened. "My name is Santoso Topekchi."

"What is your father's name?"

"I don't know. That's his problem."

As a concession to White bureaucracy, many Indians took two names. Although Santoso took a second Indian name, others added a white name as their first. Thus the son of the Kiowa, Ge-hay-tie, became Fred Gehaytie. His wife, She Who Comes in Grief, had been given the name Maude by the Christian missionaries. Her mother kept both of her Indian names and went on the books as Tehat Hauvone, the first meaning She Wouldn't Listen, and the second meaning Long Shot, the name that had been given to her husband's Kiowa father.

The Plains Indians chose their land and continued to live as neighbors as they had done since the United States Army drove them out of Texas. Their lives reflected events of the past. Santoso Topekchi married and moved his family to a farm near Saddle Mountain. His sons and nephews rode the descendants of lineback-dun horses stolen in Mexico under the leadership of his father. Tehat Hauvone clung to her Kiowa past. She and the Gehayties owned land north of the mountains on Jack Creek. Although she had agreed to live with her daughter and son-in-law, she spent as much time as possible in a brush arbor beside their house. Like most Indians, they chose not to farm their land but to lease it instead to white people.

In 1917 Samuel Byers, the son of an English immigrant, leased land from the Kiowas. That year he moved his wife and two children, a son and daughter, onto the Gehayties' fertile, creek-watered land

and started a dairy. By 1922 the birth of two more daughters and another son had increased the family to seven. As the years passed, Samuel's dairy expanded into a diversified farming operation.

On the last night of April in 1931, Cyril, the youngest member of the Byers family, faced a problem that made him squirm in his chair at the supper table. His father had announced they would start spring plowing the next day. Cyril needed desperately to be in school on the first of May. He had promised Juanita Trumpeter, one of the girls in his class at the Mount Scott School, that he would sit with her at the May Day picnic. Juanita had long black hair and dark eyes that melted his heart. Her mother, a Comanche, had given her a Spanish name to complement her father's Anglo name. If Cyril didn't show up at school tomorrow, Juanita would sit with Tonepah Gehaytie, the long-legged son of Fred and Maude Gehaytie. Cyril couldn't let that happen. He and Toney, as Cyril called him, quit being best friends when it came to Juanita Trumpeter.

After supper, Cyril remained at the table and tried to think how he could get to school the next day. In that worried frame of mind, he picked up his *McGuffey's Fourth Eclectic Reader*. When he realized he'd turned to his favorite story, "Robin Hood's Adventures," he read it again. The tale about brave Robin and his merry men hiding in the trees and riding through the glens always gave him a lift. He enjoyed reading about England, the land his Grandfather Byers had left to come to Oklahoma. Cyril especially enjoyed the part where Robin made his friend, the fat Friar Tuck, carry him on his back across a river. Friar Tuck stopped in the middle of the stream and threw Robin into the water. Robin laughed, and Cyril laughed. It served Robin right for treating his friend that way.

When he came to the part where Robin split the arrow, Cyril remembered that his friend, Toney Gehaytie, was also a good shot with a bow and arrow. This thought returned his mind to his urgent need to be at the May Day picnic. He closed the book and pondered the problem. His father would probably catch up with him if he made up a lie. However, he wasn't about to tell the truth. He would never hear the last of it if he asked to be excused from work so he could sit with a girl at a picnic. Tossing on the horns of the dilemma, Cyril grew frantic.

Finally his racing thoughts settled on a recollection. His teacher, Ernest Crain, who happened to be his cousin, had talked to the school about May Day. Cyril recalled as much of the lecture as he could, desperate for something he could use to plead his case. Dwelling on Druids, Kings of May, and English villages, he struggled to formulate a compelling argument. Absorbed in thought, he didn't notice that his mother and sisters had cleared the table and left the kitchen.

When finally he settled on a strategy, his attention returned to his surroundings. The family had gathered in the living room as it did each evening. It was time to make his move. After running once more through his prepared speech, he eased through the door into the front room.

His mother, Lola, and his oldest sister, Mary, were sewing. His sister Louise was reading a magazine called *Aviation*. The youngest girl, Marguerite, was studying the Sears-Roebuck catalog. David, their brother, was sharing the *Kansas City Star* with their father, Samuel. When Cyril quietly approached his father, Samuel lowered his paper. "Yes, Son?"

Cyril looked into his father's cool blue eyes which matched his own. "Will you excuse me from plowing tomorrow? I sure would like to go to school."

Samuel Byers snorted. "Why in the world, Cyril? Most times you're eager to miss school."

"We've been studying the druids in England, where your father came from, and Ern—Mr. Crain—said that the celebration of May Day started with them. It's the favorite holiday in some English villages. They decorate their homes and churches with spring flowers, elect a king and queen of May and dance around a maypole. We're going to celebrate May Day at school tomorrow, and I might try to get elected king of May. I'd like to bring honor to our family, seeing that we're English."

Cyril's brother and sisters exchanged covert smiles. They knew their cousin had announced a school picnic, but he hadn't mentioned election of a king or queen of May. They suspected the true motive behind their little brother's request.

Samuel shook out his paper. "That's very noble, Cyril. We appreciate your thoughtfulness, but we have weeds that need cutting more than we need to be honored. You'll plow tomorrow and there's the end of it."

Cyril's hopes fell. He'd given his best lick and failed, but immediately his mind went back to work, searching for a way to go to the picnic and sit with Juanita.

The first day of May slipped quietly into the Wichita Mountains of Southwestern Oklahoma. The lush valley carved by Medicine Creek awakened in the soft light before dawn. Elm and pecan trees pushed new leaves out of pouting buds. Weeping willow trees arched over the creek, draping graceful branches into the water. A fresh carpet of bluestem grass, primrose, and phlox covered the ground between the trees. Gnarled cedars clung to granite slopes and tinted the mountains. Between rolling foothills east of the mountains, barbed wire fences and wooded streams outlined fields of young cotton, corn, oats, and sorghum called hegari.

From time to time, the crow of a swaggering rooster pierced the quiet. In a plum thicket beside the creek, a mockingbird ran through his repertoire in praise of the new day. Crows rose from their roosting places in the tallest pecan trees—dark silhouettes in a silver sky.

Light from kerosene lamps gleamed through the windows of the farmhouses. Inside, women and girls were busy at their early morning chores. In the barnyards, men and boys harnessed mules and horses.

Although the day promised to be a good one, Cyril Byers found no pleasure in it. With lowered head, he joined his brother and father as they prepared for the day's work. He went into the barn with David and snatched a harness set off pegs on the wall. "Man, I hate having to plow today. I wish to thunder I could go to school."

David swung the harness onto a Clydesdale-type gelding. "Keep talking like that and you'll end up with one of Dad's peculiar punishments." Their father was proud of the fact that he never whipped his children, but he always found some way of teaching them a lesson.

"I wish Toney Gehaytie had to work. He'll be at the picnic."

"Afraid he'll beat your time with Juanita Trumpeter?"

Cyril buckled the hames on the horse's collar and stared at David. His smart-aleck big brother could be a real pain.

Samuel Byers stepped around his team of red-bay geldings. "David, you work the corn up by the Gehaytie's. Cyril, you do the cotton across the bridge. And mind you, boy, stay awake and cut the weeds, not that good stand of cotton."

Cyril watched his father drive his team out of the farmyard. "Stay awake, boy, and cut those weeds," he muttered to himself.

As the eastern sky glowed pink, Cyril stretched and yawned. His bare feet dangled on each side of the backbone of the weeding plow. A light breeze lifted the auburn hair sticking out from his straw hat. He lifted the reins and tapped them on the horse's back. "We're into this crappy deal again, Topper. You'll do all the work and I'll do all the bitching." Cyril often spoke to his horse using words he'd never say at home.

Topper was a small mare, one of the kind called Indian pony in southwestern Oklahoma. She had a reddish-brown body and four white-stockinged legs. At the horse sale where his father had bought her, Cyril had said he wanted the filly that was "sorrel on top." When he wondered what to name her, those words suggested Topper. Although she never offered her own opinion, Topper was willing to do whatever Cyril asked of her. She took him to school, herded cattle, let him ride her bareback along the creek, and worked in harness. This morning it would be harness work in a cotton field.

Cyril wedged the sack lunch his mother had prepared for him behind a brace on the plow and shifted the reins to his left hand. "I wish we were going to school instead of running this dern go-devil."

Deep dirt muffled the mare's hoof beats as she led the sledlike plow down a lane beside Jack Creek. Its steel-shod runners whispered in the powdered earth. Cyril's head nodded in rhythm with the pony's steps. At the spot where the lane bent into a grove of pecan trees, Topper stopped suddenly and lifted her head. She flicked her ears and snorted. Cyril stiffened, searching the trail ahead. A human figure stood in the dark woods, as still and quiet as one of the tree trunks. Cyril strained forward to get a better view.

"Who is it?" he called.

A boy with brown skin and black hair stepped into the lane. "Hey, Cy-Byers."

"Toney! What are you doing, sneaking around like an Indian?"

"I am an Indian, you clodhopper. And I ain't sneaking. I'm waiting for you." He raised his left hand and showed Cyril a bois d'arc bow and five willow arrows. "Let's go hunting, Cy-Byers."

"Ain't you going to school today?"

"I'm going to school all right. But first I'm going to kill a squirrel so my mama can fix it for me to take to the picnic. I figured you'd like to go hunting with me."

I can't go hunting. I have to run this dern go-devil. My bone-headed father kept us out of school so we could plow."

Tonepah's eyes narrowed and he cocked his head. "You mean you ain't going to school today?"

Cyril caught the meaning of Tonepah's words and bristled. "You didn't come down here on the creek before daylight to ask me to go hunting. You want to find out if you can sit with Juanita Trumpeter at the picnic."

"How can you say a thing like that, Cy-Byers?"

"I can say it easy. If you want to know, I've got a plan that will get me to the picnic."

"What's that? You going to throw the go-devil in the creek and tell your old man the hogs ate it?"

Cyril had been bluffing. Until that moment he had no idea how he might get to the picnic. But pressed by the need to answer his tormentor, he suddenly thought of a plan. "No. I'm going to start at the west end of that cotton field and plow to where you can't see because of the tall pecan trees. If Dad looks over there, he'll think I'm plowing where he can't see me. I'll leave the plow on the creek, ride over to the picnic, and be back before he misses me."

"You better not try that, Cy-Byers. If your old man catches up with you, he'll skin you alive."

"Don't try to scare me, Toney. You're worried because you know my plan will work and you won't get to sit with Juanita."

"That may be, but I agree with your old man. You ought to stay away from school and plow today. If you don't, I wouldn't be surprised if something happened that made you wish you had."

"You going to run tattle to my father?"

"You know I ain't like that. But there's more ways to skin a cat than pulling it over the head."

Tonepah faded into the shadows. Cyril shook the reins on his horse. "No telling what Toney has on his mind. Knowing him, it'll be something wild," he said to himself.

Beyond the pecan grove, each plank in the wooden bridge over the creek bounced and rattled as the horse and plow passed over it. On the other side of the bridge, Cyril guided Topper into a field of cotton and aligned the plow's runners astride the first row of young plants. Lowering the steel blades to cut the weeds underground, he clucked to Topper. With a shrug of resignation Cyril settled into the familiar routine. Back and forth across the field, up one row and down another, the go-devil traced a methodical pattern. The monotony of the work, combined with the warmth of the sun, made him drowsy. Periodically he roused himself to see how close he was to the shadows cast by the line of pecan trees on Jack Creek. He went over his plan. At noon he would hide the go-devil and ride over to the school picnic. He'd eat lunch with Juanita Trumpeter, then ride back and finish plowing.

As he finally neared the shadows of the trees, he placed a bare foot on each runner of the plow and stood up. A whirring sound rose above the familiar noise of harness and horse. It was followed by a dull thump. Topper spun in her tracks, whirling the go-devil around like trash in a tornado, and bolted. Cyril had no time to think. He flexed his knees, gripped the reins and rode the plow like a Roman charioteer. As the mare raced off at full speed, she carried the go-devil in a sweeping arc to the west. The flying plow leaped from furrow to furrow, ripping through rows of young cotton. A cloud of brown dust rose behind it. Cyril pulled hard on the leather lines to try to stop her. "Whoa Topper! Whoa girl!"

Even though the mare was panicked, she saw the barbed wire fence looming ahead and veered sharply. The go-devil flipped sideways. Thrown like a stone out of a slingshot, Cyril sailed into the west end of his father's cotton field. He landed on his chest and face, skidding under the fence. Stunned that he hadn't hit the razor sharp barbs, he spat dirt and gasped for air.

After he had caught his breath, he eased away from the fence and checked himself. He touched his chin and drew back bloody fingers. Further inspection showed no broken bones or other serious injury. He brushed dirt off his hands and patted Topper. "Holy, jumping Jehosephat! We could have been killed."

Topper had bleeding cuts where the chains that attached to the go-devil had twisted around her hocks. With trembling hands, Cyril pulled the plow forward and unhooked the chains. The runners and centerboard had survived, but the cutting wings and controls were wiped flat. He hitched up and mounted his battered chariot. Managing to head toward Jack Creek, he stretched forward and touched Topper. "Why did you bolt, girl? What I heard wasn't a rattlesnake or a heel fly."

He watched the ground slip back between the runners of the plow. Suddenly his head jerked up. "That's it, Topper. That no-count Kiowa did it."

When he arrived at the place where Topper's hooves had first chewed up the cotton, Cyril stepped off the go-devil. He searched the ground carefully, then squatted and picked up what he was expecting to find—a willow arrow. He rubbed the smooth shaft from its feathers to the rounded tip. It was one of those he'd seen in Toney Gehaytie's hand earlier that morning. Although it had no arrowhead and would not penetrate, it was heavy enough to kill a bird or stun a squirrel. Cyril tapped the missile in his hand. It could easily frighten a mare into bolting if it hit her on a twitchy flank.

Feeling certain that a pair of black eyes was watching him, he shook the arrow at the line of trees along the creek and shouted, *"Tsatalbai, b'hanti, piata tiawa."* The words were his imitation of a Kiowa phrase that Tonepah had taught him.

"You are a bad boy," Cyril said, repeating in English the meaning of the Kiowa words.

When he couldn't spot Toney among the trees, Cyril stamped the ground. "You're more than that, you stinking coyote. You're a coward who hides to shoot at someone's horse. I'll fix your wagon for this."

From across the creek Tonepah peeked through the trees. He was satisfied. He had made a quick decision to hit Topper's flank with an arrow, and his aim had been true. Now he would get what he wanted. He had stopped his rival from reaching the place where his father couldn't see him. Cyril would not eat with Juanita that day.

Tonepah untied the reins on his black and white Indian pony. "I guess that'll hold Cy-Byers for a while, Wahpah." He called his mare

Wahpah because his father had told him it was the Spanish word for "beautiful."

Tonepah held the body of a squirrel in his right hand and used his left hand to swing onto the horse's back. "Let's go get Mama to cook this squirrel."

At home, Tonepah found his sister Marie squatting at an open fire between the house and an oak-framed brush arbor. She flipped a braid of raven hair over her shoulder, pushed the coffeepot to the back of the flames, and glanced at Tonepah. "What are you doing here? I thought you'd be spending the day on the creek."

"I've been checking with Cy-Byers before I go to school."

"Oh, so you've been at the Byers' place? Did you see David?"

"Your sweetie is working in the field across the creek."

Marie quickly stood up. With one hand on her hip and the other shading her eyes, she followed her brother's pointing finger. When she did not catch sight of David Byers, she sighed. "So, what are you doing here?"

"I want Mama to cook this squirrel for me,"

"Mama's still sleeping. Skin the squirrel and I'll fry it. Why do you need it cooked now?"

"I want to have it for the school picnic when I sit with Juanita Trumpeter."

Marie reached above her head and brought down a skillet. "I thought that little Comanche claimed Cy-Byers."

"Not if he ain't there to claim her. I took him out of the running for today."

"How's that?"

"I shot his horse in the flank, and she tore up the plow. He'll be all day getting it fixed. You should have seen old Cy-Byers. He rode the runners on that go-devil like a Kiowa riding two horses at the same time."

"That must have been something to see. Did he fall off?"

"Topper turned quick, and Cy-Byers flew like a bird. It looked like fun."

Fred and Maude Gehaytie came out of the house. Maude was a tall woman who towered over her husband, a short, powerful man with a huge chest. They heard Tonepah and Marie chuckling. "What are you children laughing about?" their father asked.

Starting with meeting Cyril in the pecan grove, Tonepah told his parents everything that had happened that morning. Maude laid her hand on his arm. "Was Cyril hurt?"

"Naw, Mama. He hitched up and rode the go-devil again."

Fred pushed between his wife and son. "I've told you to leave those Byers boys alone. We don't want trouble with their old man. He's the best white renter on this creek."

Over Fred's head, Maude's eyes met Tonepah's. "Yeah. Leave those boys alone. I don't want that David Byers hanging around here trying to get Marie off by herself."

Tonepah grinned at his sister. She smiled and poked at the golden-brown pieces of squirrel in the frying pan.

Tehat Hauvone sat at the back of the arbor and listened. Tonepah's report reminded her of the long-ago times when Kiowa braves sat around campfires telling stories of their adventures on the warpath. She rapped her ash walking stick on the nearest post of the arbor. "Come talk to me, Tonepah."

Tonepah went to his grandmother and sat down. To make sure she understood his story about Cyril and the flying go-devil, he raised his voice as he told it again. When he finished, she nodded.

"You must be careful. Your friend will do something to get back at you. It's only natural for people to take revenge. Kiowas used to go to war for that reason."

"Thank you, Grandma. I'll watch out for my friend."

Cyril drove out of the cotton field, over the bridge, and up the lane with an angry scowl on his face. He brought Topper into the barnyard, slammed a block of hay into a wooden trough for her to eat, and scrambled to the top of the plank fence nearby. There he sat, awaiting his father and his fate, absorbed in thoughts of revenge.

But as the warm sun bathed his back, his seething anger gradually eased. The trill of a meadowlark vibrated in the air. To his left, a line of trees traced the banks of Medicine Creek as it wound down from Saddle Mountain. To his right, where Lake Lawtonka lapped at the foot of Mount Scott, whitecaps danced on blue water. From the old barnyard at his lineback, earthy vapors rose and enveloped him in a pungent haze.

This had been more than an ordinary run-in. Toney's attack had been deliberate, to keep him from attending the picnic. Shooting Topper was stupid and unforgivable, yet Cyril couldn't believe that Toney had intended to hurt her or him. Nonetheless, they could have been killed, and Cyril doubted whether he would ever understand how his friend could have done such a thing. Even so, Cyril couldn't bear the thought of bringing his father's wrath down on Toney's head. It would be better not to tell him what caused the wreck. The incident would remain a difference between boys—a difference he'd settle himself.

When the sun was noon high, his father's team of matched bay horses trotted briskly into the farm lane south of the barn. Samuel Byers sat on the cultivator plow behind them, his neatly trimmed auburn hair showing beneath his gray felt hat. When he pulled up to Cyril, his blue eyes turned cold.

"What are you doing here? You haven't finished the cotton."

"Something spooked Topper. She ran away and turned the go-devil upside down."

Samuel's face turned red, and his freckles disappeared.

"What do you mean, something spooked Topper? If you don't know what scared your horse, you must have been asleep. You went to sleep and let her run away, didn't you?"

Cyril could have accused Tonepah and turned his father's fury away from himself. But the anger in his father's voice and the fierce-ness of his face convinced him that he was right not to tell on the Kiowa boy.

Samuel Byers walked toward Cyril in stiff-legged strides. Then his face softened somewhat. "Are you all right? Was the mare injured?"

"We both got scratched, but we're not hurt bad."

Samuel bent over the go-devil. "You certainly did a job on it. How in the name of Pete could you sleep and let her run away?"

"I was sleepy when it happened, sir, but I couldn't have kept her from running, even if I'd been wide awake."

Samuel picked up his horses' reins. "Let's feed my team and go to dinner. We'll get you back in the field this afternoon. I'll decide on your punishment tonight." Cyril winced.

At a bench near the back door of the house, Samuel and Cyril washed with soap and water. When Lola Byers brought them towels, she stopped, shocked by her son's face. "Land o' Goshen, Cyril! What happened to your chin? Did you wash it good?"

"It's nothing, Mom. I've been hurt worse than this."

"We need to dress it, anyway."

While his mother inspected his chin, Cyril sat quietly. When she dabbed Mercurochrome on the sore, he stifled a scream. "That hurts more than the scrape."

In the dining room, Cyril's sisters were putting dinner on the table. Mary set down a platter of fried chicken. "Gee whiz. You did get a scrape. Does it hurt?"

"Not much."

Marguerite carried in a bowl of mashed potatoes. "What happened, Hot Shot? Can't you handle your horse?"

"I can handle my horse dang well, Miss Smarty Pants. You've had a horse run away with you, haven't you?"

Lola Byers arrived with a plate of Parker House rolls.

"Children, stop fighting. Watch your language, Cyril."

Louise set a bowl of cream gravy beside the potatoes, and Cyril smiled. "You should have been riding the go-devil, Louise. You'd have enjoyed zipping along at thirty miles an hour."

"Sounds like fun. So, what caused the runaway?"

It wasn't Cyril's nature to lie, yet he was determined not to tattle on Toney. "Something spooked Topper and she ran away. I fell off and scraped my chin. Can we eat now?"

His mother shook her head. "You mean: *May* we eat now? We'll eat when your father has returned grace."

"Yes, ma'am," Cyril answered quickly. He remembered other times when his mother had read his mind and was glad she didn't press him for the truth.

The family took their seats. Samuel Byers cleared his throat. "Let us pray."

That afternoon Cyril and his father repaired the go-devil, and Cyril went back to the cotton field. He spent the afternoon agonizing over missing the picnic with Juanita and fretting about his father's promise to punish him that night. At sundown he returned to the barn and unharnessed Topper. She joined the team of bay geldings eating oats on one side of the trough. Opposite them was a mixed team—a black Percheron-type mare and a chestnut gelding with Clydesdale feathers at its fetlocks. As he continued with his evening chores, David stopped him at the barn door. "Hear you got into a storm, Cy. Sorry about that."

"Thanks. Dad promised to punish me tonight."

"Hope he doesn't get too fancy."

Usually Cyril enjoyed the time he spent in the barn at the end of the day. While he hated the boredom of plowing, he looked forward to milking and feeding the animals. He liked the clean, fresh smell of the cows and the sound of streams of milk shooting into the foamy buckets. But that evening his mind dwelt on a serious problem.

After supper Cyril was in no hurry to join the family. He had no desire to be near his father, so he sat at the table after everybody else was gone. He picked up his *McGuffey's Reader,* but decided against it. After several minutes, he took a deep breath and went into the living room. His father lowered his paper.

"Son, I've thought about your problem. You need a powerful reminder to stay awake when you work a horse. I'm giving you a whole day to think about it. Saturday, when the family goes to town, you'll stay at home."

Cyril flinched. Not go to town on Saturday? This was a severe punishment. He would miss the week's episode of Buck Jones at the Ritz Theater. He wouldn't get to eat a hamburger or drink a Nehi grape soda at Wimpy's Café. But his father's was the last word, so he didn't argue or beg.

As he remembered the one who had caused this disaster, thoughts of revenge crowded his mind. As sure as Friar Tuck threw Robin into the river, he'd get even with Toney.

Cyril survived the miserable weekend. On Monday morning he dragged through morning chores and ate little of his mother's sausage, eggs, and biscuits. She looked at his food and laid her hand on his forehead.

"Are you ill, Cyril?"

"I'm all right, Mom."

After breakfast the Byers children carried their lunch pails and schoolbooks to the barn, where they found their father brushing the black mare. He laid a folded army blanket on her back and centered a saddle, which bore the stamp Haynes and Co., Saddlemakers, Anadarko, Oklahoma. After Louise and Marguerite packed their books and lunches in the saddlebags, Samuel boosted them into the saddle. David swung a McClellan saddle onto the chestnut gelding. He cinched the saddle tight, and Mary put her lunch and books in its saddlebags. Cyril tightened the girth of another McClellan on Topper. "I hate this no good piece of army junk."

Samuel Byers raised his hand. "Don't start that. Soldiers ride these saddles all the time."

"Soldiers have bigger behinds than mine, and they can get comfortable if they sit up straight. No matter how I sit, the edges of that stupid gap down the middle cut the inside of my legs. Can I ride bareback?"

"You mean: *May* I ride bareback? And the answer is no, you may not. I've told you before. If you ride bareback, there's no place to carry your lunch and books."

As the children rode out of the barnyard, Cyril moped along behind, lost in thought. What was he going to do about Toney? Not tattling was right, but now he wanted to get even. He wanted Toney to suffer. An ordinary fistfight, with equal black eyes and bloody noses, wouldn't do. They'd had a dozen fistfights. Revenge for this grief should be something special. The riders were coming to a public road. Cyril was still bringing up the rear, and ahead of him the mare and gelding walked through dry weeds in the bar ditch. He noticed the cockleburs stuck to the horses' legs and tails. Cyril grinned.

Here was the answer to his problem. He dismounted and gingerly began picking the egg-shaped seedpods covered with needle-sharp hooks. The barbs caught on his pants and pricked his fingers as he crammed handfuls of them into his pockets. Ignoring the pain, he planned how he would use his treasures. When his pockets were filled to overflowing, he remounted his horse and hurried to catch his brother and sisters.

About a mile farther on, the road passed Logan's store. Signs on its walls advertised Day's Work chewing tobacco, Camel cigarettes, Nehi soda, and Hurst's sliced light bread. On a telephone pole out front, a poster announced "Ritz Theater presents Buck Jones in *The Roaring West,* a fifteen-episode serial."

Reading the poster, Cyril remembered why he had missed last week's episode and patted his bulging pockets. Two miles beyond the store, the children dismounted at the one-room frame building that was Mount Scott School. After they had loosened the saddle girths, the Byers children tied their mounts at the end of a line of horses forming under a row of bois d'arc trees. While he was loop-knotting the reins of Topper's bridle to a tree, Cyril scanned the group of horses and recognized a black and white Indian pony.

"Howdy, Wahpah. I reckon I could put these cockleburs under your saddle blanket and let Toney do his hurting when you throw him, but I ain't mad at you. I'll take care of this myself." Inside the school building the children walked into the cloakrooms—girls on the right, boys on the left. Sweaters, caps, and jackets hung from hooks on each side of the long, narrow rooms. The odor of sweaty garments mingled with the smell of apples, peanut butter, German sausage, sourdough bread, fresh onion, bologna, and fried chicken in the lunch pails stored on shelves above the hooks.

The siblings deposited their lunches and entered the classroom. The morning sun shone through tall windows in its east wall and streamed across rows of desks. A blackboard paneled the wall opposite the windows. Maps of the United States, Europe, and the Holy Land covered most of the back wall. At the front of the room the teacher, Ernest Crain, sat at a large desk.

The older Byers children avoided using their cousin's given name and greeted him according to their mother's instructions: "Good morning, Mr. Crain." Cyril saw no difference between Mr. Crain and Cousin Ernest, but he followed the example of his brother and sisters.

When the pendulum clock on the side wall showed eight o'clock, Mr. Crain rang a handbell to call the school to order. Cyril joined the other boys and girls making their way to assigned seats. His school-mates were descended from various European and Indian cultures and ranged in age from six to fifteen years.

Mr. Crain checked the roll and assigned lessons. After that he walked in the aisles, observing the students work. Cyril stared dutifully at his book, but couldn't concentrate on the fourth-grade reading assignment. Cocklebur spines pierced through his pockets and bit into his thighs, distracting him. At ten o'clock Mr. Crain tapped on his desk.

"Recess time. Those in the first four grades, please rise."

The younger members of the school moved into the aisles. With his eyes fixed on Toney Gehaytie's head, Cyril joined them. He kept his quarry clearly in sight until they had all marched out of the building. When Mr. Crain dismissed them, the children shouted and ran to the playground.

Cyril allowed the others to pass and then raced forward and locked his left arm around Toney's neck. While holding on like a bulldog, he pulled a handful of cockleburs from his pocket and rubbed them into Toney's hair. He massaged the spiky seedpods into the thick strands until all of them caught and some even met a Kiowa scalp. Tonepah fought like a roped colt. He kicked backward and caught Cyril below his right knee with a solid blow. Whipping his body from side to side, he dropped to the ground and rolled forward. Nothing worked. He couldn't get rid of the demon on his back. Once Tonepah turned his head and thrust his face into a handful of cockleburs. Cyril pushed them against his face, scraping skin off Toney's cheek. Toney let out a scream that was part pain but mostly anger.

When Cyril ran out of cockleburs, he looked for an avenue of escape and released his victim. He would run around the building and wait for the counterattack he knew would come. This proved to be a miscalculation. Ernest Crain heard the loud cries of the victim and arrived at the front door in time to intercept his young cousin in full flight.

"Cyril, what's going on?"

At that instant Tonepah ran into sight. Mr. Crain stopped him. Tonepah could have passed for a porcupine; the cockleburs made his hair stick out all around. Deducing what had happened, Mr. Crain gasped in fury, his anger compounded because Cyril was his cousin. He grabbed Cyril's shoulder and shoved him into the classroom. "Sit down at your desk and don't move."

He motioned for Marie Gehaytie to come to him. "Take your brother out on the steps and get those cockleburs out of his hair." She had to hang on to her infuriated brother to keep him from charging into the school after Cyril.

Mr. Crain expected Cyril to be full of fear and remorse. Instead, a look of satisfaction was spread across the boy's countenance. With clenched fists Ernest stopped beside Cyril.

"Get to the front of the room and bend over a desk," he ordered.

Cyril began the long walk. He passed empty seats along the way, which gave him another reason to be satisfied. The fourth grade was still out at recess. Juanita Trumpeter would not see him get whipped.

Cyril bent over a desk in the prescribed position and looked at his brother and sisters. Their expressions showed neither condemnation nor sympathy. Their eyes told him he had asked for it, and must take his punishment.

Cyril screwed up his courage and prepared himself to receive his punishment. Suddenly his cousin rang the school bell and called in those who were still outside. He waited patiently until the students had settled in their seats.

"I wanted you all to see Cyril's punishment—especially Juanita Trumpeter."

The children giggled. Cyril's mouth went dry. Public association of his name with Juanita Trumpeter's was more than he could bear. His inborn stoicism failed him, and he blushed.

Ernest Crain walked to where Cyril waited and stood behind him. Cyril looked back at his teacher-cousin.

"How many?" he asked.

Ernest raised the ruler. "Ten hard ones."

Cyril avoided Juanita Trumpeter's beautiful brown eyes, which were fixed on him in loving sympathy. He braced his body and counted. "One, two, three—I will not cry—four, five, six—cockleburs for a Kiowa scalp, worth the pain—seven, eight, nine— nearly finished—ten."

It was over. He'd survived the worst that life had to offer—a whipping in front of Juanita Trumpeter and the whole school. His revenge diminished the humiliation. Throughout the morning Cyril listened to Toney's yowls of pain each time Marie yanked a cocklebur out of his tangled hair, and smiled.

In the afternoon the teacher continued his slow walk in the aisles. Once, as he passed Cyril's desk, he bent low and said, "Stay after school."

Cyril's hand went to the seat of his pants. He thought he'd had all the beating he needed in that area.

After school, when the other students had gone, his cousin stood in front of Cyril's desk. "I asked David to tell your parents you'd be late today."

"I don't need any more punishment, Ern—Mr. Crain."

"I only want to talk. It's not common for a boy to take a whipping the way you did today and not protest or cry. This was more than a playground fight, wasn't it?"

Cyril hesitated for a moment, and then said, "Yes."

"Do you want to tell me about it?"

"I haven't told anyone about it."

"Why not?"

Why hadn't he told on Toney? Cyril squeezed his brows together and was silent for a moment. "Toney did something that hurt me and my pony, but I'm not sure how he could stand to do it. I haven't told any grown-ups because I don't want to get him in trouble."

"Sort of you and him against the grown-ups?"

"Right."

"And today you took the law into your own hands?"

"Something like that."

"If I knew the whole story, maybe I could help."

Cyril was not sure he was ready to share the details of the arrow attack with anybody. As long as the difference was between Toney and him, he would feel safe. If he told an adult, the secret might get back to his father.

When Cyril did not answer immediately, Ernest folded his arms. "That's all right. If you don't want to talk about your problem, I understand."

"I've thought about this a lot, and I need to talk to somebody about it."

"I'll help if I can."

Starting with when Toney stopped him at the trees by the cotton field, Cyril told Ernest everything. He included the go-devil wreck, the tragedy of missing Buck Jones on Saturday, his anger at Toney for being so stupid, and the discovery of the dry cockleburs on the way to school that morning.

Ernest did not interrupt Cyril's story, nor did he speak for some time after it was finished. Finally, he moved to the desk across the aisle. "You and Tonepah are good friends, but you sometimes misunderstand each other. Why do you think that happens?"

"Maybe because our families aren't alike."

"I don't believe that's the reason. I know Fred Gehaytie. Like many men, he is impulsive. When Tonepah quickly makes a decision to do something, he's following in his father's footsteps."

"But how could he shoot my horse? Didn't he know he might kill her, or me?"

"You've already told me you don't believe he meant to kill you, and I agree. I believe he shot your horse on a sudden impulse."

"What does that mean?"

"It means he didn't plan it ahead of time."

"Like not looking before you leap?"

"Right."

"Dad's always getting on to me for doing that."

"I know, but he also has impulsive outbursts."

"Yeah. Sometimes he flies off the handle."

"Your fathers are alike. Perhaps you and Tonepah are not so different."

Cyril gathered his books. "I guess we aren't."

As he rode home, Cyril went over in his mind what Ernest had said. He agreed that he and Tonepah were alike. There had been many times when he had leaped before he looked.

At home, he went directly to the barn and joined his father and brother, who were milking cows. Cyril lifted a clean pail off a hook on the wall. "Sorry I'm late."

Samuel Byers continued milking. "David tells me you had to stay after school."

"Ernest wanted to talk to me."

"I hear you had business with Ernest earlier in the day. What about the cockleburs?"

"Toney shot Topper with an arrow and made her tear up your go-devil and the cotton field. I got even with cockleburs."

Samuel Byers leaped to his feet, kicking over the milk bucket. "Why didn't you tell me that?"

"Well . . ."

Samuel thrust his contorted face at Cyril. "You take too much on yourself, boy. That Kiowa made a stupid, dangerous attack on you and your horse. How dare you hide the truth and think you'd take care of this yourself? You're just like those kids who run free on the creek. You boys think you don't have to pay attention to adults. I'm going right now to have it out with Fred Gehaytie and his stupid son."

Cyril saw his brother standing behind their father. The fear etched on David's face convinced him that the situation was serious. Their father was having one of those impulsive outbursts Ernest had talked about. Silence was the only safe course to follow.

At the moment when Cyril thought the storm had passed, his father turned on him again. "And you had to get a whipping in front of the whole school to make you tell the truth."

No longer able to bear the attack in silence, Cyril returned his father's hot glare. "The whipping is not what made me tell the truth. I thought you would understand, like Ernest. He says I was right in believing Toney didn't mean to kill me. He thinks Toney shot Topper because he's impulsive, like his father."

"Oh, yeah? Ernest is forever apologizing for people. Remember this. I'll show you impulsive if you ever lie to me again. And another thing. I don't want you hanging around that savage Kiowa anymore."

Cyril was frightened and angry, but decided to hold his tongue. This was no time to voice his disagreement with what his father was saying. How he would deal with his father's orders remained to be seen.

An Ocean Between

During the five weeks since Cyril had taken revenge on Tonepah for his attack on Topper, the boys had not been together. Cyril had never been sure whether his father was serious the night he ordered him to stay away from Tonepah—"that savage Kiowa," he had called him. He may have meant the words he screamed, or perhaps they were outbursts of impulsive rage. Either way, Cyril had decided not to test the matter. All through the school term he had avoided Toney on the school grounds. He also hadn't ridden on the creek, which he would have done if he'd wanted to see Toney. Tonight, Cyril felt strange.

Although he was in the living room with his family, he felt apart from the group. He watched rain pelt against the panes of the window. The mournful wind sighed at its frame and made him feel lonely. But there must be more to his loneliness than weather—he yearned for something. Once, when his parents had left him at his grandmother's house overnight, he'd felt this way. That time he'd missed his home. Suddenly, Cyril understood—he realized he was missing Toney. He remembered the day he rubbed the cockleburs in Toney Gehaytie's hair. Ernest Crain had reminded him that he and Toney were good friends, even though they sometimes misunderstood each other.

Cyril began planning how he could see his friend. A cautious approach would be best. His father hadn't mentioned the Gehayties since the incident, and Cyril was not going to ask if he could visit them. If he could get permission to ride on the creek, he'd have an excuse to be away from the farm. He crossed the room and stood by his father. Samuel Byers lowered his newspaper. "Yes, Cyril?"

"May I ride on the creek tomorrow?"

"That'll be all right. Be back in time for evening chores."

The next morning after breakfast, Cyril pulled two large biscuits apart and laid a round sausage between the halves. While he was wrapping the sandwiches in waxed paper, his mother brought a chocolate cake from the pantry and cut two slices. "Carrying two sandwiches and two pieces of cake is a good idea. You never know when you'll run into someone who's hungry on the creek."

Cyril's eyes darted to his mother's face. Sure as shooting she knew he planned to see Toney.

Lola Byers ignored her son's sudden glance and handed him a brown paper sack that held the sausage sandwiches and cake. "Stop by the garden and get some fresh onions and tomatoes. I folded some salt in paper for you."

Down at the old barn, at the bottom of the slope, Cyril caught his Indian pony. "We're going to visit Toney, Topper." He cinched his McClellan saddle on the mare's back and swung into it. "Mom knows what I'm up to, but she's not letting on. If my father gets mad, I'll take whatever he dishes out. The day Ernest whipped me in front of Juanita and the rest of the school, I learned a lot about taking whatever I deserve."

On Jack Creek upstream from the barn, Cyril stopped at a cottonwood tree and stood in the saddle. He stretched as high as he could and wedged the sack lunch in a forked branch. "That'll keep it safe from ground varmints. Let's go see Toney and Wahpah."

Cyril followed the creek another half mile, then stopped across from a small, square house, its unpainted roof rising to a peak above faded green walls. Beside the house stood a brush arbor, fresh elm branches covering its post-oak frame. Cyril recognized Toney's mother, Maude Gehaytie, standing at a fire near the arbor. As she leaned over a steaming pot, two braids of black hair swung forward. Inside the arbor, colored blankets outlined the forms of sleeping people. Beyond the arbor, a pen built of split rails held a gray-roan horse and a black and white Indian pony.

Cyril urged Topper through the shallow water and up to the fire. Maude raised her eyes. Cyril returned her steady gaze. "Where's Toney?"

Maude pursed her lips and thrust her chin toward a blanket-covered figure at the edge of the arbor. Cyril walked Topper over near the figure. "Let's go swimming, Toney."

Suddenly the blanket flew up and a hand grabbed his ankle. In a single motion, Tonepah stood and hoisted Cyril's leg up out of the stirrup, heaving him over the other side of his horse. Cyril fell to the ground headfirst. When he could focus his eyes, he saw Maude's face. A faint smile played at the corners of her mouth. Cyril stood and faced Toney, whose close-cropped black hair and light tan face showed over Topper's back. "I didn't come here to fight, Toney. Get your old ugly pony. We can outrun you to the island."

Tonepah reached for a bridle and glanced at Wahpah. "You can't outrun us nowhere, Cy-Byers."

The boys kept their mounts side by side as they rode onto a dirt road. Wahpah and Topper eagerly bounced on their front feet. Soon they'd be running their fastest. Keeping their eyes on a sand plum bush, the riders held their prancing ponies. At the bush they both shouted, "Go!"

The ponies leaped forward, digging into the dirt and extending their necks. The boys bent low as they urged them on. Wahpah's legs flashed black and white, matching Topper's white stockings stride for stride. For half a mile, their hooves pounded the hard-packed ground with the three-count beat of a racing gallop. When their course dead-ended at a crossroad, the ponies crossed it and flew over a wide ditch. They swung left into a field of saw grass and headed for Jack Creek. Although they were rushing at heavy underbrush, neither boy drew rein. At the creek Topper and Wahpah leaped into the water. The boys slid off their backs and grabbed their manes as the mares swam furiously toward a sandy island. Their front hooves touched ground side by side.

Tonepah dropped to the sand. "I *said* you couldn't beat us!"

Cyril fell down beside him. "You didn't beat us either, Toney. Boy howdy! That was fun!"

"Yeah. A real kick!"

The little mares drank from the creek, then trotted off to nibble elm leaves at the far end of the narrow island. The boys lay on their backs.

In a while, Cyril raised himself onto one elbow. "What did it look like when I came off that go-devil?"

Tonepah sat up. "It was beautiful, Cy-Byers. You rode that thing like a wild man. When it flipped, you looked like a bird. You could've flown over that fence if you'd raised your arms. How did it feel?"

"It was swell. I rode scared, but I enjoyed the ride."

"You seen Juanita this summer?"

"Naw, not since school let out. Topper and I walked her home the last day of school, but I never found out who she sat with at the May Day picnic. Was it you?"

"You know Cy-Byers, girls are the beatin'ist things. I told Juanita about the trouble I had getting a squirrel for her and me, and getting rid of you, but she turned me down flat. She said it wasn't nice of me to shoot your horse, and she wasn't going to eat with me."

"Have you seen her lately?"

"Yeah, I saw her at a powwow at the Millers' the other night. She and Johnny Wolf are mighty friendly. I don't think you and me should be fighting over her."

"We've sure been doing that—you shooting Topper and me putting cockleburs in your hair."

"Yeah. And me trying to bust your head open by throwing you off your horse this morning."

"Everybody wants to get even, Toney. You remember the story we read about Friar Tuck throwing Robin Hood in the river after Robin Hood made him carry him?"

"I remember. And my grandma told me the Kiowas used to go to war to get even. I reckon we're all alike."

"I don't know about that, Toney. You and I are alike, but we're some different, too."

After the boys swam the mares back across the creek, they turned west and followed the tree-lined bank to Lake Lawtonka. Thinning out ahead of a gentle south wind, wispy clouds were reflected in the blue water. Whitecaps flicked on low waves raised by the breeze. On the lakeshore, wide stretches of wet sand twinkled in the morning sun. A few yards back from the water, willow trees grew in green clumps. On their ride down the beach, Cyril and Tonepah pointed out odd items they spotted—a single leather boot, an orange crate, a broken bottle. They passed tin cans and many dead fish. Most were small—sunfish and perch—but some were large—crappie, catfish, and bass.

Tonepah pointed up the shore to a moving animal. "What's that?"

"Looks like a dog."

They rode closer. A coyote was anchoring the body of a large bass with its paw and ripping at the flesh with its teeth. "Let's chase him!" Cyril suggested.

The coyote began to move away from them.

Tonepah raised his hand. "Wait! We don't want to lose him. I'll keep his attention. You ride on the other side of those willows and sneak as close to him as you can. When you get behind him, ride out and head him this way."

"Okay. I wish we had a rope. Maybe we could catch him."

"I wish I had a bow and arrow."

Cyril rode out behind the willows. Tonepah took up a position a quarter of a mile from the coyote. Not close enough to frighten it away, but close enough to hold the animal's attention. To pique its curiosity and distract it from Cyril's approach, Tonepah waved his hands over his head and rode slowly back and forth across the beach.

Then Cyril charged out beyond the coyote and chased him up the beach toward Tonepah. Tonepah whirled Wahpah around and joined the pursuit. The coyote tried to dodge in front of Wahpah, running away from the lake. Tonepah rode forward to block him. When he angled back, there was Topper, pounding the ground behind his tail. The chase led into the woods where fallen trees barred the way. The coyote tore through the timber without missing a stride. Topper followed at breakneck speed. Each time she jumped a log, Cyril made sure he was with her. When the coyote ducked under a fence and disappeared over a hill, the boys slowed their sweating ponies.

Tonepah took a deep breath. "Man, oh man, what a ride! It must have been like that when my grandpa hunted buffalo in Texas."

Cyril gasped and nodded. "That was the cat's meow! It makes me think of the fox hunts in the Cotswold Hills of England that my grandfather told us about. There'd be great chases with lots of people riding horseback over the fields and jumping fences."

"Your grandpa hunted foxes in England?"

"Naw, fox hunting was for rich folks. He never even rode a horse till he got to the United States."

Tonepah swiveled in his saddle. "How about that? I thought running the coyote was like hunting buffalo in Texas. You thought it was like hunting foxes in England."

"Like I said, Toney, we're some different, but there's one way I bet we're alike."

"What's that?"

"Our stomachs. You didn't eat breakfast. Ain't you hungry?"

"Starving."

"I know where there are two sausage sandwiches and two big pieces of chocolate cake. You interested?"

"Don't talk dumb, Cy-Byers."

While Cyril retrieved the sack lunch, Tonepah settled in the shade of the cottonwood tree. Cyril handed him one sandwich and took a bite of the other. With his mouth full of sausage and biscuit, he sat down in front of Tonepah. "So, your grandfather hunted buffalo out in Texas?"

"Yep. Our tribe lived there forever."

"How come they left?"

"You know damn well why they left. Your white people's army whipped them and threw them off the plains."

"I've read about the Red River wars, but I never thought about your folks fighting in them."

"They fought in them all right. After the battle of Palo Duro Canyon, my grandpa saved the Two Mountain band of Kiowas."

"How did he do that?"

"The horse-soldiers tore up the camp and drove away the horses. Grandpa hid enough horses for the band to make their getaway."

"Is that so? Was that Old Lady Hauvone's husband?"

Cyril winced at what he had said. He had called Toney's grandmother by the white people's name for her. He touched Tonepah's arm. "I'm sorry. It slipped out."

"Don't worry about it. We know that's what you all call her. She's a great woman. She tells good stories and gives good advice. After I sent you flying on that go-devil, she warned me to watch out for you. I should have listened to her better."

"Was it her husband who saved the Kiowa band?"

"No. White soldiers killed her husband, my grandpa Jessee Hauvone, at a place called Tahoka Lakes. My old man's pa was the one who saved the horses at Palo Duro Canyon."

Cyril handed Toney a piece of chocolate cake and unwrapped the other. "The way I figure it, the difference between our grandfathers was as wide as an ocean."

"How's that?"

"While your grandfather was hunting buffalo and fighting the United States Army in Texas, my Grandfather Byers was going to college over in England."

"Why did your grandpa come to Oklahoma? I don't reckon the U.S. cavalry threw him out of England."

"I'm not sure why he came to this country. Maybe he had itchy feet. Before he got here, he moved around and did a lot of things."

"Like what?"

"He saw the fire that burned Chicago and fought Sioux Indians in the Black Hills of South Dakota for their gold. Why he even drove a wagon across the Texas plains while the Comanches and Kiowas were still on the warpath."

"That took guts."

"Yeah, I know. What happened to your family? When did they leave out there?"

"They damn near starved to death one winter, so their chief brought the band in."

"Brought them in?"

"He brought them to Fort Sill and surrendered to the soldiers. The ones that didn't die nearly froze to death in that old stone fort."

"Your family lived at Fort Sill?"

"Yep. I was born there."

"I didn't know that. How come you were born at an army fort?"

"I would have been born at home, but when it was time for Mama to have me, something funny happened. She had trouble and they sent for the medicine man. He came, but he wouldn't have nothing to do with Mama.

"He told Papa something strange was going on and he had to take Mama to the hospital at Fort Sill. When Papa argued, the medicine man told him that while he was on the way to our house, Tsain-tai, a Kiowa medicine man who'd been dead for thirty years, appeared to him in a vision. He said Tsain-tai told him to make sure I was born at Fort Sill. Our medicine man warned Papa not to tell anyone about what he had said. Papa didn't argue anymore. He took Mama to the hospital at Fort Sill and I was born."

"You believe that medicine man stuff, Toney?"

"There's a lot of things we don't know about, Cy-Byers."

"Why were those medicine men so interested in you?"

"Grandma Hauvone said that many years before I came, Tsain-tai told her I was coming. He told her the Great Spirit would send me to lead the Kiowas. She got the message wrong and thought he was talking about my cousin Paul. Paul died when I was little."

"My brother and sisters told me about the time when Paul died. Your grandmother walked past our house on the way to Paul's funeral. Her singing nearly scared them to death."

"Yeah. She told me about that. She said your red-headed sister was the one who straightened her out about Paul and me. She wasn't a bit surprised when Papa told her what the medicine man said the night I was born. She claims that me being born at Fort Sill is a sign that I'll become a great leader."

"I wouldn't be surprised. I'd follow you—well—most of the time," he said.

"Thinking about you and them damn cockleburs and your grandpa fighting the Sioux for their gold, it looks to me like picking on Indians runs in your family."

"My grandfather didn't pick on the Sioux as much as they picked on him. One day he was digging for gold and they rode in and damn near caught him. They chased his tail all the way to the fort. If General George Crook and the United States cavalry hadn't rescued him and the others with him, he'd have been a goner."

"So the horse-soldiers killed my grandpa and saved yours."

Cyril was silent.

"If your grandpa was stealing gold from the Sioux, how come you ain't rich?"

"My grandfather said the Sioux decided he didn't need none of their gold, and the cavalry decided he didn't need to be fighting the Sioux, so he left the Black Hills empty-handed and peaceful."

Tonepah stood up and brushed the seat of his pants. "Why did you come to my house today?"

"No particular reason. I was riding on the creek and decided to drop by. Anyway, that's what I'm going to tell my father."

"What do you mean?"

"Until after I put the cockleburs in your hair, I never told him what caused the go-devil wreck. When I finally did tell him, he got so mad he ordered me not to hang around with you no more."

"So what changed his mind?"

"His mind may not be changed. If he hears I've been with you, I don't know what he'll do. It's time I go find out."

Cyril swung onto Topper and rode down the creek. Tonepah hopped onto Wahpah and rode behind him.

When Cyril rode into the barnyard, it was dusk. His father and brother were filling the hay troughs. Cyril opened the barred wooden gate and turned Topper in with the rest of the stock. David waved. "Did you have a good time?"

"Yeah, real good."

His father stepped out of the barn. "What have you been up to?"

Cyril stiffened. Was that suspicion in his voice? No matter. While riding home, he had decided what he would say. He picked up his saddle and walked toward his father. "Toney and I jumped a coyote down on the lake. You should have seen him run."

"I'm glad you boys got together again. I've been wondering if you were going to carry a grudge for the rest of your life."

Cyril stared at his father. What in the world was the man talking about? Didn't he remember telling him to stay away from Tonepah?

After Samuel Byers returned to the barn, David poked Cyril in the ribs. "How about that? You thought you were going to catch hell."

Cyril shook his head. "I'll never understand grown-ups, especially our father."

The Lineback Duns

In 1934, 20 million acres of the Great Plains region of the south-western United States were gripped by fierce winds and killing drought. The Wichita Mountains lay in the center of a dust bowl that stretched from North Dakota to central Texas. In late December of that year, Cyril and Tonepah were riding their small mares, Topper and Wahpah, on a powdery dirt road south of Saddle Mountain in Oklahoma. A stiff west wind blew dust into the air all around them. Cyril rubbed his eyes with the back of his hand.

"Maybe we should have stayed with the Downeys like they wanted."

Tonepah pulled a red bandanna from his hip pocket and wiped his face. "Yeah. This dirt is bad, and the wind's getting cold." Wahpah tossed her head and threw her long black mane from the right to the left side of her neck. Topper arched her back and laid back her ears to say she didn't like the cold wind that was blowing her white mane forward. For several miles they rode in silence. Then Cyril pulled up, stopping Topper short. "Do you reckon it's going to snow? We ain't had a rain or snow this winter."

"Them clouds coming up behind us could have snow in them."

The day turned dark, as the boys rode on, hunching their backs against the cold. Like windblown leaves, the little mares scuttled ahead of the rising gale.

At the top of a rise, Tonepah faced his friend. "You're right. We should have stayed with the Downeys or started home sooner."

"We'll have to go to someone's house."

"The Topekchi place is next, but it's ten miles farther on." Sunset found them engulfed in a sandstorm. Whipped by the fierce winds, they urged their mounts into a gallop. Obedient to their riders, the mares bowed their necks and plunged ahead through the swirling dust.

Cyril felt moisture on his hand—snow. The clouds had caught up with them and were loosing their loads. The wind-driven snow began to pelt his neck and ears. Within minutes the wind was blowing out of the north, and the sandstorm had turned into a snowstorm. Before they'd gone another two miles, a mountain blizzard enveloped the night riders. Cyril urged Topper to catch up with Wahpah. "We'd better slow down," he said.

"Yeah, and stay together. A fellow could get lost in this."

"I hope we don't miss the Topekchis' gate."

The snow piled up as the mares carried their riders through the moonless night. They rode in the ditches so as not to lose the road. After several hours had passed, Cyril asked, "Don't you reckon we're near the Topekchis'?"

"I don't know where we are," Tonepah admitted.

"We better find something soon, I'm freezing."

Cyril was hungry as well as cold, but he realized he could do nothing but ride on. As his body and mind grew numb, he slumped on Topper's back. Then, somewhere in the raging storm, he heard a familiar sound, a horse's whinny. Not trusting his senses, he strained to hear it again. Topper raised her head and Cyril felt her body vibrate in answer to the call. Tonepah called out. "Did you hear that, Cy-Byers? We've made it to the Topekchis'."

Tonepah found the wooden gate and opened it. The boys rode into the yard of the Topekchi home. In a barn beyond the house a horse whinnied, and the mares answered. The front door opened and a teenage youth raised a kerosene lantern above his head. "Who's out there?"

"Tonepah Gehaytie, Robert. Cy-Byers is with me."

"Man alive! What are you guys doing out on a night like this?"

"We stayed too long at the Downeys' and the storm caught us."

"Get down, and come in."

Cyril rode into the light of the lamp. "We need to get our horses under cover. Have you got stalls for them?"

"You bet. Ride on down to the barn. I'll get a coat and meet you there."

At the barn tall, square-shouldered Robert Topekchi opened the swinging doors. Cyril and Tonepah led their horses into a wide aisle. A tawny-colored horse with black mane, legs, and tail and a broad, brown stripe down its back thrust his head over a stall gate. The mares forgot their fatigue and offered their nostrils to the gelding to exchange breath. After a few moments he showed his delight by whinnying and stamping the wooden floor. The mares responded with similar excitement. Cyril tightened his hold on Topper as he admired the gelding.

"So this is the guy that saved our necks?"

Robert Topekchi hung the lantern on a hook above the aisle. "What do you mean?"

"We were making for your place but couldn't see anything in the storm. We had no idea where we were. If your horse hadn't heard ours and whinnied, we would have ridden past your house."

Tonepah let Wahpah reach out to smell the lineback dun again. "If he hadn't heard us, we could have frozen to death on that road."

Robert rubbed his horse's neck. "His name is Leon del Concho. I call him Leo. Like all lineback duns, he's a great animal. Put your mares in the stalls and feed them. Then we'll go to the house and get supper for you."

At the kitchen door Robert Topekchi's parents, Santoso and Virginia Topekchi, and his younger brother, William, met the boys. Santoso Topekchi's graying hair, plaited in a single braid, suggested middle age. When his wife, Virginia, smiled at the boys, her whole face lit up. William, who was younger and smaller than Cyril, peered around his mother's hip.

Shutting the door against the bitter wind as his son and guests entered the house, Santoso said, "Welcome, boys. You picked a bad night to come calling."

Cyril stepped into the warm room. "Thanks, Mr. Topekchi. We were worried that we wouldn't make it at all."

"What horses are you boys riding?"

"We've got Indian ponies. Tonepah rides a piebald, and my horse is a sorrel with four white stockings."

"You didn't need to worry. Those little Indian ponies will get you through anything. Some of us rode them to Mexico in 1900. They carried us out of danger many times."

Virginia Topekchi laid her hand on her husband's arm. "Will you please let these cold boys get in the house before you start talking horses?"

The smell of frying ham and baking biscuits reminded Cyril he was starving hungry. When Mrs. Topekchi was ready, the travelers sat down to scrambled eggs, thick slices of ham, gravy, and fluffy biscuits spread with fresh butter. Mr. Topekchi and his sons joined Cyril and Tonepah at the table. Cyril spooned brown gravy on his ham. "You say you rode Indian ponies to Mexico, Mr. Topekchi?"

"We sure did. Five of us left Fort Sill and went all the way to the Conchos Valley in Chihuahua."

Tonepah glanced down the table past Cyril. "You went there in 1900? Then you weren't much older than we are. Why did you go?"

"Because I was tired of sitting around doing nothing. My cousin Tauk-see went because he got a message from the Great Spirit saying he had to. We got our cousins, Wo-tank-ah and Tenny-sau to join us and talked Papa into taking us there. We found out that Papa had another reason for going."

"What reason was that?"

"He wanted to make the world remember who the Comanches are. At first he was just out to show us what it was like in the glory days, but he ended up making sure the Comanches would never be forgotten again.

Cyril broke open a biscuit and poured blackstrap molasses on the two halves. "So what were you going to do in Mexico? What was your cousin Tauk-see's message?"

"Well we'd talked Papa into taking us to steal horses, but it wasn't until later that we learned the Great Spirit had sent Tauk-see to save a Mexican girl from being forced to marry a brutal old man four times her age."

Cyril and Tonepah finished their meal, and Virginia Topekchi cleared the plates. Santoso, Robert, and Will led their visitors to the front room of the house where they gathered around a large potbellied stove. Robert opened the stove door and shoved in an oak log. Cyril took a seat on a hide-covered, straight-backed chair near the stove. "So you went to Mexico to steal horses and ended up saving a Mexican girl?"

Santoso settled on the blanket-covered sofa and clasped his hands around his knee. "All of us didn't save the girl. Tauk-see did that alone—well, not exactly alone. He had help from that Mexican bandit, Pancho Villa, and his fighting men. But that's another story. I was going to tell you about the horses."

Tonepah raised his hand to stop Cyril's next question. "You said we shouldn't worry if we were riding Indian ponies. Tell Cyril why they're called Indian ponies."

"In the olden days the Comanches got horses from several places—farms, ranches, and other Indians. In time we learned that the animals that ran wild on the western prairies were strong and tough. The Mexicans called them mustangs. Many of them are small, so ponies describes them best. Because white people saw Indians riding those little western horses so often, they began calling them Indian ponies. We Comanches are proud to have our name connected to them. As I said, the five of us that went to Mexico in 1900 chose Indian ponies to take us there."

Cyril tilted his chair against the wall. "You said the Indian ponies saved you from danger?"

"Yeah. One time one of them got into quicksand, and the others helped pull him out. Then there was the time we escaped being caught by running them flat out down the main street of a town. On two occasions we galloped ahead of cowboys and cavalry for hours, and the ponies never gave up on us. Another time we rode without water for two days and most of three nights, and the mustangs carried us through."

"Were the horses that you stole in Mexico mustangs?"

"No. The Mexicans weren't raising Indian ponies. They had hot-blooded horses out of stallions from Spain. Andalusian they called them. We were after those high-bred horses for their size, beauty, and speed."

Cyril lowered the front legs of his chair. "Did you get many?"

"We got a good herd back across the Rio Grande, but then the damned horse-soldiers got after us. By that time the telegraph was working in West Texas, and the army forts along the border sent messages to each other telling where we were and where we were heading. We weren't on our Indian ponies. We were riding four beautiful lineback-dun mares we'd stolen at a hacienda called Serpentigero, the place of the snakes."

Cyril scratched his head. "Four? But there were five of you, weren't there?"

"My cousin Tauk-see had gone back. The night before the soldiers chased us, he talked Papa into letting him take a stallion marked exactly like the mares back to Mexico."

"Your cousin went back?"

"Not to stay. He went back to save the Mexican girl. We figured he was committing suicide, but he insisted he had to go after her."

Tonepah shook his head. "Your father just gave him the stallion and you all went off without him?"

"There's something you need to know. Before we left for Mexico my father had gone to Medicine Bluff to seek power. He came back from the bluff believing he'd been given power to take us to Mexico. On that night Tauk-see asked him for the stallion, my father felt the power leave him. He took his medicine bag and pipe and went into the hills to make medicine. He knew that if he didn't have the power working with him, everything would go wrong.

That night when he came back to camp, he called us around and told us he had the power to get us home without being killed. And he had been given another power, a power that would make people remember who the Comanches are.

He said it would be all right if Tauk-see took the stallion and went back to Mexico, but he must return the horse to him when he was through with it. We didn't find out what Papa had on his mind until we got back to Fort Sill."

"So the four of you headed back to Fort Sill with that bunch of horses you'd stolen?"

"Yeah. The next morning, but we hadn't gone far when a cloud of dust appeared on the horizon south of us. Papa said it was the United States cavalry. We ran ahead of them through the early morning, then another bunch started raising dust east of us. Up to that time we'd each been leading our own horse and riding a lineback mare. After that second troop started after us, we threw our own horses in with the herd and drove them all ahead of the cavalry. And for the rest of that morning, man, did those lineback duns prove they were as tough and fast as any Indian pony."

Outside the storm increased in ferocity. The wind rose and a sudden blast blew the door open. Robert hurried to slam it, and Santoso stoked the fire with another log. Cyril scooted closer to the stove. "When you left off, Mr. Topekchi, you were running ahead of the cavalry. What happened after that?"

"Papa finally realized we weren't going to get home with a large herd of horses, so he worked out a plan. He told us to cut out our Indian ponies and then scatter the herd on the plains. We split up and rode through the tracks made by the herd. By the time the cavalry got to the spot where we'd ridden into thousands of hoofprints, they couldn't tell which tracks to follow. That part of Papa's plan worked and we got away. We didn't learn what else he had on his mind until we got back to Fort Sill."

Tonepah raised his palms to the stove. "What was that?"

"You've seen one result of his plans—standing in a stall in our barn tonight."

"Robert's lineback-dun gelding, the one that saved our hides, was part of your father's plan?"

"That's right. He and every lineback dun you've seen Comanche boys ride. Tauk-see took that lineback dun and went back to Mexico, and the rest of us came home. Everyone celebrated. We hadn't gotten away with a lot of horses, but we had proved a point: Comanches were still brave and we could still ride. At the campfire that celebrated our return, Papa laid out his intentions to the people. He told them that he'd left a lineback-dun stallion with his nephew in Chihuahua, but he was sure Tauk-see would return it to him. Then he planned to breed the four mares we'd ridden and give a lineback-dun colt to each boy born into the tribe. When people saw them on those horses, they would know they were Comanche."

Santoso grew silent and Cyril cleared his throat. "That was a good plan, Mr. Topekchi, but your father didn't have the stallion. Your cousin still had him in Mexico."

"You listen good, Cyril Byers. That's exactly what my father's brother, Po-tauh-see, said, but Papa told him that he'd left his stallion with a brave warrior, a true Comanche. He was sure Tauk-see would bring the stallion to him."

Cyril rocked forward. "My family has always known that you can tell a Comanche farm by its lineback-dun horses, but I never thought about why. So your cousin did get back with the stallion and now every Comanche boy gets a lineback dun—"

Tonepah stopped Cyril with a tug on his sleeve.

"What about the girl in Mexico?"

"He brought her home, too, Tonepah. You probably know her as Mrs. Carmen Potasie. She and Tauk-see live east of Meers."

Virginia Topekchi carried in a pot of coffee, cups, and sugar. She set a plate of cookies on a table in front of the sofa. Cyril took the cup Santoso offered him. "I know Mrs. Potasie, but I didn't know she was from Mexico. How did your cousin get her to Fort Sill?"

"After my father unfolded his plan, the people saw that he offered a way to be sure that the world remembered who the Comanches are. But when they heard that Tauk-see had gone back to the place of the snakes, everyone figured he was dead. The old ones remembered that the owner of Serpentigero had once butchered a Comanche and hung his head on the ranch gate. They kept telling my father to forget his stallion. Everyone was sure he'd never see the horse or Tauk-see again.

"My father never gave up. He told his brother, my uncle, Po-tauh-see, that his son Tauk-see was a good warrior. He was sure his nephew would follow orders and bring the stallion to him.

"We'd been home from Mexico four weeks when I heard a commotion in the village. I rushed out and found people shouting and pointing south at a horse carrying two people. With Carmen Cavarubio sitting behind him, Tauk-see rode in on my father's lineback-dun stallion. Everyone flocked around the horse to welcome them. My father took the reins of the stallion and paraded him and his riders around the village."

Santoso's eyes twinkled and he laughed. Seeing his amusement Cyril smiled. "What is it, sir?"

"When we got a good look at Carmen, some of the other young men and I joked about how long it had taken Tauk-see to get home. We said we didn't blame him for not hurrying, since he was riding with Carmen Cavarubio's arms around his waist. They heard an indignant snicker from the kitchen where Virginia Topekchi was sitting.

Santoso ignored his wife's irritation. "The welcoming lasted all morning, until Uncle Po-tauh-see and my aunt stopped my father to insist that Tauk-see and Carmen be allowed to dismount. Carmen had been on that stallion so long that they had to rub her legs before she could walk.

Of course when we held a campfire for them that night, Tauk-see told us the whole story about returning for Carmen and the rescue."

Santoso took a long sip of his coffee and sat quietly. Cyril waited a while, then dunking a cookie in his, asked, "What did happen, Sir?"

Santoso roused himself out of his thoughts and chuckled. "I was remembering when Tauk-see and I sneaked into the yard at Serpentigero. That was when he found out that the Great Spirit had sent him to save Carmen. When he walked to the house and climbed up to a second-story window, I thought he'd gone nuts. That night he helped steal the horses at that hacienda and rode with us until we crossed the Rio Grande with the herd. Then he decided he had to go back for the girl.

"He returned to Serpentigero and stole Carmen from under the nose of the old man her father was going to make her marry. Set her behind him on my father's stallion and spirited her off on her wedding day. Carrying double, that fine horse took them to safety ahead of fifty armed men. As they were escaping, Pancho Villa and his fighters appeared from nowhere and stopped their pursuers from killing Tauk-see and recapturing Carmen."

"Stopped them?" Cyril questioned.

"They killed all they could and chased the others back to Hacienda Serpentigero."

Cyril listened in fascination.

"Did Mrs. Potasie talk at the campfire?" Tonepah asked.

"She wasn't Mrs. Potasie yet, but Carmen did talk to us that night in her own language. Comanches who understood Spanish told us she said many nice things about my father and those of us who helped Tauk-see get to Mexico. Also, she had high praise for Doroteo Arango, a Yaqui Indian who helped them escape. That was Pancho Villa's real name. Tears came to her eyes while she was telling us how much she appreciated Tauk-see and his beautiful lineback-dun stallion."

"But what about the soldiers from Fort Sill?" Tonepah's thoughts were racing ahead. "Didn't you ever get into trouble over that raid?"

"They came around, but we took care of it the way we always did. We told them it was the Kiowas who did it."

Tonepah laughed. "My folks told me that happened a lot."

Santoso nodded, his eyes sparkling. "Of course," he added, the Kiowas would do the same thing to us."

"And now we know the Comanches by the beautiful horses they ride," Cyril said.

Robert touched Cyril's knee. "The lineback duns do more than tell people who we are, Cy-Byers. They give us good saddle mounts and running horses. My gelding descends from one of those four mares that were extremely fast. He may be the fastest horse in Comanche County."

Unable to respond to that claim, Cyril was grateful when Mrs. Topekchi interrupted them. "It's time we went to bed. You boys can sleep double in the bed we have for you."

The next morning the storm had passed, and the sun sparkled on the new-fallen snow. Robert Topekchi went with Cyril and Tonepah to saddle their mares. Cyril tightened the girth on Topper. "That's quite a thought, Robert, that yours is the fastest horse in Comanche County."

"I'm not just bragging, Cy-Byers. He's outrun everything I've matched him against. Maybe when the weather clears, I'll get down your way and you can see him race."

The winter of 1934 passed and the spring of 1935 was in bloom. Cyril rode Topper toward the bridge over Jack Creek, a meeting place for boys in the Mount Scott community. There they would fish or talk or race their horses. Cyril saw Wahpah tied to the bridge and smiled. Tonepah was sitting on the guardrail. Cyril tied Topper beside Wahpah. "What's going on?"

"I'm waiting for Robert Topekchi. He sent word that he's coming this way. I was hoping you'd get to see him and his horse."

Cyril climbed the guardrail and sat beside Tonepah. "I've thought a lot about him saying his horse might be the fastest in Comanche County. You reckon that's true?"

"Maybe. We've heard he's beat every horse around Saddle Mountain so bad none of the guys will race him anymore."

"Listen. Someone's coming."

They cocked their ears at the sound of a horse approaching at a gallop. A rider they didn't recognize topped the hill east of the bridge. His mount was a black stallion with a white diamond on his forehead and white stockings on both hind legs. His flowing tail stretched out behind him. Long strides carried him swiftly toward the creek. The rider didn't draw rein as his horse clattered over the wooden bridge. Cyril nudged Tonepah with his elbow. "That guy is either dumb or he's got a lot of nerve, galloping downhill like that and not even slowing for the bridge."

"Yeah. He's just showing off for us."

The rider, a white man, turned his horse around and rode back to the bridge. "Howdy, boys. What do you think of my stallion?" the stranger asked.

Cyril pursed his lips and shrugged. "He'll do."

"Do, hell! He's the fastest horse in Comanche County."

"You might get an argument about that."

"Not from the likes of you and your little ponies."

Cyril bristled. "Our ponies might run faster than you think."

"Oh yeah? Which one's yours?"

"Mine's the sorrel with four white stockings."

"This stallion would blow that little mare plumb off the road."

Tonepah touched Cyril's thigh. "Leave it alone, Cy-Byers. You know damn well that stud can outrun Topper."

"He said he'd blow her away. I don't believe he can do that."

The stranger rode close to Cyril. "You got anything more than your mouth that says your pony can run? I'll bet you four bits you can't stay close for a mile."

Cyril stiffened and Tonepah pulled on his arm. "You ain't got four bits to lose."

"I got two bits. Will you lend me a quarter?"

"You're nuts, Cy-Byers. Why throw your money away?"

"If he wins, he'll be able to say he outran one of our ponies, but if one of us doesn't race him, he'll call us yellow." The man jerked the bit in his prancing horse's mouth. "Are you going to bet or talk?"

"I'll bet. We'll run from across the bridge to the next section line. Toney will hold the stakes."

"And who'll start us?"

"Toney can do that, too."

"Not on your life. I found you two sitting on that rail as thick as crows. I'm not fool enough to let a pair of connivers cheat me out of four bits."

Both boys jumped to the floor of the bridge, ready to fight. They weren't accustomed to being called liars or thieves and didn't intend to put up with it. But the sound of a horse trotting toward them interrupted their plans.

Robert Topekchi rode his lineback-dun gelding around the bend of the creek. "Hello Toney and Cy-Byers. Mrs. Gehaytie told me I'd find you here."

Cyril turned his back to the stranger. "Howdy Robert. How's our friend Leon del Concho feeling today?"

"Leo's fine. What are you guys up to?"

"You got here in time to help us get a race on, Robert."

"Who's going to race?"

Cyril pointed at the rider on the black stallion. "He says his horse is the fastest horse in this county. I was about to give him a chance to prove it against Topper, but he didn't want Toney to start us."

The black stallion crowded in beside the gelding, and his rider held out his hand to Robert. "I'm Carl Sanders. I was about to give these boys a lesson on running horses. Of course it ain't going to be

132

much of a test for my horse, but it'll be worth the dollar stakes the Indian boy holds."

Cyril went to untie Topper. "So you'll accept Robert Topekchi as starter?"

Carl Sanders looked back at the youth whose hand he had shook and studied the horse he was riding. "Is this Robert Topekchi? I've heard about him and his fast horse. What a shame you didn't ride your good horse today, Topekchi. Maybe you and me could've raced and you'd find out what a fast horse really is."

Robert's eyes narrowed beneath his lowered brows. He nodded. "So, Carl, you've got the fastest horse in Comanche County. You must be real proud."

"He's so much better than any of the others we've run against it's pitiful."

Cyril rode across the bridge and reined Topper to a stand in the dirt road. "Come on. Let's have a look at your speedy mount."

Carl worked the black into position beside Topper. Riding twenty-five yards beyond the pair, Robert turned the lineback dun to face them and removed his hat. "You guys ride toward me. When you're even, I'll throw my hat down. When the hat hits the ground, start racing."

The riders understood the instructions. Tightening the reins and squeezing with their legs, they passed the message to their horses that they were going to run. Rocking from front to back, the black stallion and Topper danced toward Robert, who held his hat above his head. Anticipating the start, Topper broke Cyril's grip and rushed past the starter. Robert called them back. The next time both racers bolted to run, with the black ahead. On the third try, Robert saw that they were side by side and threw down his hat. Topper used her quick stride to leap ahead of the stallion, but her advantage was short-lived. In two strides the other horse caught Topper and steadily pulled ahead. Cyril lay along Topper's back and urged her on. The black lowered his body and stretched his stride. The first quarter of a mile would determine the outcome of the race. The black was best. His longer legs left Topper behind as his larger hoofs pounded the road in a steady three-beat gait. Topper rapped her smaller hooves in the dirt with a more rapid rhythm but shorter strides. Even though he was beaten, Cyril didn't quit. He kept Topper as close as possible to the fleet stallion. Then a sound behind him caused him to glance back.

Robert Topekchi's lineback dun was tearing down the road after them. Evidently, Carl Sanders saw the dun coming; he shouted at his horse. He whipped him across the withers with his reins. Sensing that the dun was still gaining, he cursed and flapped his legs against his horse's sides—to no avail. Two hundred yards from the section line where the race was to end, the lineback dun passed the stallion. Beyond the finish, Robert eased his horse into a slower gallop, and Cyril pulled Topper along beside them. Carl Sanders never slowed his horse but rode on out of sight.

Tonepah caught up to Cyril, who had slowed Topper. "Does that give you an idea how fast Leo is, Cy-Byers?"

"I've never seen anything like that in my life! Who'd believe Robert could start us and then turn around and catch us."

Robert rode his gelding back to join them, a triumphant smile on his face. Cyril gave him an admiring salute. "That was some ride, Robert. You made a believer out of me."

Tonepah pointed down the empty road. "And also out of Mr. Carl Sanders. He thought *he* had the fastest horse in Comanche County."

"Yeah. Looks like Carl didn't want to stick around and teach us any more about fast horses."

Tonepah rattled the coins in his pocket. "He didn't even wait to pick up the four bits he won beating Topper. What are we going to do with it?"

Cyril rubbed Leo's neck. "We ought to give the stakes to Robert. He was the winner, and I'd be glad for him to have my part."

Robert stroked his horse's mane. "I've got a better idea. Why don't we ride down to Bert Shanklin's store and treat ourselves to ice cream?"

A Stabbing at the Indian School

Without his beautiful red and white mare, Topper, Cyril Byers was lost. His good friend and constant companion had gone to visit a stallion. Despite the morning's bright sunshine, he sulked inside the back door of his farm home. In those days, the middle 1930s, any boy in the Wichita Mountains whose horse was taken away would have felt the same.

Cyril tugged on a lock of auburn hair falling across his freckled forehead and peered through the screen. His gaze slipped down a gentle slope to a weathered barn. Empty pens beside the stable reminded him that Topper was not there and he kicked the door. "Doggone it, there ain't nothing I can do without her."

His mother stepped into the kitchen. "Cyril, cut that out! It's not the door's fault you don't have your mare. You should have thought of this before you sent her to be bred."

"Did I have a choice? Dad was so all-fired excited about breeding Topper to Seth Miller's skewbald stallion he didn't give me time to think it over."

"Your father's excited about the colt your flashy mare and that beautiful brown and white stallion will get."

Cyril stepped onto the back porch and let the screen door slam behind him. He slouched down the wooden steps and drifted toward the barn, wondering how Topper was getting along on the Miller farm, east of Lawton. He was glad she was still in Oklahoma, but for all the use she was to him she might as well have been in Mexico.

Lowering his eyes he disregarded the tall, leafy trees on Jack Creek behind the barn. He ignored the light brown cows grazing on the green slope beyond the empty pens. At the barn, he climbed the plank fence and sat on the top rail. Cupping his chin in his hands, he plunged deeper into the black hole that self-pity had dug in his mind. He couldn't go anywhere or do anything. He was sure nothing exciting could happen while Topper was gone.

The sound of footsteps behind him stirred him out of his funk. It was his father. "You can quit moping, Cyril. I have good news."

"What?"

"Seth Miller sent word. Your mare has completed her visit with his stallion."

Cyril spun around and dropped to the ground. "Hot diggity. When can we go get her?"

"That's a problem. I need to pick up a new bull in Wichita Falls today, and I promised Hiram I'd help with his calves on Saturday. I can't bring her home before the first of next week."

"But she's been gone for two whole weeks."

Samuel Byers studied his son's long face. "Well, why don't you come with me this afternoon. I'll drop you off at Seth Miller's and you can ride Topper home."

"That'd be great! Let's go!"

"Not so fast, son. We need to repair the trailer and eat dinner first."
In the equipment shed, Cyril was helping his father when his mother appeared in the doorway. "It's dinnertime. You two are going to eat, aren't you?"

Samuel tightened his grip on a large wrench he had locked onto the head of a bolt. "As soon as we fix this trailer."

Cyril held a smaller wrench. "Mom, have you heard the news? Topper is ready and I'm going to the Miller's with Dad to ride her home."

"Aren't you going after her with the trailer, Sam?"

"I plan to drop Cyril off on my way to Wichita Falls."

"It'll be dangerous for him to ride that road by himself."

"Now, Lola, you know the children ride all over this country by themselves."

"It's not the same. He'd have to pass those beer halls between Fort Sill and the Indian school. That's where that crazy Kiowa killed that man."

"Queno Hinauho didn't kill anybody. He's in jail in Lawton awaiting trial for *attempted* murder."

"Same thing. The mean fool got drunk and stabbed someone in a bar. Thinking about Cyril near a place like that, I'd worry myself sick."

"Cyril won't be stopping off in bars."

"Don't get smart with me, Sam. I don't want our son taking such risks."

Cyril saw his chances slipping away and had to think fast. "I have an idea, Mom. Why don't I get Toney Gehaytie to go with me? We could take Wahpah in the trailer, and then Toney and I could ride home together."

Samuel released his wrench, tossed it on a workbench, and wiped his hands with a cloth. "I like that idea, Cyril. That'll ease your mind, won't it, Lola?"

Lola Byers pushed her wavy, brown hair away from her damp forehead. "I'll still worry, but I guess the two of them would be safe enough." Pleased, Cyril went to his mother and hugged her. After dinner, Samuel hooked the trailer behind his Oakland touring car. Cyril scooted in the front seat beside him. They drove to the Gehayties' and found the family in the brush arbor beside their house.

Cyril spotted Tonepah and jumped out. "Toney, you and Wahpah come with us. We're going to bring Topper home. We can ride back from the Millers' together."

On bare feet, Tonepah loped across the yard to meet Cyril. "I hear you, Cy-Byers. Let's go!"

Fred and Maude Gehaytie walked out of the arbor. Samuel Byers tipped his gray felt hat to Maude and shook hands with Fred. "Cyril's mare is ready to come home. I'm going to drop him at the Miller place, east of Lawton. He wants Tonepah to ride home with him. We could take Wahpah in the trailer."

Fred Gehaytie looked at his wife, then nodded. "That's fine. The boys will like that ride." Samuel told the Gehayties he'd give the boys money to buy something to eat at Cox's store. He didn't mention the bars they'd have to pass nor his wife's fear of men like Queno Hinauho.

Tonepah led his piebald Indian pony to the open trailer, "All right, Wahpah, get in."

Studying this strange contraption, a new thing in her experience, the mare didn't move. Tonepah stepped into the trailer. "Come on, girl, it won't hurt you." With her best friend tugging gently on her halter rope, the little mare picked up her dainty feet and joined him.

At the Miller farm, Cyril hopped out of the car while it was still rolling. He ignored the sharp reproach his sudden dismount brought from his father and ran toward a man who stood in the yard. "Where is she?"

Seth Miller led them to Topper. Cyril crawled between the wooden planks of the stall and threw his arms around her neck. "I've missed you, girl. These last two weeks have been like forever without you."

Tonepah unloaded Wahpah and came to watch the reunion. After a few minutes, both boys and the men went to admire a brown and white male horse nibbling hay at a feed trough in the next pen.

Seth Miller pushed his floppy straw hat back from his suntanned face and exposed his pink pate. "What do you think of him boys? Ain't he a beaut?"

"He's fine, real fine, Mr. Miller," Cyril replied.

Seth hung his thumbs inside the front of his bib overalls and beamed. Samuel Byers handed him a check. "I hope we get a colt half as good looking as that stallion of yours."

"Thank you, Sam. Whatever it looks like, I'll bet it gets a lot of color out of my stallion."

Samuel laid his hand on Cyril's shoulder and they headed for his car. "I need to get on to Texas, and you two have a long ride ahead of you. We better get under way."

The boys saddled and bridled their mares. When they were mounted, Samuel Byers reached in the front seat of his car and retrieved a short, stiff whip. He handed it to Cyril.

"Here's the quirt your mother wanted you to carry, Cyril." Winking, he added, "Remember now, stay out of bars, and don't mess with any drunks you meet along the way."

Cyril tipped the whip to his forehead in a salute, then slipped its leather strap over his saddle horn. Waving, the boys set off.

Cyril and Tonepah rode out of the tree-shaded driveway of the Miller farm toward a graded dirt road. Ahead of them bright sunlight bathed the rolling hills and tree-lined creeks of southwestern Oklahoma. Cyril pointed in the direction of the Wichita Mountains. "Look yonder. Ain't Mount Scott beautiful?"

A lacy haze dimmed the arching outline of Mount Scott, giving its granite surface a soft appearance. "Yeah. It sure does," Toney said, following Cyril's gaze homeward.

"This is great, Toney. I'm glad I thought about us making this ride together."

"Me too, Cy-Byers."

Toney was eyeing the whip hanging from Cyril's saddlehorn. "Your mother wants you to carry that quirt?"

"It's more than a quirt. Here—feel how heavy it is. The handle is filled with lead. My grandfather used it in Texas when he broke mules to ride."

Tonepah hefted the quirt. "Man, this thing *is* heavy. You could drop a bull with it."

"One time it saved my grandfather's life. He used it to knock a mule down before it slammed his head into a tree limb."

"You don't need it for Topper. Why did she want you to bring it?"

"My mother was worried about us making this ride. She thought it would be good for us to have a weapon along—just in case."

The boys noticed that their horses were bouncing on their front feet as if they expected something to happen. Tonepah patted Wahpah's neck. "They think we're going to race, Cy-Byers."

"Yeah, but we better not. We have a long way to go."

The mares settled into a walk near each other. Tonepah pushed Topper away from Wahpah with his foot. "Mr. Miller sure is proud of his stallion."

"Seems like it."

"He thinks you're going to get a colt that is really colored up. You excited about getting a colt, Cy-Byers?"

"Toney, I'll tell you the truth. In the beginning I was tickled pink about getting a colt. But after going two whole weeks without Topper, a colt didn't sound all that great. I missed Topper and I hated not being able to do anything. I like excitement. When I can't get out and around where things are going on, I get antsy."

Meeting a blacktop road, the pair nudged their horses into a trot. Near Lawton they came to a double-span steel bridge over Cache Creek. Wahpah and Topper, two country mares a long way from home, were not sure they liked those long, high arches. Built of thick planks laid between angle irons, the bridge had narrow gaps in the roadway every few feet. Through the slits, the horses could glimpse the roiling waters in the creek below. Although they didn't refuse to cross, they were fearful and rose up on their front hooves to test their footing before each step. They crossed the bridge as if it were thin ice.

Safely over the bridge, Cyril and Tonepah rode into Lawton and turned north along the east edge of town. On the wide streets downtown, cars darted in and out, fighting for lanes. Cyril, in the lead, stopped to admire the quieter street in front of them. It was wide and straight and so long that he couldn't see where it ended. The freshly oiled surface of fine gravel was as smooth as a carpet. The temptation to run was great. He shortened his reins and waited.

"Toney, I ain't ever seen a road like this for running, and I don't expect to ever see a better one. Let's race."

"I was thinking the same thing, Cy-Byers. It's a good road for fast horses. Let's do it."

When the boys tightened their reins and lay forward onto their horses' backs, the mares chomped their bits. They knew what was coming. Keeping their eager mounts side by side, the boys studied the street ahead. Tonepah pointed. "See that big smokestack? We'll race to the road that goes by it."

"Okay. We'll start at the flowers in that yard."

When they had reached the flowers, Cyril raised his hand. "Now!" The horses clawed the gravel. The boys locked their legs on the mares' sides. For a quarter of a mile they tore down the road, picking up confidence and speed as they ran. Neither horse gained an advantage.

Suddenly a terrifying sound assaulted the boys' ears. A motorcycle policeman was coming after them, siren screaming. It sounded like a machine from hell. An icy knot formed where Cyril's stomach should have been. When Tonepah looked back, he accidentally pulled Wahpah into Topper. Both horses skidded as their riders yanked the reins and then dived to opposite sides of the road. They whirled and planted their forefeet. The motorcycle pulled up between them. Forcing air against their nostrils, the mares made huffing sounds like locomotives.

A tall blond man wearing shiny black, knee-high boots and a blue uniform lowered the kickstand on his motorcycle and leaned the machine on it. "Well, what have we here, a pair of Barney Oldfields?" Tonepah had never heard of the racecar driver Barney Oldfield, so he stared blankly. Cyril had heard of him but couldn't imagine why the policeman had stopped two riders on horseback.

When Cyril saw the smile on the man's face, he realized the policeman was kidding. He hopped off Topper and fell in with the joke. "Gee, officer, I knew we were fast, but I didn't think we could break the speed limit."

The patrolman's face turned serious. "I started after you because I thought this fellow with you might be Queno Hinauho."

"That's the guy my dad said is in jail for trying to kill someone."

"He was, until he escaped last night. Every peace officer in Comanche County is looking for him. I thought I'd found him."

Tonepah slid off Wahpah and joined Cyril. "I ain't Queno Hinauho, and I don't want nothing to do with him. I know that guy—he's one mean Kiowa."

"Do you boys plan to leave town?"

"Yeah," Cyril answered. "We live out in the mountains and we're going home."

"I'm warning you, this is a serious matter. You're fixing to ride through the area where Queno hangs out. He has a girlfriend at the Indian school, and we expect him to try to get to her. Also, he likes those beer joints out by Fort Sill. If you see him, don't mess around with him. Get word to the police."

Outside the city limits of Lawton, Cyril and Tonepah came to a fork in the highway. One branch turned west toward the town of Cache. The other continued north toward Fort Sill, an army installation where thousands of soldiers were stationed to learn to operate artillery guns. The travelers chose the road north, which took them past a building with a neon sign that said The Pink Pig. Attached to the building in a haphazard manner, smaller signs extolled the pleasures of beer, music, and dancing. Cyril drew rein. "There's one of the bars my mother worried about. Wonder if that's where Queno Hinauho stabbed a man?"

Tonepah caught the foul odor of spilled beer and stale cigarette smoke. "I don't know about that, but it smells bad enough that anything could have happened here."

The boys rode on toward Fort Sill. On their left, a five-strand barbed-wire fence separated the highway from a pasture. A railroad embankment flanked the highway on the right. In a while they came to an unpaved parking lot in front of a two story building, another bar. This one was called Waldo's Tavern. Its faded stucco front needed painting. Cyril slowed Topper to a walk. The sound of slurred voices and high-pitched, whining music drifted across the parking lot. From time to time shouts and raucous laughter rose above the singing.

Tonepah stopped Wahpah beside Topper. "You ever been inside a bar, Cy-Byers?"

"Nope. Have you?"

"Naw. But I've always wanted to see what one looks like."

Tonepah guided Wahpah past parked cars—Model A Fords, Chevrolet coupes, and a Model T. He stopped at the corner of the building. "Look at these high windows, Cy-Byers. I bet we could see inside if we stood on our horses."

"Get away from there, Toney. That's the kind of place my folks told us to stay away from. Queno might be in there."

"If Queno Hinauho was in this bar, someone would've already called the police. I'm going to take a look."

"I don't think we ought to do that."

"You're afraid, Cy-Byers. I piker you to go look."

"I'm not afraid and no one pikers me. Let's go."

Topper and Wahpah allowed themselves to be arranged under the row of high windows. Standing on their horses' backs, the curious boys raised on tiptoe to look through the dirty glass. Inside, young men and women crowded a small, smoke-filled room. Some sat at tables, holding bottles of beer and singing. Others danced in a narrow space between the tables and a wooden bar. A jukebox, flashing red, yellow, and green lights, blared music. Khaki uniforms identified the men as soldiers. The women wore short, bright colored skirts and tight-fitting blouses.

"Wow," Tonepah whispered, "look at those girls' dresses."

Cyril stared through the grimy glass. "Yeah!" Shifting his position for a better view, his feet slipped off his horse. His fingertips caught the windowsill as his body slammed against the side of the building. A few people in the bar heard the noise. Then a soldier spotted Tonepah at the window.

"Window peekers! "Let's get 'em!"

Soldiers and young women spilled out of the tavern and gathered around the boys. One soldier grabbed Wahpah's bridle. "We got ourselves a pair of snoopers."

Another soldier grabbed Topper's loose reins. "And their little old horses."

Like scared rabbits, the boys began to bolt, but the crowd blocked the way. Two soldiers grabbed them. Unsteady on his feet, the soldier who held Topper's reins grabbed her mane. "I always wanted to ride a horse."

"Me, too," the soldier holding Wahpah replied. "Never had no chance to ride a horse in Brooklyn."

The soldier beside Topper hopped onto her, slid over the other side, and landed on his head. His friends laughed. The one who had caught Wahpah swung onto her back, sat straight for a second, then lurched over and fell to the ground. Everybody laughed again. This was great fun. For a quarter of an hour the soldiers took turns trying to ride the horses. Some stayed on long enough to ride a few steps.

Cyril realized he was at the mercy of drunk strangers and shuddered. He had done wrong by peeking into the bar. He felt guilty and afraid. Tonepah's face showed that he shared Cyril's alarm. Like fools, they'd gotten themselves trapped. Powerless in the grasp of men much stronger than themselves, they watched helplessly.

Then their chance came. Caught up in the fun, Cyril's captor had loosened his grip. Glancing across the circle of noisy drunks, Cyril saw that Tonepah's guard had also relaxed his hold. Their eyes met and they nodded. Two soldiers fell off the mares at the same time. Cyril and Tonepah rushed forward, grabbed their horses' manes, and swung onto their backs. Ignoring the reins, they locked their heels into their mounts' flanks. The mares bounded away tearing the reins from the hands of their captors. Using their knees like rudders, the boys guided them around to the rear of the building and then back through the parking lot. Scattering the crowd of startled soldiers and young women, Topper and Wahpah carried their friends out onto the highway.

Across the pavement Cyril and Tonepah caught up their reins, and took control of their horses. Cyril released his grip on Topper's mane and fished the quirt out from under the front flap of the saddle where it had become lodged during the fracus. "Holy jumping Jehoshaphat! I'm glad we're out of that."

They continued north. Tonepah turned his head. "Look! We may not be out of this yet. They're starting their cars." Some of the soldiers were coming after them.

The boys charged off again. But the cars began to gain on them. Leaning forward to lie low on their horses' backs, Cyril and Tonepah put their lips near the little mares' ears. They crooned rosy compliments and made all sorts of promises to urge their mounts to move faster.

A soldier drove his Model A coupe up beside the racing horses. "We've got you now, you little twerps!" He aimed the car at the horses. The boys turned their steeds toward the ditch, but the Model A roared after them onto the berm. They could hear the men and women in the cars laughing and shouting.

Cyril and Tonepah kept riding in and out of the ditch. The barbed-wire fence and the railroad embankment kept them trapped in the right-of-way. The first car was followed by others careening down the highway after them. The riders pressed on, but flesh and blood could not stay ahead of the cars forever. Salvation came in the form of a low railroad trestle that opened a gap in the embankment. Laying their heads on their horses' necks, the boys ducked under the trestle and disappeared in a boggy swale between the railroad and Cache Creek. The drunks realized the game was over and broke off the chase to return to the bar.

Cyril blew the sweat off his upper lip. "What a bunch of two-bit jerks. They could've killed us."

"Yeah, those damned sons of she-dogs were really showing off in front of the girls."

"We've lost a lot of time. We'd better get a move on."

The boys rode along Cache Creek for two miles, then turned back toward the railroad track and rejoined the paved road. The horses trotted north as the shadows lengthened. By dark they were within sight of the Fort Sill Indian School. Cyril and Tonepah were familiar with that school where children of several Indian tribes went for an education. Both had visited there with their parents.

Near where the school road left the highway and passed through a rock arch, Wahpah and Topper suddenly shied. Surprised by their sideways leaps, Cyril and Tonepah urged them forward. Then the boys heard the eerie sound that had spooked their horses, low and mournful like something in pain. A voice moaned, "Help me!"

Neither boy moved or spoke. Again they heard the voice. It was coming from under the arch. Tonepah and Cyril walked their horses toward the sound. They found a girl curled up on the gravel, clutching her stomach. "Help me." she said. "Queno stabbed me."

The boys slipped off their mounts and knelt beside the girl. "I know this girl," Tonepah said. "She's Dorothy Gray. She's a Kiowa."

"Queno. That crazy Queno Hinauho came to my dorm and forced me to go with him. We got here and he stabbed me."

Tonepah leaned closer. "I'm Toney Gehaytie, Dorothy. You know me."

"Help me, Toney," she moaned, and went limp. Blood oozing through her dress looked black in the moonlight.

Shaken, Cyril stood up. "What in the world can we do?"

Tonepah straightened. "We could take her to the school hospital. I know where it is."

"But if we push her onto a horse's back and carry her two miles, we'll probably kill her."

"You're right. We need help."

"You stay with her, Toney. I'll ride to Mr. Bear's." The president of the school lived not far away on the campus.

"Why should I be the one that stays with her? I don't know nothing about hurt people."

"You're both Kiowas. She might be scared to death if she came to and no one but a white boy was with her."

Guiding Topper beyond the arch, Cyril pointed her toward the school buildings half a mile up the road. For the fourth time that day he asked the little mare for her best and she gave it to him. As he rode, the quirt slapped against his knee. Slipping its leather thong over his right hand, he held the quirt along Topper's neck. "No worry, girl," he assured Topper, his words bursting in rhythm with her gallop. "You know I'd never use this on you. I know you're giving me all you've got."

Once on campus, Cyril headed for a brick house, the home of John Bear, president of the Fort Sill Indian School. Cyril had visited there before.

He charged Topper up the wide wooden stairs at the front of the house. Her hooves clattered on the porch. A large man wearing a white shirt and black pants jerked open the door. "What in heaven's name?"

"Mr. Bear, come quick. Toney Gehaytie and I found a girl who's been stabbed. She's out at the gate."

John Bear studied Cyril. "You're one of the Byers boys. What are you saying? Who's been stabbed? Is it one of our students?"

"Toney says she's Dorothy Gray. She says it was Queno Hinauho that stabbed her."

"Damn it, he did come back. And now he's stabbed Dorothy?"

Grabbing a coat in the front hall, he ran down the steps and stopped. "I forgot. My boys took the car to join the hunt for Queno. I'll have to call the hospital to send someone."

Cyril waited by the porch. Mister Bear had said his sons were hunting Queno. Did that mean he was still nearby?

John Bear returned. "All right, the hospital will send help. I asked them to pick us up. They have to come by here anyway to get to the gate. Tie up your horse, and we'll wait for them."

"A policeman in Lawton had warned us this afternoon that Queno had broken out of jail. Do you really think he's still around here?"

"Queno was on the campus this afternoon, drunk and raising cane over by the girls dorm. We called the sheriff's office, but by the time the officers got here Queno had disappeared. The girls said he staggered off toward Cache Creek. Some of the men are looking for him on the creek. My sons and a deputy sheriff are driving the highway in case he'd try to get back that way."

Cyril peered into the night toward the rock arch where he'd left Toney. "I'm going back. Toney didn't want to stay there by himself, anyhow."

"Don't leave. You might run into Queno out there."

"I'm sorry, Mr. Bear, but I've got to get back to Toney."

Before John Bear could stop him, the boy sprang to his horse's back and whirled her around. Cyril leaned toward his mare's ear again. "We're running for Toney, Topper. Just one more time, Girl, please?"

Topper responded. Racing as fast as her weary legs would carry her, she brought her rider into view of the gate. Cyril caught a glimpse of two people struggling. The taller figure waved wildly. The smaller one was dodging the flailing arms. "It must be that murdering Queno," Cyril said to Topper. "I've got to help Toney."

Cyril's first urge was to rush in, but instead he stopped his horse under the arch. In the shadows he could make out Tonepah and the older Kiowa now.

"You little son of a bitch, get out of my way or I'll kill you."

"Leave her alone," Tonepah shouted.

Queno raised his right arm. Moonlight reflected from the knife in his hand. "I stabbed the bitch, and I mean for her to die. And now I'm going to cut your throat, you bastard." With his other hand Queno grabbed Tonepah's hair and jerked his head back.

Cyril charged through the arch, straight at Queno. Holding the quirt by the whip end, he swung with all his strength at the drunken

Kiowa. The leaded butt of the whip struck Queno behind his left ear. He dropped like a sack of sand.

Tonepah gasped. "Thanks a million, Cy-Byers! I thought I was a goner."

"Man, I'm glad you're all right. So this is Queno Hinauho."

"Yeah. He must have been passed out somewhere in the grass when we came through here. I guess he must of come to."

"I'll say—how's the girl?"

"Still alive. She's moaned some."

"Mr. Bear called the hospital. Someone should be here soon."

"Dorothy's hurt bad. He stabbed her in the back and the belly. There's a lot of blood."

Tonepah picked up Wahpah's reins and bent over Queno.

Cyril dismounted and stood beside him.

"He's awfully quiet," Tonepah said. I think you killed him."

"I sure hope not."

A pickup rattled into view, its dim headlights jiggling in the dark. When it slid to a stop, John Bear and two young men dressed in white stepped out.

Mr. Bear hurried over to Cyril and Tonepah. "Here we are, boys. These hospital orderlies will take over now." He looked down. "Good Lord, there are two bodies here."

"She's not a body. She's still moaning," Cyril said.

Tonepah touched Queno with his toe. "This guy's Queno Hinauho. We're not sure about him. Cy-Byers hit him with a leaded quirt to keep him from killing me and stabbing Dorothy again. He hasn't moved since Cy-Byers hit him."

The hospital attendants examined the girl, then carefully laid her in the bed of the truck. While one of them covered her with blankets, the other examined Queno.

"He's still breathing, but man, he's really out."

Propping Queno in the front seat, the attendants jumped in on either side of him.

"Hadn't you better restrain him?" Mr. Bear asked worriedly.

"We can't take the time," said the one behind the wheel. He fished under the front seat and came up with a tire iron, which he handed to his partner. "If the son of a bitch comes to, you might need this." The driver leaned out the window. "I'll come back for you, Mr. Bear."

John Bear gripped both boys' shoulders. "You've done a good night's work, boys. I hope we got here in time to save Dorothy. That was a brave thing you did, Cyril, going back for your friend.

"Old Toney was doing all right. He just needed a little help to finish things off," Cyril said, winking at his friend.

"You two are a long way from home. What are you doing here?" Tonepah led Wahpah to the center of the road. "We're supposed to be taking Cyril's mare home from visiting a stallion, but we're having trouble getting her there."

Cyril joined Tonepah. "I reckon we'd better get under way."

John Bear cleared his throat. "Boys, your trip is over for the night. You can't leave before you give statements to the sheriff. Have you eaten?"

Cyril shook the coins in the front pocket of his pants. "My father gave me some money. We were going to stop at Cox's store and buy some cheese and crackers and a soda pop."

"You should have supper at my house," John Bear said.

"My mother will worry about us."

"I'll call and tell her you're here."

"We don't have a phone."

"Then I'll call Bert Shanklin's store and ask them to send word to your families."

The pickup truck bounced into view again. The young man who had driven it before opened the door. "I can take you back now, Mr. Bear."

John Bear put his foot on the truck's running board. "How's the girl?" he asked.

"It doesn't look good. He stabbed her six times." Then he turned to Cyril. "Queno's not hurt bad. He came to before we got to the hospital, but he was still groggy and couldn't give us any trouble. We called Sheriff McLarty, and he'll be out to get him."

John Bear opened the passenger door of the truck. "You boys go put your horses in the stables. Then come to my house."

Cyril and Tonepah rode slowly. At the school stables they watered their tired horses and threw them blocks of alfalfa hay.

When they returned to the school grounds, the main campus was a beehive. Electric lights burned in the houses. Groups of people stood in the yards and on the porches. Everyone was talking about the terrible events of the evening. Cyril and Tonepah approached John Bear's house. John Bear called to them. "Come on, boys, the sheriff needs to talk to you."

Two white men who wore cowboy boots and wide-brimmed hats left a knot of men. The older one nodded to them. "I'm Sheriff Hans McLarty, and this is Deputy Foster McLong. We need to hear your stories." The boys took turns telling the officers what had happened. When they finished, Deputy McLong asked Tonepah, "You know Queno Hinauho?"

"I know him."

"And you got a look at him at the scene?"

"He tried to cut my throat."

The deputy turned to Cyril. "And you saw him there, too?"

"I saw him trying to kill Toney. I didn't get a good look at him until after I hit him with my quirt."

"But you'd recognize him?"

"Yes, sir."

"You need to come downtown and identify the man we've arrested as the one who said he stabbed Dorothy Gray and who tried to kill Tonepah."

The deputy drove, and Cyril and Tonepah sat in the back seat of the sheriff's cruiser. Sheriff McLarty laid his arm on the back of the front seat. "If the girl dies, the lawyers will try to get him electrocuted for murder. If she lives, we'll charge him with two more attempted murders. He should go to prison for a long time."

Cyril leaned forward. "How many years would he be in prison?"

"I couldn't say for sure. But for my money I'd say that if he don't get the hot seat, he ought to be in prison until four days after hell freezes over."

After Cyril and Tonepah identified Queno, Deputy McLong returned them to John Bear's home. Members of the faculty and others who lived at the school were gathered there. John Bear's sons, T.W. and Junior, had returned. Excited conversation filled the room. When the boys entered, the talking ceased. Every eye settled on Cyril and Tonepah. John Bear met the boys and then turned to face the roomful of people.

"My friends, I want you to meet two brave boys, Cyril Byers and Tonepah Gehaytie." Applause erupted and loud cheers went up. Both boys stared at the floor, not sure how to respond.

John Bear raised his hand. "You've heard what they did, and I'm sure they appreciate your thanking them for it. But they've had a long day and haven't eaten. So, if you'll excuse us, we'll go to the kitchen and get them some supper."

A tall, fair woman joined them and John took her hand. "Boys, this is my wife, Mrs. Bear." John led them to the kitchen. "Can we find them something to eat, Ida?"

In a short time Ida Bear placed a tray heaped with scrambled eggs, crisp bacon, and toast in front of the hungry wayfarers. The boys loaded their plates and feasted on the midnight breakfast. Then they bedded down in John Junior's room upstairs.

When the boys came down the next morning, John Bear sat reading the *Lawton Constitution.* He handed Tonepah the newspaper. "You're famous, boys." Tonepah read the headline: "Girl Stabbed Six Times Survives." Another headline, in smaller print, said: "Saved by Passing Riders." A third divided the article: "Boys Capture Knife-Wielding Assailant."

Carrying a glass of orange juice in each hand, Ida Bear came through the swinging door from the kitchen. "You're certified heroes, boys, but I guess heroes get hungry. Start with this juice."

"Thank you, ma'am," Cyril said as he took one of the glasses and strained to read over Tonepah's shoulder. "Gee whiz, our names are in the paper."

Tonepah pointed at the page. "Where'd they get our names?"

"After you were in bed last night, reporters called." Ida Bear explained, handing Tonepah the other glass of orange juice. "We gave them your names and told them what you'd done, but we didn't want them to bother you so late. They'll be back this morning. By the way, Cyril, your mother called. She doesn't want you to ride home. She'll send your father as soon as he returns from Texas."

After Cyril and Tonepah finished breakfast, they heard voices out front and peeked through the curtained windows. Reporters, photographers, and curious onlookers were gathered on the steps and lawn. John Bear rose, "Come along, my young friends. Your public awaits. The sooner we start, the sooner we'll finish."

When the trio emerged from the house, people surged onto the porch. John Bear raised his hand. "If you'll stay calm, I'm sure these boys will pose for your pictures and answer your questions."

He motioned to Cyril and Tonepah to come forward. "Boys, these are the newspaper reporters. They want to interview you."

A young man with a card in his hatband that said "Press" spoke up. "Why don't you tell us your stories in your own words?"

Tonepah poked Cyril in the chest. "You first."

Cyril faced the reporters, but before he had gotten very far, another reporter butted in. "You're the kid that hit the killer behind the ear with a lead pipe, aren't you?"

Cyril raised his left hand and showed the crowd his quirt. "I never hit anyone with a lead—"

"They say you rode back to the scene of the crime," a second man interrupted, "even though you knew the killer was there. Wasn't that pretty stupid?"

"I didn't know he was there. And, no, it wasn't stupid. I went back because of my friend."

Another man pushed the others aside. "This one's too fresh. Let's talk to the Indian kid."

He pointed his pencil at Tonepah. "You risked your life to save a girl. How does it feel to be a hero?" Tonepah stared silently at the man, who impatiently tapped his notebook.

"Would you have risked your life for a white girl? What would you have done if she'd been white?"

"In that case I reckon I'd have gone for help, and Cy-Byers would have stayed with her."

This answer made no sense to the man. "You saved her because you're both Kiowas, didn't you?" Tonepah sensed what the man was hinting at. "The guy that was trying to kill her was also a Kiowa. I kept him away from her because she was a girl that was bleeding to death, and I wasn't going to let him get at her again. Anyone would do that."

The questioning seemed endless. The boys heard the same questions over and over until they grew weary of trying to give answers the reporters could understand or would accept. When it became clear that the ordeal had gone on long enough, John Bear called a halt and asked the crowd to leave. Relieved, Cyril and Tonepah went to feed their horses.

Although they had talked far into the night before, the friends found plenty to chat about as they ambled toward the stables, Cyril still carrying his grandfather's quirt. They agreed that the questioning of the reporters was tiresome, but still felt proud of what they had done. Suddenly, Tonepah stopped and nudged Cyril. Five boys were milling around the stable pens. Among them Cyril recognized Indians from three tribes.

"There they are!" an Apache boy shouted.

As the boys crowded around Cyril and Tonepah, a tall Comanche stepped in front of them. "You think you're something, don't you?"

Tonepah stared at him. "What do you mean?"

"Saved a beautiful maiden and got your name in the paper. We've heard all about you wise guys."

"Get out of here. We don't want trouble."

A fat Kiowa pulled Tonepah around. "You're a pair of smart-alecks, ain't you? Some guys like to show off."

Trying to grab his quirt, an Apache snatched at Cyril's hand. "What are you carrying that little switch for?"

Tonepah jerked away from the one who had pulled on him. "You better not mess with him or that little switch. He nearly killed Queno Hinauho with it last night."

Everything went quiet. A broad-shouldered Kiowa stepped toward Cyril. "So you're the one who hit my cousin."

"I hit Queno Hinauho."

"I'm Walter Hinauho, and I don't like white boys hitting my kinfolks. We're going to clean your plow."

Tonepah moved between the Kiowa and Cyril. "Your cousin stabbed Dorothy Gray six times and was aiming to cut my throat."

"This ain't about what Queno did. A white boy hit my cousin with a leaded quirt."

"He did what he had to do."

"Why don't you shut up, Tonepah Gehaytie? This is between Cyril Byers and me, not us Kiowas."

The tall Comanche held up his fists. "We aim to teach this blue-eyed redhead a lesson."

As the five boys started toward him, Cyril held the quirt ready and worked his way along the iron-pipe corral. Tonepah slid along beside him. "There are five of you and two of us, and you'll probably whip us, but I'll tell you this: If you keep coming, some of you are going to be mighty sorry."

The two friends were backed into a corner, but they were armed with a formidable weapon and prepared to battle for as long as their strength lasted. Looking into their blazing eyes, their enemies saw nothing but rock-hard determination. Walter Hinauho stretched out his arms to hold back the others. "I ain't going to fight another Indian over this." His friends swiftly stepped back. Keeping their eyes on the others, Tonepah and Cyril eased out of the corner. Shoulder to shoulder, they walked to the barn while their would-be attackers left.

When they returned to the Bear home, some stragglers from the earlier crowd remained in the front yard. The sight of them made the boys groan. Neither wanted to answer more questions. Cyril saw his father and the two boys ran toward him. "Dad!"

"It's good to see you, son. Are you two all right?"

"We're okay," Tonepah said, "but I sure don't want to talk to those people no more. I've never answered so dern many stupid questions in my whole life."

Samuel rested his hand on Tonepah's shoulder. "We'll get out of here quickly. Let me run speak to John Bear, and then we'll go."

Samuel Byers returned with good news. "Mr. Bear talked to the hospital. The doctor says Dorothy Gray will make it. The boys bumped shoulders and grinned at each other.

With the horses safely loaded in the trailer, Tonepah and Cyril slid into the front seat of the car beside Samuel Byers. As he drove toward the mountains, the boys told him about finding the stabbed girl, fighting Queno, answering a thousand dumb questions, and facing five bullies. When they finished their stories, Samuel Byers looked stern. "I promised your mother you wouldn't mess with drunks you met along the way. And here you not only fight with a drunk, but the very outlaw she feared you'd encounter. He shook his head, "And now you've picked up other enemies besides."

Neither boy tried to apologize or defend himself, and Samuel Byers drove on in silence. They were glad they hadn't mentioned Waldo's bar or being chased by the drunken drivers.

In a few minutes he glanced at them again. "Well, what was the worst of it?"

Cyril shifted on the seat. "Finding Dorothy Gray stabbed and lying in the road."

Tonepah scooted forward. "Yeah, that was the worst."

"But if you want to know what scared me most," Cyril went on, "I'd say, it was the bullies at the horse pens this morning."

Samuel Byers braked to turn a corner. "How could that be?"

"When we were so busy getting help and fighting Queno, I didn't have time to worry. But facing off with five bullies who'd made plans and laid for us gave me plenty of time to get scared."

"If they were laying for you, why didn't they get you?"

"Toney talked them out of it."

Tonepah peered around Cyril "They didn't like the odds. Three against five didn't suit those cowards."

Samuel Byers raised his eyebrows. "How do you get three?"

"Me and Cy-Byers and that heavy quirt he carries. When we backed into that corner together, and they saw we aimed to fight as long as we could stand up, we looked like too many for 'em."

"How'd your horses come through all of this? They looked worn out to me."

Cyril rubbed his neck and shoulders. "Wahpah and Topper aren't the only ones worn out. I won't care if I don't have no more excitement for the next year."

"*Any* more excitement," Samuel Byers corrected.

Cyril smiled to himself, finding an odd comfort in the familiar reproof. It made him feel closer to home.

And home was exactly where both boys wanted to be.

Tehat's Honoring

Two weeks had passed since Cyril and Tonepah had helped to rescue Dorothy Gray. Cyril had said he didn't want any more excitement for a year, but his mother was of a mind never to let him leave the farm again. She had insisted that he stick close to home. Considering his near miss with death, he understood. But he was tired of sticking around the farm and wanted to see Toney again. He approached his mother in the kitchen, where she was baking bread.

"Mom, I want to go see Toney."

"I don't want you gallivanting all over the country anymore."

"I want to go to the Gehayties', not all over the country."

"All right, you may go to the Gehayties', but don't go any place else."

Cyril rode to the Gehayties' and tied Topper to a crosspiece of their brush arbor. Tonepah was finishing breakfast. "Hey, Cy-Byers. Where you been?"

"My Mom's been having conniptions since we got home. She hasn't wanted me out of her sight."

"My folks haven't been that bad, but they're pretty excited about what we got into."

"How's that?"

"Everyone's telling my folks there should be a powwow for you and me."

"A powwow? Like when Chief Hunting Horse and the other Kiowas have a fire at the Indian church at Christmas?"

"Right. There'll be singing and dancing at the fire. They'll want you and me to dance."

"I'd be scared to death, dancing in front of Indians."

A rapping sound came from the back of the arbor and someone spoke in Kiowa. Tonepah stood up.

"Grandma wants to see us. Come on."

Cyril followed Tonepah to the pallet under the arbor where Tehat Hauvone waited for them. He'd never been this close to Tonepah's grandmother before. Tehat Hauvone sat erect, watching them with keen interest. Her two white braids were tucked beneath the red blanket around her shoulders. Deep wrinkle lines rayed out from her nose and mouth. Her flashing black eyes leveled on Cyril, who forgot his manners and stared. She was frightening and fascinating. Tehat spoke and Tonepah interpreted. "She wants to look at you."

"Why's that?"

"Because you're the one the Great Spirit sent to save me."

Being in Tehat's presence gave Cyril a tingly chill; now she was speaking of him in the same breath with God. "Tell her I don't believe that God sent me anywhere."

Tonepah didn't bother to translate for his grandmother. "Forget it, Cy-Byers. She's sure I'm supposed to live to lead the Kiowas, so she thinks the Great Spirit takes care of me."

The boys returned to the front of the arbor, and Cyril untied Topper's bridle. "Your grandmother scares me. All Indians scare me. I couldn't dance at a powwow."

"You're not afraid of me."

"You're different. We do things together."

"You'll have to dance, Cy-Byers."

"We'll see."

Cyril didn't want to argue with his friend, but he couldn't imagine himself dancing in front of a crowd, any crowd, let alone this one.

Since Samuel Byers had brought Cyril and Tonepah home from the Indian school, the climate inside the house had been just as stormy as that outside. Blaming him for what happened to the boys, Lola Byers had hardly spoken to her husband. The older children had talked of nothing except the attempted murders and their little brother's brush with death.

Today, life on the Byers farm was returning to normal. The summer sun was out and Samuel was repairing the family car. Ever since he had hit high center on a rutted farm road in Texas, oil had been dripping beneath his automobile. He drove the Oakland touring car onto the driveway beside the house and slid under it. Several oil-pan bolts were loose, and he began tightening them.

Footsteps crunched on the gravel drive, and he turned toward the sound. A pair of khaki pant-legs and scuffed, brown oxford shoes appeared between the car and the ground. Samuel lowered his wrench. "What's up, Fred?" He knew his Kiowa landlord well.

"We need a beef."

"Just a minute."

The khaki pants and oxford shoes didn't move. Samuel tightened the last bolt, scooted from under the car, and stood. After wiping his right hand on his pants, he extended it to Fred Gehaytie. "What's this about a beef?"

"The people want to give a barbecue for your son and mine. We need a beef."

"I'd heard something was planned for the boys. So it's to be a barbecue?"

"Folks in Lawton are getting up speeches to be said at the Indian School, but we want Cyril to come to a barbeque and powwow in his and Tonepah's honor."

Samuel laid his wrench in his toolbox. He had not expected Cyril to be invited to an Indian Powwow. "Seems strange. People want to do something for my son, so they ask me for a beef."

"That's the way Kiowas do. When a boy is to be honored as a man, his family gives gifts to make sure he's accepted."

"What are you giving?"

"Sixty Indians will be on the creek for the barbecue. We're buying ice cream for them."

"Sounds fair. Hiram Oswalt and I are running some beeves together on his place. If he'll give you half a beef, I'll give you the other half." Samuel knew that his father-in-law, Hiram Oswalt, would give the Indians a beef if Fred told him it was for Cyril.

Like everyone in the Mount Scott community, Fred knew that Hiram Oswalt was partial to his grandchildren. He offered his hand. "Thank you, Sam Byers. Hiram's like us. He takes care of his grandchildren."

Later, the authorities at the Fort Sill Indian School contacted Samuel Byers with details of their plans to honor Tonepah and Cyril. On Saturday morning of the following week, the Indians would hold a barbecue on Cache Creek. At three o'clock that afternoon a program of music and speeches would be given in the school auditorium. At the supper table that night, when Samuel mentioned the plans, Cyril flinched. The memory of reporters yelling dumb questions at him was too fresh in his mind.

"I don't want to go to the Indian school and answer no—I mean, any—more questions."

Lola Byers touched her youngest son's hand. "You won't have to answer questions. These people want to do something nice for you and Tonepah." The other Byers children agreed with their mother.

His brother ruffled Cyril's hair. "You'll like what they do, Cy, especially the Indians."

The next day, Cyril met Toney on Jack Creek. "You heard any more about what they're planning for us at the Indian school?"

"Yeah. Before the speeches and the powwow, we'll have a barbecue. You won't believe the food: barbecued beef, brown beans, sliced onions, pan-fried bread, ice cream, and tons of other stuff."

"Mom says we won't have to answer questions."

"Guess who'll be there."

"Who?"

"Juanita Trumpeter."

Cyril brightened. "That's good. I hope I get to see her."

"I told you that 'cause we're friends. I don't want you hogging her time."

"I wouldn't do that."

"Not much you wouldn't."

Cyril quickly accepted Tonepah's offer of a ride to the barbecue with the Gehaytie family. He was pleased that he'd be there with Tonepah and Juanita. Still, he worried about having to dance in front of the other Indians.

On the following Saturday morning, while the Byers family was still at the breakfast table, the Gehayties' car pulled into the driveway. Cyril jumped to his feet and started for the door. His mother caught his arm. "Just a minute, young man. Brush your hair and put on your shoes. I'll bring your jacket to the program for you."

"Aw, mom, do I have to wear shoes? We'll be playing on the creek. Shoes will slow me down."

"Leave your shoes in the car while you're playing. But don't forget to put them on when you go to the auditorium."

Cyril swiped a brush through his hair and hurried outside. His father was talking to Fred Gehaytie, who sat at the wheel of a 1929 Model A Ford. Its motor chugged patiently. Maude Gehaytie sat in the middle of the front seat with Tonepah beside her. His teenaged sister, Marie, and Tehat Hauvone sat in the rear. Tonepah hopped out and opened the back door. "You can sit by Grandma, Cy-Byers."

Samuel Byers went over the arrangements with Fred. The Gehayties would bring Cyril to the auditorium after the barbeque. "Afterwards he'll go back to the creek with us, and we'll bring him home tonight," Fred offered. Samuel Byers nodded in agreement.

As Samuel backed away from the car, Fred let out the clutch and the car jumped backward. Then he shifted into first, spun the steering wheel to the right, and floorboarded the gas pedal. Gravel flew out behind the car as the Model A roared out of the yard. At the end of the lane, Fred spun the steering wheel to the left. The car skidded sideways onto the graded section line. Thrusting his chin out like a racehorse at the finish, the resolute Kiowa barreled down the road. He zoomed through water crossings, sped down hills, and scattered chickens, dogs, or turkeys at each farmstead they passed. Cyril rode with both feet jammed against the front seat and gave himself up to imminent death.

Assuming they shared his alarm, Cyril stole a sideways glance at the other passengers. Tonepah was smiling, obviously happy. Maude's countenance was rock hard. Even if she'd wanted to object, her clinched teeth would have kept her from speaking. Cyril peeped at Marie, who looked as if she might break into joyous song. Cyril couldn't read Tehat Hauvone's face, but he remembered the stories he'd heard about this survivor of the Red River Wars. No, he thought, she wouldn't be frightened. She'd be enjoying the ride in this fine automobile.

Fred turned south on Highway 277 and picked up speed. Dust hovered around Cyril's face and his nostrils filled with the smell of oil and water overheating. Cyril watched the countryside stream past like scenes in a speeded-up movie. Ahead of them a pair of cream-colored Belgian horses pulled a loaded hay wagon onto the highway. Cyril's eyes bulged. The team ambled to the center of the highway, then suddenly dashed forward, snatching the heavy load out of harm's way. It wasn't the first time the driver of the wagon had seen Fred Gehaytie's Model A.

At the Indian school road, Fred wheeled in without braking. The right side of the car lifted as it knifed into the graded drive on two wheels. They passed the rock gate, where the boys had found Dorothy Gray lying in a pool of blood and Queno Hinauho had tried to kill Tonepah. When the Indian school came into view, Fred finally slowed down. Cyril's audible relief sounded something like a prayer.

Ahead of them, white brick buildings etched silhouettes in the morning sky. In twos and threes, well-dressed boys and girls walked on the paved sidewalks of the tidy school. Cyril and Tonepah studied the faces of the children. None of the bullies who'd cornered them at the horse pens were on the walks.

Fred skirted the main campus, then turned onto a dim trail that angled down to Cache Creek. In a grove of pecan trees across the creek, tents and tepees had been set up in a semicircle. Strings of smoke from small cook fires plumed upward. Men, women, and children milled around the temporary dwellings. Fred turned off the engine and pointed to a group of men.

"They're unwrapping the beef. I'll go help."

Tonepah threw open the car door and bounded down the creek bank to a log that bridged the stream. "Come on, Cy-Byers. Let's go find the guys." He disappeared on the other side of the creek. Marie followed her brother.

Still shaky from the hair-raising ride, Cyril got slowly out of the car. He followed Fred and Maude Gehaytie down the slope. Then he realized he had forgotten to take off his shoes. He climbed back up the bank and sat on the running board of the car to remove his shoes and socks. Tehat Hauvone had just gotten out of the car and stood silently looking at him. Her gaze swept from his bare feet to his red hair. He could tell from her eyes that she didn't much care for what she saw. Tightening her red blanket, she raised her chin and with regal strides marched down the slope. Cyril remembered that she thought the Great Spirit had sent him to save Tonepah and wondered why she'd looked at him as if she hated him. Could it be because his skin was white? Was he the only one, or did she look at all white people like that? Suddenly, he wasn't sure he wanted to be with her or any of the Indians that day.

At the log bridge, Cyril took in the scene on the other side. He'd seen a similar arrangement of tents and tepees before but only from a distance. Each Christmas when Chief Hunting Horse and the other Kiowas gathered at the Methodist Indian mission across Jack Creek from his home, they built a temporary camp. Cyril had visited in the church but not in the camp. He'd never been near an Indian tepee, but he was curious about such dwellings and the people who lived in them. As he crossed over to the encampment, he found that his curiosity overcame the trepidation he had felt under Tehat Hauvone's scrutiny.

The savory aroma of food cooking on oak fires greeted him. Laughing and shouting, small children dashed in and out between the tents and tepees. Hanging here and there in the trees, highly decorated, V-shaped cradleboards held sleeping babies in their laced-up pockets. Cyril paused to admire the beadwork and silver ornaments on several of them. Pictures on the canvas dwellings also caught his eye. Paintings of buffalo, deer, antelope, and wolves adorned some of them. Horses, with and without men on their backs, embellished others, along with silhouettes of eagles, trees, and Spanish dagger. One teepee was not canvas. Its tanned hides were painted red. Curious, Cyril walked closer and bent down to peer in the opening. An old man rounded the teepee and raised a warning finger. "Don't touch it."

"I was only looking. It's a real teepee ain't it?"

"Yes, it's a real teepee, an old teepee. It is the home of Land of Pure Water, Chief Buffalo Horse's widow. One of the Grandmother Bundles used to be kept in it. You must not come too near because power from the Grandmother Bundle may still be in it."

My friend Toney Gehaytie told me about the Grandmother Bundles. This teepee is like a church, ain't it."

"Yes." The old man nodded. "Like a church."

"Thank you for the warning. I believe I'll move on."

Even though his red hair announced from afar that he wasn't one of them, the people he passed nodded to him in friendly acknowledgment. Searching for one girl in particular, Cyril studied the people at each campsite. He recognized several classmates from the Mount Scott School, but not the one he had in mind.

Near the edge of the camp, he heard female voices in the woods. Hoping Tonepah and the other boys might be nearby, he hurried around a nearby tent. Women and girls were gathering armloads of fallen tree limbs and carrying them to a pile in the center of the clearing. There they were building the fire for the powwow where Tonepah said he and Cyril would dance. Cyril had heard the Indians sing their enchanting songs around such fires at the Indian Methodist church. He'd often wished that he could join them. But now that Tonepah had definite plans for him to take part in a powwow, he wasn't sure. Maybe he'd hide and let the Indians do their own singing and dancing.

Cyril walked over to where Fred Gehaytie and some other men were tending the beef. They had shoveled away dirt and lifted large chunks of canvas covered meat from a trench. For hours, since long before daylight, the wrapped meat had lain above coals in the depths of a long pit where oak logs burned. Fred Gehaytie and a Comanche man slipped their gloved hands under one chunk and lifted it to a table. Fred carefully pulled back the thick canvas that covered it. Tempting aromas rose from the well-cooked beef. The Comanche man saw Cyril eyeing the meat and drew his knife. He trimmed off a sliver, speared it with his knife and held it out to Cyril. Cyril accepted the savory offering eagerly. Permeated with the tangy taste of burned oak, the meat was delicious.

Cyril walked on and found some women at nearby tables busily preparing food. Sweat glistened on their foreheads and upper lips. Some of them were speaking quietly in a language Cyril didn't understand. Crossing the clearing, he came upon a group of older people seated with their backs against the trunk of a fallen tree. They spoke the strange language in even quieter tones. When Cyril paused in front of them, he saw that one was Tehat Hauvone. She had fixed her eyes on him. Her gaze puzzled him. Did it express approval, or was she accusing him of something? He had no idea why, but he felt guilty.

Guessing that Tonepah had crossed to the other side of the creek, Cyril started for the footbridge. When he saw Juanita Trumpeter standing in front of a tepee with a tall woman, he pulled up short and averted his eyes. Juanita walked over to him. "Hello, Cyril."

"Hello, Nita. How are you doing?"

"Fine. Are you having a good time?"

"It's great here. Do you want to walk with me?"

The tall woman cleared her throat. "We need to help with the cooking, Juanita." Cyril glanced at the her. She was pretty, almost as pretty as Juanita.

Out of nowhere, a pair of arms wrapped around Cyril's neck. Tonepah had chosen that moment to find him and begin a wrestling match. Suddenly both boys were rolling on the ground, looking up regularly to make sure Juanita and her mother were watching. When they saw that their audience had disappeared, the demonstration fizzled and the boys stood up. Cyril brushed his hands. "Man, where'd you go? I've been looking all over for you."

"Yeah, I saw where you were looking. Did you think I was hiding behind her skirts?"

Cyril rolled his eyes. A group of boys had gathered around them, and Cyril turned his attention to them. "What are you guys up to?"

An Apache loosened an imitation, pearl-handled Colt revolver in his tooled leather holster. "We're playing cowboys and Indians. Who do you want to be?"

"Buck Jones."

"I'm Buck Jones."

"Then I'll be Ken Maynard."

A tall dark Kiowa boy wiped his nose. "I'm Ken Maynard."

"And I'm Tom Mix," Tonepah concluded.

Cyril studied his brown-skinned playmates. "I've always sort of wished I was a Kiowa. I reckon I'll be one of the Indians."

The boys laughed and play resumed. For the next hour the wooded banks of Cache Creek resounded to the make-believe sounds of gunshots and the plaintive groans of the dying wounded.

Maude Gehaytie called them to dinner, ending the game. Cyril ran eagerly with the others to the tables, where they found glazed pots of brown beans and platters heaped with baked potatoes. On another table, ears of boiled corn lay in stacks like cordwood. Blue-gray enameled trays held mounds of sliced barbecued beef. Fresh tomatoes and sliced purple onions gave the tables a festive appearance. The aromas were overwhelming for a boy who'd been chasing cowboys all morning. Cyril's stomach rumbled, but he had to wait.

Reverend Rollie Ballew stepped into the space in front of the fallen tree where the old people sat. "Gather around everybody."

As the boys started toward the fallen tree, Cyril asked Tonepah. "How come he's speaking English? Those old folks were speaking Kiowa or something when I walked by them."

"He's Kiowa like us. The Comanches and Apaches wouldn't understand him if he spoke our language."

Reverend Ballew motioned for silence. "Friends, everyone is welcome on this day as we come together to honor the bravery of Tonepah Gehaytie and Cyril Byers. Together, as you know, they rescued Dorothy Gray. Not all of you may know, however, that in the process, Cyril Byers also saved the life of his friend and fellow rescuer Tonepah Gehaytie, who as he protected Dorothy Gray was nearly killed himself by the murderous Queno Hinaho. Fred Gehaytie has asked me to tell you that the beef we'll eat is a gift from Cyril's father, Samuel Byers, and his grandfather Hiram Oswalt. Fred also wishes me to announce that he and Maude have supplied the ice cream we'll have. As a special gift, they have brought dishes to serve it in made by the Navahos in New Mexico. You may keep your dish after you eat the ice cream. Murmurs of approval went up from his audience. Reverend Ballew continued, "And now, let us bow in prayer." Some bowed. All remained silent.

Reverend Ballew raised his right hand. "God, we the people who walk the Jesus road come to you today with thanksgiving. Hear us now, because of your Son. We thank You for this food you've given us to feed our bodies. We thank You for the sun and the rain which helped this food to grow. We are happy when we follow Jesus. Turn us back when we stray from the straight trail that He has marked for us. Amen."

Cyril had expected a much longer prayer. When he raised his head and opened his eyes, he was astonished to see that men and boys were lining up to be served first. He'd always thought women and girls should eat first, except for mothers who served the food. Reverend Ballew guided Cyril and Tonepah to the head of the line. "Here we are, boys," the reverend said. "You can get in line behind me." Serving themselves right after the preacher and before the other men and boys was an honor. The boys filled their plates and hurried to join the Gehayties and Tehat Hauvone under the trees.

Fred Gehaytie raised his plate.

"Now this is what I call eating. Just look at all the good food we have. This must be like in the old days when they were getting ready for the Sun Dance."

Cyril dug his fork into hot barbecued beef. "What was the Sun Dance?"

"I thought Tonepah had talked to you about the Sun Dance and the Grandmother Bundles."

"He told me that the Sun Dance was given to the Kiowas by an Arapaho man, but he didn't say anything about food."

"The traders would come the day before the Sun Dance, and the people did everything they knew how to entertain them. There would always be lots of food left over."

"Where was the Sun Dance held?"

"Mostly here in the Wichita Mountains, or on the headwaters of three rivers up north, the Arkansas, Cimmaron, and Canadian."

Overhearing her husband, Maude Gehaytie turned to them and nodded. "Yes; we've seen a list of where they held the Sun Dances each year for over fifty years."

"Why did they hold them?"

Tonepah fished an olive out of a jar. "I told you before, Cy-Byers, it was religious. My grandparents went to the dances to get power to do things. It was a way to make themselves better."

"Did they have preachers there, like we do at revivals?"

Fred paused and reflected. "The priest of the Sun Dance was a powerful man. I'm sure Tonepah has told you that the Kiowas worshipped the buffalo."

"Robert Topekchi told me."

"Then you know how sacred the buffalo hunt was. The priest of the Sun Dance was so powerful that it was he who chose which men's society would police each buffalo hunt."

"I've heard about the men's societies."

Maude handed Cyril a piece of fry bread. "Women had societies, too," she interjected. "They came together for different reasons. One society, the Bear Women, was so secret and so powerful it raised terror in the hearts of the other Kiowas."

Cyril stole a quick sideways glance at Tehat. It would be hard to imagine a Bear Woman who could be more terrifying than Toney's grandmother, he thought to himself. He raised a slice of beef toward his mouth. Its tangy odor reminded him of the fire that cooked it and a question he'd meant to ask Toney.

He took the bite, chewed carefully, and swallowed. "Explain something to me, Tonepah."

Tonepah also swallowed. "What now, Cy-Byers?"

"Why do Indian fires smell different?"

Everyone laughed. Fred looked around the camp.

"Since Rollie Ballew went Christian, we don't let on to him about it, but a lot of Indians sprinkle cedar incense in their fires to keep off evil spirits. Another relic of our heritage that we find hard to let go."

After the meal, everyone disappeared into their tents and tepees or returned to their cars to rest. That didn't surprise Cyril. A nap after eating was standard practice in his home, especially in warm weather. He joined the Gehayties, who were spreading blankets on the ground. He and Tonepah found shade under a tree away from the others. Tonepah spread his blanket beside Cyril's. "How you doing, Cy-Byers? Have you quit being afraid of Indians?"

"I'm doing better. Still can't say whether I'll dance in front of them."

"You'll do fine."

The boys chatted a while and then slept.

When Cyril awoke, the camp was buzzing. The people had re-placed their ordinary clothes with brightly colored skirts, blouses, shirts, sashes, and shawls. Beaded moccasins or polished boots had replaced oxford shoes and slippers. Colorful blankets of various hues appeared, wrapped around a woman's body or artfully draped over a man's arm. Cyril knew his family would say that the Indians had put on their Sunday-go-to-meeting clothes. Remembering his own shoes, he went back to the car and put them on.

Dressed in their finest, everyone left for the auditorium at the In-dian school. In a rainbow they mounted the slope on the west bank of Cache Creek. Cyril looked over the crowd and turned to Tonepah. "Where's your grandmother?"

"She stayed at the campground so she can rest up for the big do-ings tonight."

"Maybe I ought to skip the powwow tonight. Your grandmother doesn't like me and I'm scared to face her and the other Indians."

"Will you quit it with that scared stuff. She's my grandma and that's my family you're talking about. No one's going to bite you."

Just outside the auditorium, a young white man stepped sud-denly in their path. "My name is Paul Preston. I represent the Lawton Chamber of Commerce. They've sent me to be in charge this after-noon. Where are the boy heroes?"

No one answered, and he referred to a clipboard. "Where are Tonepah Gehaytie and Cyril Byers?"

Fred Gehaytie gave him an impassive glance and laid his hands on the backs of Tonepah and Cyril. "These are the young men we've come to honor."

Preston pointed at Tonepah. "Stay with your family. You Gehay-ties go stand on the right side of the walk, behind the Lawton High School band."

He placed his hand on Maude's shoulder as if to propel her in the right direction. The severely modest daughter of Tehat Hauvone squared her shoulders, raised to her full height of six feet, and shot him a withering glance.

Hastily Preston drew back his hand. Maude and Fred led their im-mediate family to line up behind the band in front of the auditorium door. As soon as the other Indians had filed past them into the building, Paul Preston redirected his wits toward Cyril. "Come with me," he commanded. Your parents are over here."

This man reminded Cyril of the newspaper reporters who had badgered him and Tonepah. In no hurry, Cyril watched Preston dash across the lawn, waving his clipboard. "Mister Byers?"

Samuel and Lola Byers stopped. Preston waited for Cyril. "Here your folks are. "Hurry up."

Without even glancing at him, Cyril walked past Preston to his mother.

Lola smoothed Cyril's hair with her hand. Preston caught up to them. "Come on. I want you on the left side of the walk behind the band."

Cyril ducked under his mother's arm. "That mug's been pushing us around since we got here."

"Never mind. Slip on your jacket. I'm glad you remembered your shoes."

The Byers family took their place behind the band. Paul Preston appeared between the Gehayties and the Byers. "When you go in, the Byers will follow me down the left aisle then file into the first row. You Gehayties go to the right side and come into that same row from the other end."

Without waiting for a reply, he turned his attention to the band director. Samuel Byers leaned toward his landlord. "With that pompous ass in charge, it's going to be a long afternoon."

Fred Gehaytie nodded agreement. "It's already been a long afternoon."

The drum major of the Lawton High School band blew a blast on his whistle, threw back his shoulders, and thrust his baton downward. A Sousa march filled the air and the band filed into the building, followed by Preston, the Byers, and the Gehayties. The closed room was stifling. The band led the honorees and their families to their seats, then, continuing to play, marched on to take its place beside the stage. Twelve people sat on the platform. Cyril recognized two of them, Mr. John Bear and Reverend Ballew. He guessed that the man and woman on the end of the first row were Dorothy Gray's parents.

The band finished; the audience grew quiet, and Paul Preston stepped to the microphone. "May I have your attention? Speaking for the people of Lawton and the staff of the Fort Sill Indian School I welcome you to these ceremonies. We're gathered here today to recognize Tonepah Gehaytie and Cyril Byers."

A monologue followed in which he mentioned famous persons in Lawton, Comanche County, Oklahoma, and the United States. At last he turned and pointed to the men seated behind him.

"I'm sure we look forward to hearing from some of the dignitaries seated on this stage. Their interests and expertise extend around the world."

He'd managed to circumnavigate the globe without mentioning Tonepah or Cyril more than once. He sipped from a glass of water.

"And now, allow me to present to you, Mister John Bear, the outstanding President of the Fort Sill Indian School."

John Bear walked to the microphone. "It is my pleasure to welcome you to the Fort Sill Indian School. We gladly join the people of Lawton to recognize two brave boys, Tonepah Gehaytie and Cyril Byers. What they did to save the life of Dorothy Gray speaks well for their upbringing. The fact that they come from different cultures shows how similar all people really are. Bravery is not limited to one culture. I have observed that these boys are the best of friends. I watched one of them ride into a dangerous night to be with the other one. He found his friend fighting against terrible odds to save a girl. Together they succeeded. Their friendship emphasizes something I have said for years. The past is past. Indians and Whites must put old animosities aside and should work together as friends to make the world a better place. As an educator I advise our people to pin their hopes on the schools. I tell them that sometimes Indians are too proud of being Indians. We need to be sure that pride never stands in the way of our learning and contributing or helping others do the same."

Paul Preston mounted the podium. "Thank you, Mr. Bear. We'll now hear from Sheriff Hans McLarty, whose prompt action when he arrested Queno Hinauho brought honor to his badge and comfort to the community."

Hans McLarty strode to the front. "Thank you for those kind words. The Sheriff's duties aren't easy. We're grateful for the assistance these boys gave us in recapturing Queno Hinauho. All peace officers in Comanche County join me in this expression of gratitude."

The mayor of Lawton and the Comanche County judge followed with words of thanks. Colonel Matthew Keller, Provost Marshall at Fort Sill, congratulated the Wichita Mountain area for producing such stalwart representatives as Tonepah and Cyril.

The heat rose, hand-held fans blossomed and handkerchiefs mopped at sweaty faces. Trapped in the oppressive heat and suffocated by the droning voices, the honorees grew restless and sought outlets for their shackled energy. They discovered they could glimpse each other by leaning forward or backward and looking beyond their parents. From time to time, when their eyes met, they made faces. Their parents ignored them.

When the band struck up "America the Beautiful," the people came to life and moved in their seats, grateful for a break in the proceedings. The respite lasted until the band had played "The Battle Hymn of the Republic," which proved, however, to be introductory to the remarks of the main speaker, Alvin Gorman, United States Senator from Oklahoma.

During his introduction of Senator Gorman, Paul Preston advised him to hire a smooth operator, such as himself, to come work for him in Washington. Ignoring the suggestion, Alvin Gorman rose to speak.

The senator's speech followed the pattern of political speeches everywhere. His friends found grounds for hope in it. Members of the other party thought it was hogwash and nodded off. When he said, "And in conclusion . . . ," Cyril began to pay attention. The Senator pointed at the honorees. "Tonepah Gehaytie and Cyril Byers are the very kind of good citizens I want behind me as I enter this campaign to lead you against dangerous foes. I ask you to return me to Washington, D. C., to continue the fight against those who oppose the recovery acts I've helped the President set in motion."

Cyril didn't know what Washington, D. C., had to do with a pair of country boys in Oklahoma, but he reckoned it must be a great honor to have your name mentioned in the same breath with it.

Paul Preston praised the speech and speaker effusively, almost forgetting to announce that Mr. Bear wished to speak again.

John Bear returned to the platform. "I want to introduce Hautie and Mildred Gray, the parents of Dorothy Gray, the girl whom Tonepah and Cyril saved."

Cyril had guessed correctly. A couple in the front row rose and walked to the speaker's platform. John Bear asked Tonepah and Cyril to come stand beside him. Hautie Gray stepped to the microphone. "We are most thankful to these brave boys for saving our daughter's life."

Mildred Gray bent forward and hugged Cyril and Tonepah. "We do thank you, Tonepah and Cyril," she said, her eyes brimming. "Dorothy wanted to come today and thank you herself, but the doctor said it's too soon for her to be out. She's recovering well at home."

Cyril felt the Grays' sincerity and warmth.

After they returned to their seats, the band played and the drum major spun a baton. In a moment he took up a second. Twirling two batons at the same time, he captivated the audience. When he threw one of the fancy sticks to the high ceiling, then caught it behind his back without missing a twirl, Cyril and Tonepah grinned and nodded to each other. Twirling a baton was swell.

The display ended, and Paul Preston called on Reverend Ballew to dismiss them with a prayer. Remembering the short prayer Reverend Ballew had given before dinner, Cyril was hopeful. The Reverend didn't disappoint him and Paul Preston pronounced the meeting closed. The band played as it lead the audience out of the building. On the front steps, Lola hugged Cyril and place her other arm around Tonepah's shoulders . "We're proud of you, boys."

Samuel shook Tonepah's hand and clasped Cyril on the shoulder. "We'll be leaving you with the Gehayties now, son. They'll bring you home after the powwow.

"Dad, Toney wants me to dance at the powwow. I ain't—I'm not sure I can do that."

"You'll do all right. You're the one who always wants to go join the Indians at the mission."

Back at the campground, the Indians uncovered the food and gathered for another meal. Leftover barbecued beef, brown beans, sliced onions, pan-fried bread, and ice cream were enough celebration for Cyril. He didn't need a powwow.

When supper was over and night was falling, a man lit the pile of wood in the center of the clearing. The dry brush on the bottom caught quickly and the flames licked upward. The people came to the fire. Joining the Gehayties, Cyril watched others take seats on the circle of logs. In a while two men appeared carrying drums, rings of wood covered with tightly drawn deer hide. The drummers seated themselves and began a four-count beat accompanied by their voices: "Hi ya, hi ya, hi ya, hi ya." Despite his fear that he might have to dance, the drumbeat and the singers' chanting thrilled Cyril. They were the same rhythm and words he had heard that many times before had made him wish he could join the Indians at the mission.

Somewhere in the circle, a young man stood and started to move his feet in time with the music. Soon another one joined him, then others. Before long, young men filled the space between the logs and the fire. Cyril watched their feet. Standing on the toes of one foot they dropped their weight onto the heel, then drew the other foot forward and repeated the action. Toe, heel, toe, heel, they moved forcefully around the fire. When others began clapping, Cyril joined them. Glancing at those seated on his side of the fire, he saw Juanita Trumpeter looking in his direction. Was she smiling at him or at Tonepah, who sat beside him? In a while the dance ended and the young men went to a nearby tepee.

Then the drummers started again, and the young women came forward. Their dance step was different. They slid one foot forward and brought it to rest, then slipped the other foot forward next to the first. Using that motion, they glided around the circle. Their heads, arms, and hands were also part of the dance. Their eyes turned left, then right, searching. Their arms rose and their fingers flicked in the firelight, beckoning. No one answered and they danced on, repeating the movements like actors in a play. After ten minutes the drums went silent and the women took their seats.

After a rest, the drummers returned to their music. Older men and women now formed a line of dancers. The beat of the drums filled Cyril's ears. Unconsciously, he began bouncing his body in time with the drums. Until he saw Tonepah circling the fire with the heel and toe step, he hadn't been aware that his friend had left the log where Cyril still sat. As Tonepah circled the fire, the other dancers motioned him forward. Each time he passed a couple, they took seats on a log. Soon Tonepah was dancing alone. Admiring Tonepah's movements, Cyril became aware that he was doing more than dancing. Like the young women, he was acting a part. Moving his feet in time with the drums, Tonepah raised his hands as if holding bridle reins. Bouncing first on one foot and then the other, he moved in a good imitation of a trotting horse. Rounding the circle he looked at the ground, then quickly raised both hands with the palms turned outward, the picture of fright. Still showing fear, he spun on one foot and planted the other in front of his body. His hands seemed to lock on something above and behind him. A reenactment of a vicious encounter began. The dancing boy struggled with an unseen enemy. Suddenly, Cyril realized that Toney was fighting for his life. He was battling the killer Queno Hinauho. Cyril watched Tonepah with increasing fascination, pleased that he understood.

Tonepah circled the fire once more and came back to Cyril. Again, he acted out riding his pony, finding the girl, and fighting Queno. Enthralled, Cyril riveted his attention on his friend. Then he felt a pair of hands on his shoulders. It was Fred Gehaytie. "You must dance, Cy-Byers."

Cyril stepped hesitantly toward the fire. His knees felt like water. He almost thought he would pass out from self-consciousness. Then he saw that the people looking at him, clapping and singing, "Hi ya, hi ya, hi ya, hi ya." They were encouraging him, urging him on. They expected him to continue Tonepah's reenactment. The time had come for him to tell his part of the story.

Cyril joined Tonepah, who raised his hands, recreating his fight with Queno Hinauho. Cyril followed the beat of the drums with his feet and watched his friend recall the horrifying events of that terrible night. At the proper moment, he took up the reins of his phantom pony, dug his heels into its sides, and drove into the imaginary battle between the two Kiowas. Moving his hands as if grasping his quirt, he raised his right hand high over his head. His arm whirled in an arc and struck a blow behind an unseen ear. The force of his effort turned Cyril around to face the audience. Eyes lit up and heads nodded. His act had pleased the audience.

So this was the point of the evening's activity. The powwow was the Indians' way of honoring Tonepah and Cyril by giving them the chance to tell the story of their deeds. This was a good way to honor people—much better than gathering in a closed room, sitting on hard chairs, and giving long speeches. That thought gave Cyril another reason to wish he were Kiowa. Caught up in the frenzied atmosphere of friends, fire, and throbbing drums, he let himself go. When Juanita Trumpeter smiled at him, his pleasure increased. She was also smiling at Toney, but that didn't matter.

When the drums stopped, Tonepah caught Cyril by the shoulders. "You did good, Cy-Byers."

"Thanks, Toney. That was great."

"The people liked your dancing. One of them wants to see you." Cyril followed Tonepah around the circle until they stood in front of Tehat Hauvone. When he found himself under her fierce gaze, Cyril's proud flush faded. She spoke in Kiowa. Tonepah interpreted: "She thanks you for saving me, the one chosen to lead the Kiowas."

Cyril stared at the streaks of lightning that sparkled in her dark eyes and felt helpless. Again she spoke and Tonepah translated her words into English: "She says you're the only white person she doesn't hate."

When she spoke again, Cyril thought he saw a glimmer of kindness cross her timeworn face. Tonepah laughed. "She thinks the Great Spirit made a mistake by sending you to a white family. When you danced and showed what you did in the fight, it came to her that you should have been born a Kiowa." Cyril felt the deep honor of her words and accepted them in silence.

As the fire burned down, the powwow broke up and the Indians started home. When Fred Gehaytie floored the gas pedal of his Model A and aimed it at the Wichita Mountains, Cyril ignored the speed. Tonepah laid his head on his mother's shoulder and went to sleep. Cyril made a pillow of his own right arm and tried to do the same. But eyes in the darkness disturbed his rest. At first they were the loving eyes of a Comanche girl who smiled only at him. Then the scene changed and he looked into the face of an old Kiowa woman whose eyes seemed to demand more than he could deliver. He wanted to let his thoughts dwell on Juanita Trumpeter, but he couldn't shake the memory of Tehat's Hauvone's firm gaze.